IT TASTED
THE FLESH . . .

It tasted the sweet, decomposing meat. It nibbled on the skin, tearing chunks out with pointed razor-sharp teeth. Its thick black tongue savored each morsel, stretching out the pleasure of the foul human flesh.

Already the internal organs were swollen with putrification. It pulled down on the legs, jamming the stake upward, tearing through the inner fabric, draining the blood with ritual satisfaction. It flowed red down the smooth sides of the pole, out of the bowels, leaving behind just the meat: the tasty, bloodless meat.

It ripped open the stomach, gorged itself on the contents, pulled out the viscera with clawed hands, stuffed the torn scraps into its mouth: chewing, drooling, groaning with ecstasy.

Its power was at last restored.

But its desire for more only whetted.

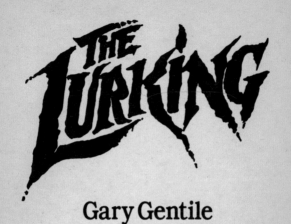

THE LURKING

Gary Gentile

Jim,
Not to be read
alone at night.

Gary Gentile

CHARTER BOOKS, NEW YORK

THE LURKING

A Charter Book / published by arrangement with
the author

PRINTING HISTORY
Charter edition / June 1989

ISBN: 1-55773-224-8

Charter Books are published by The Berkley Publishing Group,
200 Madison Avenue, New York, New York 10016.
The name "CHARTER" and the "C" logo
are trademarks belonging to Charter Communications, Inc.

PRINTED IN THE UNITED STATES OF AMERICA

10 9 8 7 6 5 4 3 2 1

PROLOGUE

It stalked through the woods on two monstrous, bulging legs, with an easy lope that carried it quickly and effortlessly, almost sibilantly, across crystalline sphagnum moss and beds of frosted pine needles. It waded through cold cranberry bogs, crunching the ice along the shallow edges with splayed, hamlike feet. It reached into the lower branches of an aspen, swung from one to another on massive, muscular arms. The barrel chest was carpeted with thick black wiry hair.

It alighted soundlessly, rustled through the bushes like the wind.

It was hungry.

It had just woken up, and it was hungry.

Somewhere in that interminable, moonlit pine forest was food: nourishment for a growling stomach, fodder for a craving, black soul. It searched for what it knew it must eventually find. Hunched over, nostrils flaring like fire hoses, it sniffed the leaf-covered soil. It groped with dirty, bearlike hands, feeling the frozen ground with calloused digits. It picked up a scent.

The sunken patch of ground was filled with mulched leaves and covered over with rimed pine needles, appearing level with the surrounding land. But sharp eyes picked up the depressed contour, trained olfactories detected the

1

effluvium from underneath, sensitive fingertips felt out the soil that grew no grass, subtended no roots.

Blackened talons pierced the solidified crust, ripped out chunks of sand that were rock hard. The debris was tossed helter skelter with maddened fury. Below the frost line the digging became easier, more frantic. It was close. It could smell the tantalizing nearness of death.

In fading moonlight it scrabbled through silicon granules, deep and loose, touched artificial fabric. The rasping inhalations alternated with animal grunts. It tore through the last barrier, ripped desiccated flesh with hardened nails, pulled bloodless entrails to its quivering mouth, sucked in the life-giving tissue, chewed lustily, swallowed, reached out for more, pulled apart the rib cage, snapped bones, gorged itself, tore the body into pieces, stuffed its mouth, sucked off putrid fingers, leaned back on its haunches, momentarily sated.

The sky lightened from deep purple to pale blue. The brightest stars shone untwinkling. Faint shadows climbed down from a stand of cedars and crept along the ground. A jay called forlornly from the treetops. A twig snapped.

It was instantly, menacingly alert.

Something stepped out of the pines, shuffled through shrubbery into the glade. It was a lower life form clad in red, unaware of its surroundings, totally oblivious to its presence. The red, bipedal creature carried a stick that glinted metallically in the morning's first light. It stopped, glanced around, took two steps, stopped, repeated the formula.

It was revolted by the odor of life, by the blundering, by the interruption. It crouched, watching as the creature approached nearer, nearer, plodding with slow steps, within reach, almost on top of it, looked down, gasped—

It let out a beastial, bloodcurdling growl as it leaped to its full, unhunched height, towering over the startled creature. It grabbed for the tiny head, surrounded it with huge paws, dug dew claws into widened eyes. The stick rumbled and belched smoke, fell to the ground. Blood spurted from crushed sockets. Teeth gnashed at the ex-

posed, white neck, rending and tearing. Limbs came free with frightening ease, and the creature fell apart like a plastic doll, dangling in its grip.

That was all it could stand. It dropped the twitching creature, reeking with life and still flowing blood. It trampled over rotting logs and dried moss. It ran away from the dying creature, away from that terrible condition known as life. It ran through the woods, seeking more death for its insatiable hunger. It needed more death. It could survive only on death.

It hated life. And worse, it hated the memory of life.

Golden beams of sunlight vaulted through the pine trees, glistening on dewdrops only recently melted. Bright flowers bloomed, scenting the air with the freshness of spring. Pitcher plants and jack-in-the-pulpits arched in the swamps, surrounded by bright green moss.

Two canoes floated lazily along the swiftly running creek, their reflections cast back perfectly by the clear, dark cedar water. A paddle dipped into the shallows, dragged for a moment along sand tainted with iron oxide. A cupped hand plunged in beside it, brought up water infused with tannic acid from leaching cedars.

"Hey, it don't taste too bad."

"Bobby," Karen squealed from her position in the bow, "how can you drink water that's been on the ground?"

From the other canoe came a splash as the flat of a wooden blade hit the surface of the creek. "Try some."

The cold cascade washed over her, dampening her pink sweater and blue jeans, stinging her face and hands. "Bobby, make him stop."

Bobby was laughing too hard to say anything. He submerged the empty canteen and let it fill as the canoe glided on its own. The creek wound like a snake, and he had only moments before he was forced to drop the canteen in front of him and wield his paddle. He barely missed crashing into the bank at the outside of the turn. Sticks and lower limbs scratched across his face as he forced the canoe back into the current.

"Karen, why the hell don't you put your paddle in the water once in a while?"

Karen slid off the seat onto her knees, and ducked her head down below the gunwales. Her high-pitched voice was muffled. "My arms are tired."

"How come your jaw isn't tired? It's the only muscle you've exercised all morning."

After the branches scraped over her back, she sat up. "It wasn't my idea to go rowing."

From the bow of the other canoe Mary drew hard to port. "Let's stop for lunch. It looks flat up there under that pine tree."

Ralph followed her lead, steering the canoe with an exaggerated J-stroke. "That bank looks kinda steep. Can we get the cooler up it?"

"We'll have to, unless you want to picnic in the boat. It's the only spot I've seen that isn't covered with briars and brambles."

Aluminum scraped on mud covered rocks. Mary touched a sneakered toe to the bank, tested it with her weight. "Feels okay." She leaped out and dragged the boat halfway up. She waved to Bobby and Karen. "Come in on the upstream side."

Ralph stood up, tossed his paddle to the top of the eight-foot ledge, and picked up the cooler by the end handles. He had taken only one step when the other canoe crashed into his stern. He braced himself on the gunwale, but dropped the cooler over the side. It splashed, and floated upright.

Bobby was livid. "Karen, can't you do anything right? I told you to pry."

"Well, I don't know what to do. This is stupid anyway. Why didn't we go to the shore instead of renting canoes?"

"Because all you ever do is go to the shore." Bobby poled the canoe up to the bank. "Hey, Ralph, did we lose any beer?"

"No, the lid didn't open. But I heard some bottles break."

Mary released the bow painter and pulled the boat onto

the landing. The aluminum keel carved a groove in the mud. "Come on, Karen. Don't be a sissy."

"But I'll get my shoes all dirty."

"It's hard enough to stand on." Mary held out her hand. "Come on."

Karen stood up shakily, grappled for Mary's fingers, and stepped delicately over the gunwale. Her sneaker sank into the mud. "*Aaagh*, I got water in my shoe." Mary pulled her hard, and Karen flew into her arms. Her muddy foot slurped after her, but the sneaker stayed stuck. "Oh, now look what happened," she whimpered.

"I'll get it." Bobby climbed over the thwarts, carrying the blankets and lunch pack.

Karen clung to Mary with both hands. "Hurry, it's filling up with water!"

The canoe wobbled slightly, but did not tip. Bobby plucked the sneaker out of the mud, let it drain, and tossed it on the upper bank. "I'll start a fire and dry it out."

Mary let go of Karen, and scrambled up the sandy wall. "Let me have the cooler, Ralph."

Ralph held the plastic box over his head. Glass and ice rattled around inside. "Can you reach it?"

She bent low, grabbed one handle, and pulled it up. "Take my hand." She helped Ralph up to the ledge.

Karen hopped around on one foot, leaning against Bobby. The boy tossed up the blanket and pack. "Come on, Karen."

She wiped back strands of hair that had fallen out of the tortoiseshell comb. "What am I supposed to do?"

Bobby whistled a familiar British chanty. "I'll put my hands on your London derrière, and give you a push. Ralph will pull you up."

"He's too high. I can't reach."

"Grab that root. No, the white one. It's thicker."

Ralph dropped down to his knees, stretched out a hand. "Just a little closer."

She was halfway up when the root pulled out. Bobby could not hold her, and she fell onto her bottom. "Oh, no," she wailed. "My pants."

Bobby took the root from her, squinting. "Hey, Ralph, this isn't a root. It's a bone of some kind."

"Prob'ly deer."

"Hey, there's more of 'em here." Bobby scrabbled in the loose fill of the ledge. He exposed more white, but did not pull them out. He brushed dirt away with the flat of his hand.

"Do you mind?" Karen cried, from below. "You're getting dirt in my hair."

Part of the bank collapsed. Several cubic feet of loamy soil covered Bobby's basketball sneakers, and filled up Karen's lap. A gleaming white stone, the size of a canteloupe, rolled against her stained sweater and was partially covered up again in the swirling dirt.

Karen cried like a baby. "Now look what you've done."

Ralph and Mary could not help but smile broadly. Bobby broke out into gales of laughter.

"Stop it. Stop it, all of you. It's in my hair." Karen kicked out with hands and feet. The rounded dome of the stone grew larger as the sand filtered away from the edges. She pulled it off her lap. It was so light that it came right up to her face. She stared at it for a moment, her face frozen in horror.

An earthworm crawled out of the eye socket, several teeth fell out of the upper jaw. The skull glared hideously.

Karen dropped it, and screamed.

And kept screaming.

CHAPTER 1

Sand spit out from under the knobby, off-road tires of the dust-covered Jeep. From the passenger seat Elaine Adams directed the long lens of a single lens reflex at the short leaf pines that rose sixty feet into the clean, clear air and blue sky.

"There they are, Cliff. Over there." Elaine pointed a steady white finger across a clearing where half a dozen police cars spread out like a wagon train under attack.

"I see them." Cliff's voice was deep and full-throated. He spun the wheel with the ease of power steering. The CJ-7 bounced off the sandy trail, four-wheel drive engaged, and slewed along the soft ground toward the police round-up. "Who does he think he's signaling with that bubble gum machine on the roof?"

There were no sirens wailing, but the spinning lights on two of the cars continued to flash, another burst into miniature novas as strobe lights vied for attention in the noonday sun.

"Stupid cops. Out here in the middle of the woods and they still have to make a spectacle." The Jeep hit a moss covered log and bounced suddenly. "Cliff, slow down, you're not in the Maine woods. I'm trying to change lenses."

"Sorry, hon." He applied the brake gently.

Elaine shoved the telephoto lens into the gadget bag,

7

aligned the bayonet of the 28-millimeter lens onto the camera body, and twisted it into place. When it snapped, she brought the rubber eyecup in front of one bright blue eye, squinted, pressed the shutter release halfway, and checked the digital readout for metering instructions. "This'll make a good shot."

New brake shoes halted the Jeep without a squeal. Cliff engaged the emergency brake, and climbed out of the roofless cab. Thick brown hair was blown back over an upright forehead. "Yeah, but it's not exactly Sunday supplement stuff."

"News is news." Elaine climbed over the doorless sill, dragging her camera and gadget bag with her. "Jake'll love it when I come back with something spectacular. And it'll look great on my by-line."

"Uhn-huhn." Cliff hitched up his jeans and tucked in his red-checked flannel shirt as he poked along cowboy fashion toward the police entourage. "Well, just remember that murder mysteries aren't your field."

"A murder is *any* journalist's field. It's part of the business." Elaine chugged along with short steps to fit her five-and-a-half-foot frame. She pulled curly, shoulder length hair out from under the collar of her bulky insulated vest. "This may get me out of the supplements and onto the front page of the dailies."

"I still think you should have called Janice and let her have the story."

"That minx? This is one time I'm going to scoop her. The braggart."

Cliff held up a well-manicured hand. "Don't start talking like that or you'll end up sticking your foot in your mouth."

"I've got plenty of room."

"And small feet. But I'm glad *you* said it."

"I just wanted to beat you to it. Hey, that big galoot over there must be the sheriff."

"Lower your voice, Laine."

"Come on, these local yokels aren't as tough as Philly cops." Elaine switched on the motor drive and started clicking off shots. "If they have to do anything more than give road directions they'll be calling in the Stateys. And I want to get some pix before the real police get here."

Cliff ran his hand along the side of a battered and rusted, faded red pickup truck. "What are those kids doing here?"

"I don't know, but that girl looks like she's been crying for a week. Maybe they know something about it." She snapped three pictures before she got her finger off the shutter release. "Damn this motor drive."

The sheriff was big and round, with a pot belly that rivaled a wood-burning stove for girth. His gruff voice thundered loud and clear, in a slow drawl that could have been a forty-five rpm record played at thirty-three. "I don't know. Just git somebody on the radio and tell 'im to call the cor'ner."

"He don't know these backwoods roads," said a deputy.

"So send Hopper out ta the road ta meet 'im. Do I hafta tell ya everything? Less you wanna take these bones back in your trunk."

"Yes, sir. I mean, no, sir. I'll get right on it."

The sheriff turned slowly, throwing his hands in the air. "Goddamn rookies they got today can't walk an' chew gum at the same time. Hey, you. Get outa there."

Elaine looked up, but continued toward the group of youths milling in a stand of white cedars. She addressed one of the boys. "Hi. I'm a reporter from the *Bulletin*. Do you know anything about finding a body?"

"Yes, ma'am. We were canoeing along the river and—"

"Oh, Ralph, please don't go through it again. I don't want to hear it." The girl put her hands over her ears.

"Where is it?" She snapped pictures left and right. "How did you dig it up?"

The other boy pointed. "We weren't really digging. We were just trying to get up the bank."

"Hey. I'm talking to you." The sheriff lumbered toward the tall pine tree like a sick dinosaur, but Elaine had just seen the partially excavated pit and hurried toward it.

She sat down on the ledge, pushed herself off onto the sandy landing, and turned around. She gasped. For a moment her womanly instincts replaced her character as a reporter, and she put her hand over her mouth. Overcoming her natural aversion, she tugged the camera strap from in front of the lens and fired off a sequence. After two rapid-fire clicks the film advance jammed, and a red indicator light came on.

"Damn. Out of film."

"Hey, lady. Ain't you got ears?"

Elaine looked up at the hulking policeman. "I'll be right with you, Sheriff. Photographs first, then the interview."

"Huhn?"

She rapidly rewound the film. "I'm a reporter from the *Bulletin*. I want to get these shots before the sun goes behind those birch trees."

"Lady, I warned you." The sheriff reached down with one chubby hand, grabbed her by the upper arm, and dragged her bodily, feet kicking against the bank, right over the ledge. "I don't want you takin' no pixtures."

The sheriff's arm was slapped away, and Cliff jumped in between them. He towered over the law officer by half a head. Cliff planted two open palms hard against the sheriff's chest with a resounding slap that shoved him back two steps.

"Keep your filthy hands off my wife, bozo."

The sheriff's jaw dropped, and for a moment he stared wide-eyed, unmoving. Then his hand fumbled for his holster, but stayed there once he unsnapped the leather retainer. His fingers curled around the grip of the revolver. "Mister, you got no business here. I warned her."

Elaine was shoved out of the way as Cliff was grabbed from behind by two deputies. Elaine quickly regained her balance, and took one of the deputies by the shoulder and spun him around. "Let go of him."

The deputy dropped his hands.

"Grab him, you son of a bitch," the sheriff shouted. "You take your orders from me, Hopper, not some city slicker news hound."

Hopper looked from one to the other, then gently placed a hand on Cliff's arm.

Cliff did not resist, but continued to stare into the

sheriff's dull eyes. "You're cruising for a bruising, Sheriff. Badge or no badge, you can't go pushing people around."

"Then she better do what she's told. I'm the law 'round these parts."

"And you've been watching too many John Wayne movies." Cliff shrugged suddenly, breaking free from the grips of the deputies. "You're exceeding your authority when you start harassing women and children. If she suffers any bodily injury I'll enter a plea for your dismissal on the grounds of police brutality."

The sheriff relaxed his gun hand, let it fall to his side. "What are you, a lawyer or something?"

"Corporate attorney for Feinberg, Fenner, and Smith."

"Don't mean a thing ta me. And she still got no business hamperin' an investigation. I'm in charge here, an' I don't want nobody tearin' up the evidence."

"Excuse me, Sheriff." Elaine stepped forward and stood by Cliff's side. "But I'm using Kodachrome 64, and it's never yet damaged anything I've used it on."

"Lady, I— Hey, what are you two gawking at. I got the sitiation under control. Bridger, di'nt I tell you ta tell Hopper here ta go meet the cor'ner."

"But, I haven't called him yet."

The sheriff put his hands on his ample hips and leaned forward. "Then git on the radio and call 'im. What the hell you think we got all them fancy 'lectronics for?"

"Yes, sir. Right away, sir."

The sheriff eyed Hopper. "An' what're you waitin' for, a written invitation?"

"Well, he won't be here for at least an hour and—"

"Then go sit out on the hardtop an' wait for 'im. An' don't let no more cars come down here. I got enough trouble with tourists for one day." Hopper took off, and the sheriff redirected his attention. "Now, lady, as I was sayin', I got an investigation ta perform, I got witnesses ta interrogate, I got a body ta dig up an' relocate, I got—"

"Are you saying this is just an old grave site?"

"I ain't sayin' nothin', just that I got some bones that

been in the ground for a coupla decades an' they gotta be moved—"

"How do you know the body's been buried that long? Or that short? Are you qualified in forensic medicine?"

The sheriff huffed, and glanced away. "Lady, I was born an' raised in the pine barrens, an' I seen animal carcasses dug up by wild dogs. This ain't no different, 'cept it's human."

"But you don't know how long it's been buried here. It could be a gangland murder from the depression, or a recent drug pusher late in his payments, or an Indian from the time of Columbus."

The sheriff stabbed out with a stubby finger, barely touching Elaine on the chest. "Or a big mouthed woman that don't know her place."

"Don't touch her."

The sheriff jerked back, looked up at Cliff's narrowed brown eyes. "I wasn't touchin' her. But *you* are beginnin' to get on my nerves. Both of you. Now git outa here."

"The public has a right to know what's going on, and the media has a responsibility to its readers." Elaine made an exaggerated showing of changing the film in her camera. "You can't prevent me from gathering information—"

"Lady, I have a right to keep people out of an ongoing criminal investigation, and—"

"Then you admit this is a criminal investigation and not an ancient Indian burial site?"

"I don't admit nothin'. Used to be Iroquois 'round here coupla hunderd years ago, so this could be an ole redskin, but—"

"The Iroquois was a loose confederation consisting of the Cayuga, the Mohawk, the Oneida, the Onondaga, and the Seneca. Which tribes lived in the barrens?"

The sheriff threw his hands in the air. "Lady, I don't know. It may not even *be* an Indian. I jus' said it *might* be. *You're* the one who—"

"Sheriff, I think you should contact the New Jersey State Museum in Trenton. They have trained archaeologists there who might want to look over the site for anthropological evidence. New Jersey has antiquities laws which make it illegal to disturb a site of possible archaeological significance until it's cleared by a state representative."

She clamped down the back of the camera, raised it, and ground off three quick pictures of the sheriff's startled expression.

"Lady, I said no pixtures."

"What are you afraid of, Sheriff? That I'm going to capture your soul?"

The sheriff rolled his eyes again, stared up at the treetops for a moment. "Lady, I don't mind tellin' you, you got a ornery way 'bout you."

Elaine put on her brightest smile. "That's part of being a journalist."

The sheriff raised his finger again, stabbed it toward her, glanced at Cliff, and kept his distance. "All I gotta say is I don't want you near them remains. You wanna stand by an' watch, that's your business. But don't go gettin' underfoot. An' don't go wanderin' off in the woods. I got depities out scourin' the brush for a lost poacher an' they may tend to be a trifle trigger-happy, what with all these goings on."

"I'd like to get a few more pictures before—"

"I said no pixtures an' I mean it. That's what we got police photographers for. Now you go on an' get outa the way."

"But, Sheriff—"

"An' I ain't answerin' no questions. I said you could hang around an' watch, not work your jaw. Any questions to be ast, I'll ast 'em. I'd just as lief do this investigatin' my own way, an' I don't need no help. Now move along."

The sheriff terminated the conversation by sliding down the bank. He checked out the canoes and their contents.

Cliff placed a warm hand on Elaine's arm and led her away from the creek. "You sure handled him well."

"He doesn't scare me. Besides, the first thing you learn in journalism school is not to be intimated by ignorant louts and loudmouthed politicians. They can't hurt you with harsh language. And you can get a sharper response by being obnoxious and catching people off guard."

"Sounds good on paper, but someday I won't be around and you're going to get a poke in the snout."

"If that happens I'll sue the bastards. I know a good lawyer. But I thought you worked for Dewey, Cheatam, and Howe."

"Don't press your luck."

Elaine approached the teenagers still huddled by the cedars. A whippoorwill chirped merrily overhead. "Hi. Did that hick cop give you as much grief as he did me?"

Bobby snickered. "A lot more. You'd have thought *we* committed a crime the way he acted. Hell, all we did was tell him what we found."

Elaine took a few pictures, then retrieved a business card from her gadget bag. "I'm from the *Bulletin*. Elaine Adams. I happened to be out here on assignment when we overheard the police band on the CB. Looks like you really turned up a nest of worms."

Bobby laughed nervously. "Some of them crawled out of that skull, too."

"Bobby!" Karen screamed. "Don't be gross."

He jerked a thumb at her. "She grabbed an arm bone and the side of the bank collapsed right in her lap. Ended up with a skull between her legs."

"Bobby!"

"Cut it out, Bobby." Mary took Karen, sobbing, in her arms. "She's had enough for one day."

He scowled. "I was only kidding."

Ralph stepped forward, gesturing. "Lucky this old man happened by, or I don't know what we'd do. Hey, where is he?" He stared around, squinting. To Bobby, "You see where he got to?"

"His truck's still here."

"You mean the red pickup?" Cliff said.

"Oh, I'm sorry," Elaine said. "This is Cliff. What's this about an old man?"

"Said his name was Luke something or other. I didn't catch his last name. He was driving by and I flagged him down. Told him what we found."

"Yeah, and he wasn't too anxious to help, either," Bobby

added. "I guess he thought we found a corpse, and didn't want to get involved. Kept saying something about disturbing the Jersey Devil."

"Anyway," Ralph continued. "I finally convinced him to take me out to the road, then down to a phone booth. I called the police, and they told me to make sure this guy Luke hung around, 'cause I didn't how to get back in here. All I know is the canoe livery dropped us off on the Batsto and said they'd pick us up this afternoon where it runs into the Mullica."

Karen had her face buried on Mary's shoulder. Mary patted her back. "Shouldn't you be writing this down—for the paper?"

Elaine looked over her shoulder. The sheriff was climbing up the side of the bank, using a thick stick to push up his bulk. She unzipped an outer compartment of the gadget bag, whispering, "I've had a tape recorder going the whole time, but don't let that hillbilly cop know."

The teenagers shared a smirk.

The sheriff ambled toward the group, poling his way on what appeared to be a thick broom handle with one end burned off. He leaned his chin on the rounded, upper end. "How old're you kids?"

Bobby and Ralph exchanged worried looks.

"All right, everybody hand over your ID."

"My wallet's back in the car."

"So's mine. I didn't want it to get wet in case we dumped. This is Karen's first time in a canoe."

"Go ahead. Blame it all on me."

"I wasn't blaming—"

"Stop your squabbling. I'm likely ta run ya in just for the heck of it. You boys ain't old enough to be carryin' no booze."

"It's only beer."

"I don't care if it's cough medicine, you're still in trouble."

"Sheriff, I don't believe this." Elaine shook her head in astonishment. "These kids found a body and go out of their way to report it, and you want to make a big stink about a couple of six packs."

"Don't need no Pennsy scum over here, gettin' drunk an' litterin' up the pines with their empties."

"But they found a human corpse! Isn't that a little more important?"

"Don't change the law none. No, we gotta protect ourselves from the likes o' them. The pinelands'd be overrun with drugged up punks if we didn't keep 'em in their place." Turning to the teenagers he said, "Now, if you kids'll jus' accompany me ta ma car I'll take down all the particulars an' put a call in to your fokes—jus' to make sure you're tellin' the truth. An' you—" The sheriff stabbed a pudgy index finger at Elaine. "You keep your footprints away from that body. I'll be watchin' ya."

He turned his broad back on them all and, using the walking stick like a cane, tramped back to his car. He finally turned off the flashing strobes.

CHAPTER 2

The *Bulletin* building was a huge, brick structure that took up an entire city block. The thick concrete lower floor held the massive presses. The editorial offices were spread throughout the upper stories.

Elaine charged along the corridor, low heels clicking, and snaked around the overlapping walls leading to the darkroom. It was black as pitch inside. "Hello? Is anybody here?"

"Just me," said a disembodied voice. A tank lid slammed shut and a red light came on. "I'm all alone today."

"Sam, I've got a rush job for you." She took three rolls of film out of her leather handbag, and slapped them on the stainless steel counter.

"Miss Adams, that sounds strange coming from you." Sam was close to retirement, gray-haired and stoop-shouldered from forty years of darkroom work. He wore a perpetual smile on his face. Teeth glared weirdly in the red safe light. "It's only Monday, and your piece won't be set until Saturday."

Elaine laughed. "This is different. I just dropped a hot story on Jake's desk. It'll be going out in the early edition."

"Well, I'll see what I can do." Sam took a print out of the developer, let it drain, and dropped it in the fixer. "Miss Marlton was in on a drug bust last night, and left a couple rolls in the night drop." He pulled a long strip of film out of

17

a chemical bath, held it up high, and peered at the negatives as he ran them past the red light. "Got some good stuff, too."

"This'll beat her hands down. I've got exclusive pix of a murder victim just dug up in the pines."

Sam agitated the film in the light-tight tank. "That's a different slant for you. You take such pretty pictures of birds and flowers and nice people. I don't think you belong in the murder racket."

"Well, I'm about to change all that. I'm going to follow up this story and get my by-line on the front page."

With a plastic clothes pin Sam lifted some prints out of the fixer and placed them in the rinse bath. "Only hard part about being on the front page is staying there. You got a real secure place in the supplements. Nobody can touch you."

"And that's why I'm ready to move on. Sam, gotta go. I'll stop back later for the proofs."

"I'm pretty backed up but I'll try—"

Whatever else Sam said was lost in the distance. Elaine smoothed out her skirt, hopped the elevator to the top floor, and sauntered into Jake's office with an unconcealed grin on her face.

"So what did you think?"

Jake slammed down the phone. "What about?" He picked up another phone and punched a call button. "Henry, make that a five-star banner. . . . No, squeeze it in. . . . Okay, continue it on page two, but I want front-page coverage. . . . So stick it in the corner, one column. . . . Great." He hung up. "Elaine, I'm real busy. What's on your mind?"

"What did you think of the piece?"

He ran through the papers on his desk. "Which one?"

"The body those kids found in the pines."

"What? Oh, yeah. They just never stop turning up, do they? Happens every couple of years."

"But I was right there, on the spot. I even got pix of the remains. The skull had been dislodged, but the skeleton was partially exposed. It'll look great with the headline." She fanned her hands out in front of her, as if reading off a marquee. "Skeleton unearthed. Foul play suspected."

"What, a half rotted corpse? That isn't the kind of stuff we use on the front page. Or any page, for that matter."

"Boss, this is a real story. It'll make people pick up the paper."

"Along with headlines like 'How My Baby Got Sucked Down the Toilet,' and 'Alligator Emerges from Manhole and Nabs Senior Citizen.' Elaine, we're not a rag sheet hawking sensationalism. We're a newspaper reporting current events."

Elaine leaned on his desk, eyebrows knitted. "But Boss, what could be more current than this? It only happened yesterday, and I was the only reporter there. None of the other papers will have it. The sheriff tried to hush it up, but I picked up everything I could before he—"

"Oh, I'm not saying it's not current. I'm just saying it's not front-page beat. I got the Arabs bombing Iran. I got a possible OPEC embargo. I got a coke ring expose in Germantown. I got congressional hearings. I didn't say I wasn't going to use it, but I just don't want a bunch of bony digits reaching out for people."

"Well, how about page two. I've got pix of the kids who made the find, the sheriff—"

"Look, I'll fit it in wherever I can. Janice is working on it now. As soon as I see how much space—"

"What do you mean, Janice is working on it?"

Jake's head jerked back, his tousled hair flopped over his forehead. He loosened his dark blue necktie and opened the top button of his shirt. "She's fixing it up, so I can have copy for the afternoon edition."

"Jake, that's not fair. I won't be overwritten by that bed warmer. This is *my* story, and I want it to go out under my by-line."

"Be reasonable, Elaine. You're a nature photographer and a human interest writer. That's why you're my south Jersey correspondent. If it turns out to be an ancient Indian burial you can include it in your regional report. But a news item's got to be written by someone who knows the ropes, someone with some punch to her words. Sure, you happened to be at the right spot at the right time, but I couldn't have it printed the way you wrote it."

"But she'll hog all the credit and I—"

"It'll go out by-lined as a staff writer, nothing more."

"But I want the syndication—"

"Elaine, Elaine, Elaine." The swivel chair squeaked as Jake pushed his lithe form up from the padded seat. "We're a team here at the *Bulletin*. I've got staff writers and staff photographers out all over the city, writing pieces and snapping pix. If I had to give credit to each one on every filler and back-page street scene we'd never get this paper out on the stands."

"Jake, you don't understand. I've been stuck doing local color for as long as I can stand it, and this is the break I've been looking for—to get my by-line established in the wire services."

"But you're good at what you do. You weren't even born in these parts, yet you know more local history than any other writer. And your power of prose—for the kind of assignments you're doing—is evocative. You're irreplaceable. But you're not a Janice Marlton."

"Maybe not yet."

"And maybe never. Look, I don't know what it is with you. You're good at what you do. So work on your strong points. Don't try to be something you're not. Besides, Janice is quick. She gets the news and writes it up faster than Clark Kent. That's why she's on the dailies. I've seen how you pore over your stuff until it's letter perfect. But we're not running a slick."

Elaine was getting stiff from her standing position. She shifted her weight. "You're just not realizing my full potential. You're not being—"

The phone clattered. Jake held up his hand and jerked the black receiver to his ear. "Yeah. Yeah. Okay, wait a minute." He covered the mouthpiece and directed his attention to Elaine. "All right, you lucked out. I need Janice for another assignment. Go talk with her for a few minutes and listen to what she has to say about the rewrite. I've got to get this paper to bed."

"What about the by-line?"

Jake uncovered the diaphragm, scowled, and covered it

again. "All right, already. You can have the by-line—*if* you do the final rewrite yourself."

"You're a sweetheart." Elaine's face exploded into a gargantuan smile. "All I need is a chance—"

Jake's voice was a mild roar. "Out!" He pointed to the door, looked down, and shouted into the telephone. "Just get out and leave me—oh, sorry, Henry. I didn't mean you."

Elaine left before he recovered. She hurried through a warren of desks and filing cabinets and banging typewriters, nodding obliquely to fellow workers. She dropped her purse in her cubbyhole, then located Janice typing furiously at her computer console. Her tone was icy. "Good morning. How's it going?"

Jet black hair swirled around the quickly turning head. "Hi, babe. I'm working on your story right now. Be done in a jiff."

"Jake said I could finish it. He's got another assignment for you."

Long red polished nails dangled over the keyboard, and multifaceted diamonds scintillated with the slight movement. "Okay by me, but unless you get your little ass in gear it'll never be done for the early."

"He's already killed that idea." Elaine bent at the waist, reading the green type on the screen. "What's that? I don't remember anything like that."

"Journalistic license. I'm jazzing it up so the readers don't fall asleep before they get to the second paragraph."

Elaine felt an intense heat working up her spine. She made a pretense of scratching her temple and pulling down blond tresses, to cover a face she knew was turning a bright red. "But that isn't the way it happened."

"Nobody knows that but you." Janice's unbuttoned sweater fell aside, revealing the bulge of an ample bosom that strained her form-fitted blouse. "If you make it too realistic nobody'll believe it."

"But, what about the witnesses. They'll know."

"And they'll tell another dozen people. Meanwhile, a million readers will live vicariously through an exciting story they'll talk about all day. Weeks. And they'll keep looking for a follow-up that never comes."

"But what about the investigation. It'll turn up more news, and when we make another report we'll get caught with all that misinformation."

"Babe, there's no follow-up to a story like this. It dies at the end of the column."

"But I want to chase it down, see what the coroner reports, find out how the body got there, what killed him, who did it. I've finally found a good story. I'm not going to let it get away."

"Lois Lane says a good reporter doesn't find a story, she makes it."

Elaine continued to read from the monitor. "But adding all that crap about the Jersey Devil is pure trash. Nobody's going to swallow that."

"What? Are you kidding? They'll eat it up. We're about due for another Jersey Devil story."

Elaine threw her rear on the desk, sitting so she could look at Janice without twisting her body in half. "What are you talking about? You can't just make something up and expect people to believe it."

"Babe, I know you were born and raised in California, but don't they have magazines out there? I grew up in Vineland, and I've been hearing about the Jersey Devil ever since I was a kid. Everybody knows the Jersey Devil exists, and lives in the pine barrens."

"Well, I never heard—"

"All those historical pieces you do and you never came across the Jersey Devil? Where've you had your head, inside a clam shell?"

Elaine rolled her eyes. "I never held much stock in 'ghoulies and ghosties and long-legged beasties, and things that go bump in the night.' That's kiddee matinee stuff."

"I'm not talking about spectral manifestation. This is folklore."

"But you can't just go making up a bunch of legends about this Jersey Devil, or whatever it is."

"Babe, I'm not making it up. The Jersey Devil's been

around a lot longer than I have. Everybody around here knows about it."

"But that old man only mentioned the name, he didn't say all that stuff you put in there. I never even found the guy. He was off in the woods with the deputies. I just put it down because the kids mentioned it."

"And that's what we hang the story on. Babe, they dig up bodies in those woods all the time, and none of them are ever identified. There are unsolved mysteries in there from the time lovers had their first quarrel, or bootleggers murdered distributors who fell behind in their payments. Believe me, the sheriff's not even going to *try* to solve this case."

"But, someone should. After all, someone died for a reason, and probably not a good one. Doesn't anyone care what happened to this poor soul?"

"Hell, no. All they want to do is forget about it. They'll disinter the body and cremate the remains, and all thoughts of who it was will go up in smoke and ashes."

"But—"

"But nothing. If the authorities want to investigate it, that's their business. Our job is to make a story out of it." Janice wagged a delicate finger at Elaine. "And that's where you need some help. The first thing you have to do is trash that antique typewriter and put in for a terminal."

"It's not antique. It's an IBM Selectric, with rotating ball—"

"Same thing. Great for secretarial work, but not creative writing. You want to be able to do continuous editing while you write."

"But I don't know word processing."

"You can learn. You already know how to type, so you can pick it up in a couple days. Maybe even convince Jake to get you your own monitor and keyboard at home. With a modem and telephone link you can access your projects right from the comfort of your own living room. And from what I remember, that living room of yours in Society Hill, overlooking Penns Landing, is quite comfortable."

Elaine's anger rose, her fists clenched. This time she could not hide her skin flush. "Jealous?" she spat.

"No, babe, just envious." Janice smiled pleasantly, her voice as smooth as if she were discussing the weather. "Another thing you have to do is tell it like it is. This first line of yours is a disaster." Janice picked up the typed manuscript. " 'In the wake of what was probably the last frost of the season, with the April sun warming the pine scented atmosphere and wild magnolias and swamp azaleas struggling to catch the golden rays in recently opened blossoms, even the great crested flycatchers and Carolina chickadees remained blissfully unaware of the terror about to unfold below their newly built nests.' "

She flung down the paper, and glared up at Elaine. "I admit, John Muir couldn't have said it better. But we're not talking about a National Park vista or a pastoral waterfall. This is an article about fear, torture, and death. The word 'terror' just doesn't fit in with what you wrote. Now look at this."

Janice punched some control keys and the screen flipped to the beginning of the document. " 'Four teenagers came face-to-face with ultimate horror when they uncovered a half-naked corpse while digging for buried treasure in New Jersey's pine belt.' "

"But, that's not even close to the truth. The corpse wasn't half—"

"And they weren't divining for gold doubloons, but that doesn't matter. What's important is that you've grabbed the reader, right from the first line. You don't have time for a slow buildup. You have to hook him right from the start, with all the salient facts in the first paragraph. Then, you go on to describe the incidents more fully, but without adding any more information. You just get long-winded. The reader wants to hear more, so he keeps reading. The story gets thinner, with more description and less data, until it peters out to nothing. You throw in a few teasers to keep him interested, and he loves it."

"But, you've left out the setting. You've left out—"

"Babe, nobody gives a damn that the first Mason jars

were manufactured in the barrens, or the pineys used to trap minks and muskrats for their pelts, or they had bog iron forges during the Revolutionary War and made cannons and musket balls. Save that and your pictures for the weekend rotogravure. For a piece like this you need to wallop the reader right between the eyes."

"But you've deliberately distorted the facts."

"No, I just angled them to highlight reader interest."

"Yellow journalism."

"Babe, it's all part of the game. We want to sell newspapers, the reader wants to be entertained."

"What ever happened to reporting the facts? Or doesn't that enter into it anywhere?"

"The facts are all here. I've just made them intriguing. You tell people what they want to hear, with enough of the truth to keep it believable, then—"

"If you girls are done confabulating, I've got a paper to get out." Jake stood with arms akimbo, bent forward so his growling face and protruding jaw were thrust out at them. "If the finished copy isn't on my desk in an hour, it goes out. By tomorrow it's old news. Or the *Inquirer*'s got it."

Janice punched the keyboard as she got up. "Babe, it's all yours, now. You do what you want with it." The dot matrix printer clattered as the tractor feed spat paper out from under the bale. She took a compact and lipstick out of her suitcase-sized pocketbook, rouged her cheeks and colored her lips to match her nails. "Use my copy as a guide, and cut all those goddamn adjectives. You're not painting a picture, you're writing a story." She pursed her lips at the mirror, snapped the compact, and shoved everything into a voluminous central pouch. "What's hot this time, Jake? Besides your trousers, that is."

The editor took her by the arm and led her away. "Henry's got a tip about a hunter that got torn up either by a wild animal or hooligans with a sharpened garden rake. I know you like blood and guts—"

Over the noise of the sputtering printer Elaine shouted at the departing figures, "Want me to call Sam in Photo and tell him to rush it?"

Faintly she heard, "Kill the pix, just run the story."

"But, what about—" They were out of range, swallowed up by throngs of reporters rushing about with last minute stories. The printer halted, rolled out the last sheet of fanfold. Elaine dug her fingers into her head, then rubbed them down along her temples. She felt a headache coming on. She took a vial out of her purse and popped a couple acetaminophen, and kept them on her tongue till she got to the water fountain.

She returned to the printer stand, ripped out the paper along its perforated edge, and carried it and her original copy back to her desk. She switched on the typewriter and stuck in a single sheet of paper. Slowly, thoughtfully, she rewrote the piece with a blend of material.

An hour later, frustrated with the effort and chagrined at the result, she handed the finished product to a copy boy and headed for the ladies' room. After a couple more painkillers she hopped the elevator and got off at the photo lab.

"How did they turn out, Sam?"

Teeth glowed red in the safe light. "Beautiful, as always, Miss Adams, what I can see of them."

"Is something wrong?"

"Just that you were shooting color, and it took some time to get the chemicals to the proper temperature. I made contact prints, but they're still hanging up."

"It doesn't matter. Jake killed the pix. Damn near killed the story."

"That's the way it is in the newspaper business. You work your guts out over something you think is important, and it gets squeezed out by an ad for a clothing sale. News may sell the papers, but it's the advertising that makes the money."

"Yeah, the whole business is lousy. Maybe I *should* stick to the weeklies." She shook her head slowly. "At least I get a free hand to do what I want, do thorough research, and write it up the way it is."

Sam switched on the lights, pulled a print from the

clothesline, and held it out of the glare. "You got some pretty telephoto shots here."

Elaine glanced at them with half-lidded eyes. "Warblers and meadowlarks. That one's a green heron. They were all around the Nature Center. And that's a pitcher plant."

"The kind that eats animals?"

She nodded. "Insects. Not like in the monster movies. What about the others? The kids. The sheriff."

Sam took down another contact print. "Well, it appears you changed lenses right about here. Went to a wide angle. You should have used a fifty millimeter, 'cause most of these are too far away. Nice background, with trees and such, but no close-ups of faces. For this kind of work you need to see expressions."

"Yes, I see what you mean. They're too far away. Oh, well, just squeegee them off and I'll take them home wet. I'll see if I can use any of this stuff on my pinelands article. Maybe I can at least salvage some of my own fustian. If I hang around here any longer I'll start talking to myself."

"Doesn't matter. Nobody'll notice."

CHAPTER 3

Cliff lay sprawled on the deep-pile gold carpet in front of the blank, twenty-five inch diagonal screen, amid a jumble of papers and legal forms. His tie was missing, his collar unbuttoned, his sleeves folded up to just below his elbows. His eyes brightened. "Hi honey."

"Hi." Elaine closed the door with her foot. She laid down a double armful of newspapers and shopping bags on the mahogany Chippendale chair, and swung the handbag off her arm.

"What's in the packages?" Cliff disengaged himself from the stacks of briefs, leaving a paper doll image where he had been sitting with legs spread. "I hope *you* didn't buy dinner, too."

"No, just some shower gifts and a pair of hiking shoes."

Cliff gave her a peck on the cheek. "Planning on taking a hike?"

Elaine shrugged out of her coat, and pulled the mail out of the side pocket. She draped the sleek synthetic across an armchair, leafed through the envelopes, plucked out a letter, and handed it to Cliff. "From Uncle Hank. The rest are bulk."

"How can you tell? The label is typed, there's no return address, and the postmark is smeared."

"Because he always uses the same style envelope, and

it's thick enough to have pictures of last year's hunting trip."

"Guilty as charged." Cliff slit the top with a silver letter opener, and pulled out the three-by-fives. "What a coincidence. Here's a picture of our dinner before it was dressed out."

"I thought I smelled venison." Elaine kicked off her shoes and left them in the corner of the kitchenette. She dropped the rest of the mail in the trash, unopened, and poured a cup of coffee from the autodrip. "Want a refill?"

"Not now, thanks. Take a look at this." He sat at the dining room table and placed the photographs in front of Elaine's chair.

She sniffed the escaping vapors rising up into the exhaust fan. "How long's the zucchini been on?"

Cliff continued to study the hand-sized prints. "About half an hour. The butter's already in the double boiler. Just turn on the range."

Elaine put the element on low, swung out through the living room, picked up her handbag, and sat down with her coffee mug to her lips. "Hmmn, it's nice and fresh."

Cliff looked up and smiled. "I put it on as soon as I got home. Here, take a look." He rotated the pictures so they faced her. "It's a twelve-point buck. The biggest one I ever got."

She studied the photograph with a critical eye. "There's no contrast. You should have dragged it out into the sun."

"Elaine," he whined. "Stop judging picture quality and just look at the subject."

"Oh, Cliff, I'm sorry." She smiled as she placed a warm hand on his muscled forearm. "I didn't mean to be so critical. It's just that it's been one of those days."

Cliff smirked. "What? Another one?"

She tilted her head. "I guess it's beginning to sound like a broken record, isn't it?"

"Only when you work at the office. Whenever you're gallavanting around on assignment you're cheerful. Maybe you should do more photography and less writing. You've got the blend the wrong way. Hey, did you bring home the paper? I want to read your article."

Elaine took a sip of her coffee, then rifled through her handbag and brought out the contact sheets. "Don't bother. It's so chopped up you wouldn't recognize it."

Cliff took an eight-by-ten glossy and stared at the tiny rectangles printed the same size as the film. "It sounded good last night. That is, up until I fell asleep. I'm sorry, I just couldn't keep my eyes open any longer. And we had this report to get out today—"

"That's okay. I know how fired up I get when I start working on a story. Then Jake made me change the whole thing around. Even had Janice doing the rewrite till I screamed bloody murder—everywhere except in the story. She had the thing so bowlderized you wouldn't recognize it. Then he wouldn't print any of the pictures. Said skeletons didn't fit our image."

"Not only that, you got some of your own shadow across the femur."

"What? Let me see."

Elaine reached out for the print, but Cliff snatched it away, smiling. "Only kidding. But it's a shame it wasn't more dug up. These roots look more like bones than the bones. Honey, do you have that magnifying glass?"

"Right here." She reached behind and pulled it out of a cabinet drawer.

Cliff rubbed the glass with a fine cloth napkin, and focused it on the miniature images in front of him. Swept back hair cascaded forward as he bent close to the linen tablecloth. He turned the print back and forth. "Glare." Glossy shimmers ran over the dry surface.

After a full minute of strained silence, Elaine said, "What do you think?"

Still studying the photographs, he mumbled, "I think the zucchini's done. Venison, too."

"Oh, you." Elaine scowled playfully, winged him on the shoulder, and pushed back her chair. "I'll set the table." She spread out the elegant china and sterling silverware.

Cliff alternated the five-power lens between the last two frames. "Something just isn't right here."

"Oh, I don't know." She poked a meat fork into the roast. "It feels nice and tender. The potatoes, too."

Cliff looked up, a quizzical expression on his face. "What? Oh yes, I've had it marinating for two days. Honey, did you look at these closely?"

Elaine donned pot holders and carried the steaming roast held away from her plaid skirt. "Move that stuff over." Cliff cleared a spot, and she set the platter in the middle of the circular table. "You want to light the candles?"

"Sure." He took a wooden match from the crystal holder, struck it on an abrasive strip, and lit the tall, pink candles in the silver candelabra. "You need a hand with—"

"No, don't bother." She drained the zucchini and poured on the melted butter. "Oh, you can decant the wine. And where's the Parmesan cheese? I think we're all out."

Cliff turned off the living room lamp, and selected a bottle of red from the cherry wood wine rack. "I got another jar at the Italian market. It's still in the paper bag with the avocadoes." He placed the tall green bottle on the table, joined her in the kitchenette, and rustled through the bag for the cheese. "I got pizzelles and ice cream for dessert, too."

Elaine sprinkled the grated Parmesan cheese liberally over the zucchini. "Are you trying to fatten me up?"

Cliff patted her rear end and squeezed one cheek with strong fingers. "No, I think you're delicious just as you are." He found the wine goblets, popped the cork, sniffed, and poured.

Elaine dimmed the lights until they added only a faint glow over the sputtering candles, and joined Cliff at the table. She handed him the serated knife. "Is there something significant about having rump roast tonight?"

He took the weapons, smiling. "I don't know. I just thought I'd have a piece. Maybe two. And another for dessert."

She smiled, showing white, even teeth between thin lips that were somewhat pale without lipstick. "What about the ice cream?"

"It's in the freezer, so it'll keep. Some things are warm, and they won't."

Elaine accepted a thick slice of meat. "You know, you have a way of making the troubles of the day melt into insignificance."

Cliff shrugged, filled his own plate. "It's part of the contract. I always live up to my side of a bargain. And not just because it's the law."

Elaine split a potato and slapped butter into it. "You're a smart enough lawyer to get out of it, you know."

"Who said I wanted to. After nine and a half years I should know I made a good deal. Even the devil couldn't make me a better offer."

Elaine jerked back, her face clouded. "Speaking of the devil, have you ever heard of the Jersey Devil?"

"Of course. Everyone has."

Elaine raised her eyebrows as she tucked a fork full of zucchini into her mouth.

"Well, I mean everyone from around here. Even the devil couldn't live in L.A. with all that smog. My grandfather used to tell me stories about the Jersey Devil when I was a kid. Frightening stories that would straighten out your pubic hair—especially at night, with the lights down low, or by the fireplace. Passed down from word of mouth. And every now and then you read a magazine article about it."

"But, I never heard of it till yesterday, when those kids mentioned it."

"I remember. They said the old man talked about that body being the work of the Jersey Devil." Cliff snickered. "The pineys have a million myths about the evil demon of Mrs. Leeds."

"You . . . you know some of the history?"

"If you want to call it that. The Jersey Devil's a piney tradition that goes back to the seventeen hundreds. Supposedly born from a Mrs. Leeds—her thirteenth child, God rest her soul. There are quite a few variations on the legend, and Pop used to tell them all—sometimes one right after the other. And never mind about the inconsistencies. I even did a term paper on the subject in ninth or tenth grade. Never opened a book for it. I used all Pop's sordid tales, and the teacher never knew the difference. She thought I researched it thoroughly in the Gloucester High School library. Ha, ha, ha. I got an 'A' on it, too."

"How come your grandfather knew so much about it?"

"Honey, anyone Jersey bred knows about the Jersey Devil. Pop just knew more than most because he was a well digger, and bored a lot of ground in and around the pines. He used to say the water in south Jersey was the purest and clearest anywhere in the world. All the creeks and rivers in the barrens are potable. Of course, you've got that tea-colored cedar water, stained with tannin from the trees, and holding enough bog iron to attract a magnet. But even that's drinkable—at least, according to the bass and pickerel. And we used to pull some big ones out of there—"

"Cliff, about this Jersey Devil . . ."

"Oh, sure. Got off the subject." He cut another slice of venison and took another potato. "Well, you know where Leeds Point is, don't you? Right there near Smithville, kind of where the Mullica runs into Great Bay? Between Atlantic City and Long Beach Island. Well, that's where the Jersey Devil is supposed to have been born. The way the story goes, this Mrs. Leeds already had a dozen screaming brats when she found out she was going to have another. She either cursed it, or it was cursed by an old gypsy woman— remember, there are a lot of variations. Then, when the kid was born, it was either deformed, or it turned into a horrible apparition, growing bat wings and hooves and a forked tail, while its face grew out like a horse's head. Then it made a horrible scream, which it always makes when it reappears, ate its mother, or its siblings, or a bunch of visiting nuns, or some of the neighbors' kids—there's no real continuity— and flew up the chimney. Supposedly it comes back every seven years, visiting evil upon the land, and all that hokum.

"Over the years it's been blamed for all kinds of disasters: cows not giving milk, abnormal births, livestock found dead and torn up. However, that could have been wildcats. You still hear rumors of a few stragglers every once in a while, but mostly in the northern part of the state.

And there have been sightings—tracks. But the big scare came in nineteen-oh-nine—January, I think. Anyway, it was the dead of winter, with snow on the ground, when Leeds Devil, a nom de plume, made quite a stir. Pop was a young man at the time, and remembered it well. Always said it was the most talked about week until the signing of the Armistice.

"Well, anyway, everybody and his grandmother must have seen the thing in one form or another. Some said it was winged and hopped like a bird. Others said it was like a kangaroo with deer antlers and bat wings. Somebody even described it as a flying, two-legged cow. It was covered with either fur, feathers, alligator skin, or any combination thereof. It had a long, snakelike neck; the head of a horse, or a ram with curling horns, or a dog; it had hands like a monkey, only clawed; and it had stiltlike legs with split hooves; and a long ratlike tail. And it made all kinds of weird noises, from grunts and groans to barks and wheezes and hisses. Oh, and its eyes glowed in the dark like blazing coals, and sometimes it spewed flames from its mouth."

Elaine stopped eating, her mouth agape. "How old were you when your grandfather told you all this?"

"Five, ten. I don't know. I heard it all the time. We never had boogie man tales when I was growing up; we had the Jersey Devil. And if Pop said it might be prowling the countryside on a certain moonlit night, you can bet your ass none of us kids ventured outside after dark. Mom and Dad used to laugh at us, me especially. I was the youngest."

"I'm surprised they allowed him to scare you like that."

"Oh, he didn't mean anything by it. Besides, it kept us in line. Ha, ha, ha. How the three of us used to cower under the same blanket, all of us in Caroline's bed. Even when she and Brad were fighting." Cliff pushed his empty plate away, leaned forward, pulled the candelabra under his chin, and bared his teeth. "Pop used to scare us with a flashlight."

Elaine dragged the candles away from him. "Stop it, Cliff. Now you're scaring *me*."

"And you're an adult. Imagine how frightening it seemed

to us kids. Anyway, back to nineteen-oh-nine. The papers
had a field day with all the sightings. Possés were formed,
people went around carrying guns and knives. And not just
in Jersey. It flew across the river and was spotted in
Pennsylvania, even right here in Philly. There were all
kinds of tracks in the snow: hoofprints, giant bird prints,
three-pronged devil tracks. And dogs were afraid to follow
them. They went on for miles, sometimes in a perfectly
straight line, right up the sides of houses, or skipping from
rooftop to rooftop, along the tops of fences, even *under*
fences. And it ranged in size from three feet to twenty,
according to reliable witnesses."

Cliff changed his voice to a low, bass pitch, intoning,
" 'Where stunted pines of burned-over forest are revealed in
darksome pools, the Jersey Devil lurks.' "

"Cliff, stop it." Elaine got up and turned the dimmer
switch all the way up.

"Honey, it's only an old wives' tale. Folklore. Legend. A
hand-me-down from ancient demons and medieval gargoyles."

"I don't care. It gives me the creeps." Elaine ran her
hands along her upper arms, feeling the goose bumps and
experiencing a cold, deathly chill. "And if you ever tell
stories like that to our kids, I'll have you burned at the
stake."

"When we get around to having them, I promise you I
won't." He reached out and grabbed her by the arm, pulling
her back into her seat. "Laine, as long as you're working on
an article about the Batsto Nature Center and the Wharton
Tract, why don't you collect some firsthand accounts of the
Jersey Devil? I haven't read anything about it in years, so
we're about do for another article on the subject. And it's
right up your alley: a good, strong Sunday supplement
piece. With the way you write, the people'll eat it up."

Elaine shivered, her shoulders rolling uncontrollably.
"Well, I don't know . . ."

"Come on, it's always a hot topic in this neck of the
woods."

Elaine stared up at the white ceiling. "I suppose I could.

I've got to do some more research anyway. That's why I bought the boots, so I can do some walking around in the pines. My ankles are sore from those sneakers."

Cliff leaned back, smiling. "Good. Just do me a favor. Stay on the nature trails."

"Cliff, I said stop it. You're not going to scare me with any more Jersey Devil tales."

"I wasn't trying to. But the barrens is a big place, full of bogs and swamps that have swallowed up a lot of people. And it's easy to get lost in 650,000 acres of nothing but pine trees, when they all look alike. With a place almost the size of the Grand Canyon, I'd hate to have to send that sheriff in to look for you."

"And I'd hate to have him find me. He's so . . . irreverent. The way he treated those kids and mocked that—that poor body. He—"

"Hey, that reminds me." Cliff stretched across the table and grabbed the contact sheets and the magnifying glass. "I wanted to show you something."

"I've already been told I screwed up by using a wide-angle lens instead of a fifty."

"No, not that." Cliff moved the magnifying glass in and out. "In fact, it's a good thing you did or you wouldn't have gotten the whole body in the picture. You were standing so close. Here, take a look at it."

Still eyeing her husband, Elaine took the convex lens and the print. "I only got two shots of the—"

"That's all you need." He took a ballpoint pen out of his shirt pocket and pointed. "Now, look at this line right here."

"That root?"

"That's what I thought at first, only it's not a root. It's a broom handle, only a little thicker."

"Well, I can't quite make it out . . ."

Cliff put his face close to the print, his hair tangling with Elaine's. He touched the print with the pen point. "Look, see this end here, in the rib cage? See how it's rounded and smooth. And look here, at the other end. It's charred, as if it had been burned off."

Elaine squinted. "Oh, down by the legs. Yes, I can make it out. You think it was buried with the body?"

"No, Laine. I think it was buried *in* the body."

She slowly lowered the magnifying glass and pinched one eye. "I don't understand."

Cliff took a deep breath. "I think the person was impaled."

"You mean, like stabbed?"

"No, I mean impaled."

"It's the same thing."

"Honey, I don't think you quite understand what impaled means."

Elaine brushed blond tresses over her ear. "Sure I do. That's when you fall on a picket fence and the picket goes through you. Or when you get run through with a sword or a lance. Not a nice way to die, I guess. But at least it's fast."

Cliff leaned back again, ran his hand over his chin, and pinched his lips between thumb and forefinger. "You're right. But that's not the pure sense of the word. It can also refer to—" He gestured with his hand, index finger extended. "Have you ever heard of Dracula?"

"Of course. I used to watch all those horror movies when I was a kid. I guess a stake through the heart qualifies as impalement, too."

"No, that isn't what I meant. I meant the real Dracula, the historic figure Bram Stoker used as a basis for his vampire character."

"Dracula wasn't real. He's just a Hollywood monster: vampires and werewolves, gods and demons, creatures from outer space—"

"No, Laine. Dracula was a real person. Oh, I don't mean he was a vampire. But there was actually a man named Dracula, and he lived in Transylvania in the—"

"Is this another one of your grandfather's ghost stories?"

"No, he really lived. Sometime back in the fourteen hundreds. You did know Transylvania was a real place?" Elaine nodded, and he went on. "Well, this guy was some kind of a ruler, a prince or something. His native name was

Vlad, the same as his father. But his father was also known as Dracul, which means 'devil' in Romanian. So, Vlad junior became known as Dracula because he was even more sadistic than the old man. And that's where it was picked up and woven into the vampire legends.

"Anyway, this guy Dracula was your classic evil prince, killed *tens* of thousands of people in his lifetime. He was always waging war against neighboring countries, and had a special hatred for the Turks, who wanted to take over his territory. One famous account is about some Turkish envoys who came to his court to bargain with him. They refused to take off their hats because it wasn't their custom, and Dracula got pissed off. So, he had their hats nailed to their heads, and sent them back as an example of their snobbery."

Elaine shuddered. "Sounds like he was a mental case."

"Oh, he was a psychopath, all right. But that's nothing. One time he invited all the poor people into his court. Everyone who was sick, or lame, or too old to work, came for a handout. He feasted them until they were stuffed like Thanksgiving turkeys, and got them drunk on local rotgut. Then he locked them all up in the castle and burned it down. No survivors."

"Was that his idea of reducing poverty?"

Cliff waved his hand. "He didn't just enjoy killing people, he got off by torturing them. You wouldn't believe some of the things he did."

"Please spare me."

Cliff ticked off the items on his fingers. "He buried people alive, he decapitated them, he burned them with hot irons, he ran them over with carts, he cut off body parts (and I won't say which ones), he tied them down to hot coals, he had their skin peeled off, he ran sharpened stakes through their bodies and hung them up on trees—"

"Cliff! Cut it out before you run out of fingers."

"All right. All right." He held his hands in front of him defensively. "But the worst is yet to come. This sicko eventually came to be known as Vlad the Impaler because of his favorite pastime. He would take wooden stakes with a smooth, rounded end, coat it with oil, part a person's legs, and insert it carefully into the rectum until the colon was stretched into a semicolon. Then he would have them stood upright like a scarecrow so they gradually sank down on the pole, and let them hang there until they died. It might take hours—"

"*Cliff!*" Elaine put her hands over her ears. "Please, you're making me sick. I don't want to hear anymore."

"Honey, I'm sorry. I didn't mean to scare you, but—" Cliff pulled his chair around next to Elaine's and put his arm around her. She buried her face in the crook of his neck. He kissed her, and rubbed her back. "Honey, it's okay. But—"

Elaine shuddered, and drew back so she could look into his eyes. "Why are you telling me this? What does it have to do with the Jersey Devil?"

"Maybe nothing. But this picture—" He drew the prints closer, and handed her the magnifying glass. "Take a look at this. Right here."

She realized her hands were shaking, and forced herself to remain calm. She picked up the lens and scrutinized the photograph. "Okay, what am I looking for?"

"That white line, that thing that looks like a root. Look where it is."

Elaine squinted, her eye only inches away from the glass. "All right, so it's lying on top of the body."

"No, Laine, it's lying *inside* the body. See how it comes up between the legs, through the pelvic girdle, and is hidden by the rib cage? Notice the rounded end, alongside the sternum? Elaine, whoever this person was, he didn't die of natural causes. Nor was he murdered outright. He might have been tortured. Probably, an examination of the bones will show it. But one thing is for sure. He was impaled. That stick didn't just get there by accident—it was placed there, very slowly, and very surely. This isn't just an ordinary homicide, if any killing can be called ordinary. It's a ritual execution."

Elaine dropped the print as if it were on fire. "Oh, my God." She stared sightlessly across the room, lost in thought. "Cliff, this isn't the fifteenth century. What kind of people today would do such a thing?"

"People don't change, Laine, only the times. Society grows up, cultures mature, but certain individuals are demented. Maybe it was a witchcraft exorcism, like the ones at Salem. Or the Ku Klux Klan. It could even be the Mafia; they're pretty brutal. You might even have—"

"*Cliff!*" she screamed. Her eyes widened, and she looked directly at him for a moment. Then, she scrambled among the other contact prints, ran the magnifying glass over one, and shove it at her husband. "Cliff, look at that. Look at the sheriff. Look at what he's holding."

Cliff stared through the lens, nodding slowly. "A coincidence?"

"I don't know, but—Cliff, when did you say that ruckus was with the Jersey Devil? The one your grandfather remembered?"

"Oh, nineteen-oh-nine. Why?"

Elaine squeezed his thigh, and pulled herself close. She turned to him, her lips brushing his ear. She felt the comfort of his breath on her face. "Because, if there's any truth to the Jersey Devil legends, and it comes out every seven years—" She swallowed hard, her voice trembling over the lump in her throat. "Then this is the year it's due."

CHAPTER 4

Elaine turned off the engine, zipped up the vinyl window, and unlatched the door. The engine of the Jeep crackled as she stepped out with her camera and gadget bag. It was a brisk, overcast day and, as the heat from the six cylinders dissipated, the expanded metal parts snapped back into place. Her breath condensed in thick clouds that were quickly whipped away by the breeze.

She took a broadside shot of the Ford pickup, then another from behind. The dirt driveway went on another fifty feet to a small, square, single-story house. A thin wisp of smoke escaped from a blackened stovepipe. Brown pine needles lay scattered on the cedar shake roof. Black tar paper peeled off in strips from the outer walls, revealing bare wood underneath. Elaine placed her new Vibram soles on the pallet that served as a landing, climbed the three creaky steps to the unpainted porch, and stepped tentatively on the rotted, wooden surface.

A dirty, torn shade was drawn over the single window, and paint flecked off the sill. The door frame was canted, like a parallelogram, from uneven settling of the cinder block foundation.

Elaine knocked ever so lightly. "Hello. Is anyone home?"

There was no sound from within, but she detected the fragrance of burning cedar.

"Hello-oo." She knocked again, harder.

A dog growled behind her. She spun around, saw the mangy mutt with its hackles up.

"Nice doggy. Can you tell me if your master's home?"

The mongrel growled louder.

"Well, that's a fine how-do-you-do. I came all the way out here—"

Another dog sidled stiff-legged across the dirt, and another one behind that.

"Did someone leave the kennel door—"

Two more dogs appeared, one shaggy and one with close-cropped brown hair. They growled in turn.

Elaine, her eyes riveted on the five animals, twisted her body and rapped her knuckles on the door. "I hate to disturb you but . . . your dogs are . . . can you come out here and call them off?"

Three more scraggly curs, so thin their ribs showed through their short hair, flanked through the yard. Retreat to the Jeep was cut off.

"Please, let me in." She hit the timbers with her fist. The ancient planks vibrated with each thump and threatened to splinter. "Your dogs—"

The pack growled and grumbled, moving closer. Teeth were bared, saliva drooled from quivering lips. Piercing, dark eyes stabbed at her, and she recoiled as if from physical blows.

Her knuckles were raw, her palm numb. Harder she pounded. "Hurry!"

They closed in on her. Frantically, she punched the door one last time, then spun and jumped off the opposite end of the porch and dashed along the side of the house. Her gadget bag caught in some briars, but she tore it loose. It flopped at her side, while the camera banged at her chest. The back yard was a fenceless junkyard of rusted, broken cars and trucks, some lying on their sides like giant dead insects, others without doors and with their interiors ripped out.

To the torments of yelping dogs, Elaine threaded her way through the mass of steel, climbing over loose springs, exposed axles, jumbles of bald tires, piles of scrap metal and disjointed fenders.

"Help!"

The maddened dogs surrounded the wrecked vehicles, barking and snarling, climbing over roofless convertibles, wriggling through windowless doors. At first Elaine tried climbing high, onto the top of an overturned station wagon, but saw that height was no deterrent to the barking mongrels. Instead, she picked up a greasy spring leaf, and wielded it like a sword at the nearest predator. She did not come within feet of hitting it, but it stopped its advance, and growled.

She turned and ran through a maze of metal body parts, keeping ahead of the dogs flanking the junkyard. The tough rubber soles gripped the slick painted surfaces with the tenacity of barnacle cement. She launched herself over sharpened edges and piles of twisted debris. Her camera crashed into a headlight and shattered glass.

Then she was in the open, and running. The pine trees were widely separated, the ground was level and sandy. The dogs flowed out of the wreckage behind her, poured into the woods like a pack of starving timber wolves.

Elaine gasped for air. Low slung branches slapped her face, snagged her hair and woolen sweater. She tripped over an upthrust root, fell heavily to one knee. The gadget bag swung on its leather strap and slammed hard against her forehead. She scrambled to her feet, and threw the rusted spring leaf at the lead dog. It fell far short, but the dog slowed and barked. More ugly mongrels slunk through the low underbrush as if they were springing alive from the very soil. Then the pack was after her, and she was forced to turn and flee.

She broke through the intertwined limbs of a pitch pine, onto the flattened depression of a trail. Closed pinecones littered the path like the droppings of a gigantic antelope. She swung her head left and right, sped to where she could see the farthest. The dogs barked to her left, flitting through the trees like four-legged wraiths.

The trail veered, broadened, went straight, narrowed between two tall birches. A man stood blocking her way.

Elaine froze.

He was big. He was broad. He was ugly. His face was wrinkled like parchment; dark spaces showed where front teeth were missing; his nose was bulbous and veined. Sparse hair ringed his head like a tassel. The blue coveralls were patched and faded, the flannel shirt torn.

The dogs ran up behind her, but she could not move.

The man raised his arm, and with it came the long barrel of a .44 Winchester.

"Please, I was just—" Elaine's knees weakened, her legs shook like two rubber bands. She collapsed, whimpering. Her shins slammed down on the sand, but her body stayed upright. With tears welling in her eyes she watched the rifle lock in on her head.

The man raised it all the way to his shoulder, tucked in the butt, melded his cheek behind the breech.

"No!" Elaine thrust out her left hand as she fell forward, covered her eyes with the other. She curled into a tiny, fetal ball.

A shot rang out.

Elaine's body jumped involuntarily. She felt a warmth on her inner thighs.

Another shot split the forest. Behind her, a dog whimpered. The rifle cracked again, and again, and again.

She crouched there shivering. The barking of dogs retreated. Slow, steady footsteps approached. Her throat went into spasms. Chest heaving, she lifted her head slightly. Blond locks fell across her face. She saw the worn leather shoes, the rolled-down socks, the hiked-up cuffs, the oversized trouser legs.

He walked past her. She heard a thud. Gasping, she twisted her body, shook her hair out of her line of sight, saw him kick another dog. It lay still, its head nearly torn off, the neck a bloody pulp.

"Wild dogs," the man grated.

One by one, he stabbed the bleeding bodies with the toe of his boot. They were all inert, like hairy stones.

Elaine was barely able to hold herself up. Still on her
knees, she leaned forward on both hands, gripping the sand
with clenched fingers. "Hoo—Hoo—" She could not find
her voice, could not formulate intelligible words.

With the Winchester angled down and away, the old man
crunched pinecones underfoot as he ambled back along the
path and stopped, towering over Elaine. Yellow remnants of
teeth glared down at her.

"Ain't usta seein' wimmen so fer from an oiled road."

Elaine swallowed, and coughed. Her mouth was bone
dry. She ran her tongue around inside her gums, then licked
her lips. She cleared her throat. "I . . . I was out
looking . . . that is, I was taking some pictures—"

She leaned back, and tactfully placed the gadget bag in
her lap. She brushed the hair out of her face. Her breath still
came in gasps. She did not think she yet had the strength to
stand, so she arched her neck and looked up at him. "Those
dogs sneaked up on me after I got out of the Jeep. I knocked
on the door but—uh, do you live around here?"

The man jerked his head. "Over yonder."

"I'm . . . I'm parked over that way. Near the house
with the porch. I mean, the one with all the cars—"

He stared at her.

Elaine took a deep breath, forced herself upright, still
keeping the gadget bag in front of her crotch. "Well, uh,
thanks for getting rid of those dogs."

He was still two heads taller. He looked down. "The
barrens ain't no place fer a woman. 'Specially a purty one
like yoreself."

She managed a weak smile. "Would the dogs have left
me alone if I were . . . homely?"

"Naw. But you have a better chance if'n you run up agin
some poachers. Course, you stumble onto somebody's still,
don't matter whatchu look like. Me, I'm harmless. Been a
bachelor seventy-two years. Aim ta stay thataway."

"Do you always roam through the woods? Looking for
damsels in distress?"

"Live here all ma life. I'll die here, too. An' I seen a lot more'n you care ta know."

Elaine swallowed again, regaining some of her composure. "Well, I don't know about that. I'm a reporter, and the reason I came into the barrens was to hear stories. In fact, I was looking for a man. A Mr. Rudley. Do you know him?"

The old man nodded slowly. "That's his homestead back there aways."

"The one with the old cars?"

He nodded. "Come on. I'll walk ya. Jus' in case them dogs get a notion ta come back."

"Thanks. Very much. I certainly appreciate it."

The old man loped along, rifle sagging. Elaine waited until he turned around, then inspected her pants. The dark dungarees made the stain between her legs not too noticeable, but did not make her any more comfortable. She kept the gadget bag in front of her, and swung the camera over her shoulder.

He walked soundlessly through the woods, stepping over branches and around the underbrush. Elaine had no idea where they were going, but followed along like a faithful puppy. In a few moments they reached a dirt road.

"Them your tracks." It was not a question, but a statement of fact.

"Yes, I came in from Green Bank, and up from Ong's Hat. It was someone there who told me where Mr. Rudley lived, and gave me directions. I never would have found it, even with the topo maps, because there aren't any signposts."

"Don't need 'em. We all know where we live, an' we don't cotton to outsiders. Generally. Got too many of 'em hoppin' around in them four-wheel drive *ve*hickles, an' them motor bikes. Tearin' up the land, they are, an' scarin' off the wildlife. Usta be nice an' quiet before the city foke came."

Elaine forced a laugh. "Well, I'm a concrete jungle dweller myself. From Philadelphia. I work for the *Bulletin*."

"Won't hold it aginst ya." He walked past the bronze-colored Jeep to a cement pad in the middle of the front lawn. He picked up a rusty pail from among the crabgrass and dropped it under the spout of the well, and pumped the handle. It squeaked with each upward and downward thrust. "Guess in today's world a woman's gotta earn 'er keep."

"Actually, I barely make enough to pay my husband's taxes."

After half a dozen pumps the dry suctioning gave way to a gurgle, and water bubbled from the spout. The first spurt overshot the bucket, but then started dribbling over the lip and into the dry, dusty bottom. He stopped pumping, picked up the pail, swished the water around, poured it out on the ground where it was greedily sucked into the sandy soil, and positioned the pail under the pump head. The rifle never left his right hand.

"Never paid no taxes. Don't even have a number."

"Do you have a name?"

"Fokes hereabouts call me Jake."

"No kidding? That's my editor's name."

Jake filled the bucket, picked it up by the handle, and carried it toward the bungalow. "No relation."

Elaine followed him up the creaky stairs to the front door. "My name's Elaine. Elaine Adams."

Jake turned the knob and walked in. "Nice to meetchu."

Elaine stopped at the entrance, her mouth agape. "Jake, you walked right in."

He turned slowly, leaned the long barreled Winchester up against the doorjamb. "Live here."

"But the door. The lock."

"Ain't never had a lock. Don't believe in 'em. Bolt the door an' somebody'll just knock down the wall. Ain't got nothin' worth stealin', nohow."

Elaine was confused, her mind was racing. "But, Mr. Rudley—"

"Yes?"

"I mean, you said this is Mr. Rudley's house."

"Jake Rudley, that's me."

"But, I thought—"

"Shut the door, ma'am. You're lettin' out the heat."

Elaine jumped inside, eased the door shut, wondering how it fit in that slanted opening. "Jonathan Rudley?"

"That's what ma mama called me. Nowadays I go by Jake."

Elaine blew hot air on her hands, rubbed them together, and moved closer to the cast iron stove. "At first I thought your name was Luke, till the sher— I tried to call you, Jake. May I call you Jake?"

"Most fokes do." Jake poured water into a kettle and set it on the top of the stove. He removed another kettle, and shook it next to his ear. "Got enough hot water fer two cups o' tea."

"Uh, oh, sure. I'd love some." Elaine stared around at the meager furnishings: a cot with a single sheet and a couple of wool army blankets, a rocking chair, a wooden upright in front of a handmade table, the crude shelving made of stacked cinder blocks and horizontal slats. "As I was saying, I tried to call you—"

"Ain't got a phone. 'Lectricity neither." With a wooden match he lit a kerosene lantern that hung from a nail above the wash basin. Years of lamp black had left permanent stains on the faded, flowered wallpaper. "Earl Grey?"

"Sorry. Who?"

"Earl Grey. It's a tea."

"Oh. Oh, sure. Sounds fine."

"Have a seat." Jake found two tin mugs on the counter top that served as a kitchen work space, and plunked in tea bags from a dented metal container.

Elaine drew the upright chair in front of the stove, sat on it with her legs spread toward the heat. But when the dampness began to steam off her dungarees, and the urine odor became noticeable, she clamped her thighs together and turned sideways. "Well, Mr. Rud— I mean, Jake. This is quite a nice place you have here. Cliff stays in a hunting cabin just like it, up in Maine. Do you come here often?"

He handed her a steaming mug. "I live here."

Elaine wrapped her hands around the metal, soaking in the warmth. "You mean, year round?"

"That's the idee."

"But, doesn't it get cold in the winter?"

"That's what I got the stove fer." Jake sat in the rocker, away from the stove. "Got sugar if you want it."

"No. No, this is fine." She saw him looking below her midriff. Self-consciously, she turned so her knees were pointing away.

"Yer cam'ra's busted."

"What?" Elaine flipped it around, and saw the broken glass. "Oh, thank God. It's only the filter." She unscrewed the plastic ring. "The lens is okay. Can I— Do you mind if I take some pictures?"

Jake moved only his right foot, rocking slowly. "Don't make no nevermind to me."

She checked the film counter and rewound the Ko-dachrome. "You know, I had a difficult time tracking you down."

"Don't leave many footprints in this world."

Elaine laughed, feeling more at ease. "That's for sure. Your vehicle registration's the only identification there is on you, other than— Do you have a driver's license?"

"Usta."

She loaded a roll of high speed Ektachrome, and closed the camera back. "What happens if you get stopped? On the road, I mean."

Jake shrugged, and took a sip of tea. "Never been stopped."

"Well, anyway, I happened to get a picture of your truck the other day—the red pickup—and Sam, at the lab, blew it up so we could make out the tag number. I had it traced—we have connections with the police and the Bureau of Transportation—and found it registered to an address in Double Trouble. It turned out to be a grocery store. The owner said he knew you, but didn't know where to find you. He sent me to the post office in Green Bank. But there's only a box number there. Then I got a lead from the postmaster: he sent me to Mr. Ulmer, in Ong's Hat. That's where you sell your pelts and hides."

"You're a right smart gal."

Elaine smiled, and tilted her head. "You're not the first recluse I've had to interview."

Jake sipped and rocked.

"I wanted to talk with you because you . . . well, you helped those poor scared kids the other day—Sunday—when they found the remains."

Jake stared into his mug.

"They said you said something about the Jersey Devil. You said that was what killed the . . . that person . . ."

"Never said no such thing."

"But they said—"

"Don't care what they said. That weren't the work o' the Jersey Devil."

"But, I'm sure they said something about the Jersey Devil. I recorded it— Oh, my." Elaine looked down at her gadget bag. She pulled out the pocket recorder. "I forgot to turn it on. Mr. Rudley, er, Jake, do you mind if I record this conversation?"

"Ain't gonna make no difference. That ain't the work o' the Jersey Devil. It don't never go out'n its way to kill fokes, less'n they stumble on it an' ketch it off guard. Then it's got to protect itself. Or thinks it does."

With the tape advancing, Elaine placed the recorder back in the open side pouch of the gadget bag. "You seem to know quite a bit about this Jersey Devil."

"Ain't nobody lives in the barrens that don't know. Only way ta stay away from it."

Elaine checked the light meter readings. "How do you mean?"

"You know where it is, that's where you ain't. It owns these barrens, an' jus' lets the likes o' us stay here, long's we don't git in its way. Otherwise, it's likely to go on the rampage afore its time."

"Before its time?" Elaine lowered the camera. "What does that mean?"

"Miss, yore an outsider, an' ain't apposed to know the things that go on in these here barrens. But I'm old, an' near my time, so I don't mine tellin' ya. Nobody ain't gonna do nuthin' ta ole Jake. The Jersey Devil rules these woods, an' it wouldn't let 'em touch me."

"Them? Who are 'they'?"

Jake looked up from his tea. "The Cult. The Worshipers. The Devil's Disciples. Whatever they call themselves. They're all a bunch o' sadistic bastards, ever' one of 'em. Do more harm with their sacrifices 'an the Jersey Devil ever does. An' do it on purpose."

Elaine checked the volume control on the recorder. "Jake, what are you talking about?"

"Them Jersey Devil worshipers." He looked up from his mug, gripped Elaine with rheumy eyes. "They think they're keepin' it from goin' on rampages, but if they just left the damn thing alone it'd go its own way. Sure, it'd do some killin', but nuthin' like they do with their fire rituals."

Elaine felt her flesh crawl, and a chill run along her spine. She moved closer to the stove. "Are you saying . . . Are you saying there are people who worship this . . . Jersey Devil . . . and make sacrifices to it?"

"I'm speakin' English, ain't I?"

"Yes, but it's hard to believe that in today's world, in this age of enlightenment, that people actually believe in the devil."

"Ain't a religious man my own self, so I can't speak fer the likes o' Satan. But the Jersey Devil sure roams these woods."

"Have you ever seen it?"

"Like I tole you, nobody ever sees it an' lives to tell about it."

"Then, how do you know it exists?"

"I know. I seen its leavin's. Tore up bodies, dug up graves. That's why they make sacrifices, so it don't go 'round tearin' up the homesteads."

"Jake, I still don't think I understand. Are you talking about actual sacrifices, like nubile virgins, and all that?"

"Ain't no virgins in the barrens, leastways not past the age o' twelve. Can't say I know what a nubile is. See, the Jersey Devil can't stand livin' things. It can only eat the dead. Use'ly it can find enough meat from animals that die a natchral death: disease, old age, injuries. But sometimes, ever' seven year or so, it gets more of an appetite, an' can't find enough ta eat. Then it starts robbin' graveyards, breakin' inta crypts, crawlin' into yer homestead lookin' fer dead mice in the cellar. That's when it's likely to cause trouble, 'cause if ya bump into it accidental like, it'll tear ya apart for seein' it. The Jersey Devil's uncommonly shy. Don't want nobody ta know how gruesome it looks.

"They say it can't die, 'cept by its own hand. Rumor has it the only way ta kill it is ta 'tack it with a mirra', let it see how ugly it is, an' it'll kill itself tryin' ta destroy the reflection. That's why it only comes out at night, so it can't see its loathsome image when it bends over the crick ta take a drink.

"Now the worshipers, them fokes know the Jersey Devil can't croak, but they don't want it sneakin' inta their barn lookin' fer dead rats an' scarin' the livestock all ta hell. Some cows never do give milk agin, an' chickens, if they don't keel straight over from fright, never lay another egg. So they save up their old animals, or ketch a stray deer, an' sacrifice it deep in the woods where the Jersey Devil's likely ta find it. I seen fires in the night, but I stays away from 'em. Them worshipers lash the poor critter down an' burn it alive. Say that a roasted kill is more satisfyin' than a dead animal cooked."

Elaine leaned back in the rough wooden seat, breathing again. "Whew, as long as it's only livestock, I can handle that—the deed, if not the method. I thought you were talking about *human* sacrifices."

"That, too." Jake finished his tea, and ran his tongue over his teeth. "But only in the seventh year."

CHAPTER 5

It was dark by the time Elaine got to Winstons.

"Hi. I'm meeting my husband for dinner. Cliff Adams."

The maitre d' looked at her with a faint smile and cocked eyebrows. "Mrs. Adams has already arrived."

Elaine stiffened. She felt her face blush as the heat rushed up her body. She kept her voice smooth. "You must be mistaken."

"No. But I'll show you to their table, if you'd like."

Elaine gritted her teeth. "Yes. I'd like that very much."

"Right this way, please."

She followed the black tux and tails through the darkened restaurant, past candle lit tables and whispering couples, dodging waitresses and busboys. She recognized the long pitch-black hair from behind long before she saw Cliff sitting opposite her.

The maitre d' held out his hand in a sweeping gesture. "Mr. Adams."

Cliff looked up and smiled. "Elaine. We've been waiting for you."

"So I see."

"Hi, babe. I heard you say you were meeting the old man here for dinner, so I though I'd pop in for a drink with the happy twosome."

Cliff stood up, leaned over, and kissed his wife on the cheek. "We were just talking about you."

"I'll bet you were."

The maitre d' pulled out a chair for Elaine, and seated her between Cliff and Janice. "I'll bring another menu. In the meantime, would you care for a cocktail?"

"Don't bother. I'll give her mine." Janice smiled broadly as she handed over the menu. "I'm only staying for one more drink. A sombrero."

Elaine's grimace was icy. "Not now."

"Sir?"

Cliff reclaimed his seat, tilted his nearly empty glass. "Yes, another gin and tonic, please."

The maitre d' bowed slightly, and left.

"Babe, you should have ordered a hot toddy. I think you need it."

Elaine did not smile. "Am I interrupting anything?"

"Nothing that can't wait." Janice swallowed the rest of her drink. "We were just talking old times."

"From college." Cliff ran a finger around the rim of his glass.

Elaine nodded, lips set tightly. She did not try to hide the sarcasm from her voice. "Ah, the good old days."

"I've never had a bad day in my life. Well, except for— Cliff, do you remember that toga party in the frat house? Little what's-his-name got drunk and pulled the snaps on my toga just as I jumped back from his foul breath." Janice placed a warm hand on Elaine's, and leaned over conspiratorially. Her voice dropped an octave. "I fell back over the chair, and the robe opened up down the front like a peeled banana. I didn't have a stitch on underneath, which ordinarily wouldn't have mattered, but I had my period and the string got caught on the upholstery. Popped it right out. Oh, God, I was so embarrassed. I was as red as—well . . . But we sure had our fun."

"I'm sure you did."

A thin, waspish waiter arrived with the drinks. He handed them out with delicate precision.

"I've changed my mind. I think I'll join you." Elaine looked up. "Vodka Collins."

"Right away." The waiter's voice was high-pitched and cooing. "Have you decided on an entree?"

Cliff pursed his lips. "I haven't even opened the menu."

"Take your time. I'll be right back with your cocktail." The waiter scurried off.

"I'm not really that hungry," Elaine said.

"Well, I'm starved. Been traipsing all over Jersey today." Janice tasted her drink. "But I'm in on another drug bust in about an hour, so I don't have time for a big meal. I'll catch a burger on the way."

Cliff snorted. "Janice, how do you know when and where the police are going to make a raid? Isn't that privileged information?"

Janice waved him off with her hand. "Of course it is. But I'm privileged. I've got contacts in the police department. And the first thing you need to know to be a good reporter is how to get an inside story before it breaks. Fortunately, most police officers are male, and there are two ways to get a man to talk: either sleep with him, or bully him." She winked. "I've found you get more bees with honey."

Elaine humphed. "I'll bet you've got a regular hive going."

"My, but we're acerbic tonight. Bad day at the office? Let's face it, babe, we both got what we have in the world in exactly the same way. It's just that I don't believe in cramming all my eggs into one basket. I like being a number one reporter, and writing headline stories. But to do that I've got to know what the hell's going on. And if the best way to keep on my toes is to lie on my back—babe, I'm horizontal. It's nothing to be ashamed of. I enjoy it. You should try enjoying it, too."

Cliff opened his menu absently. "Janice, I don't think—"

"Well, maybe I just hold myself in higher esteem. Just because I'm not willing to sacrifice my virtue—"

"What sacrifice?" Janice laughed. "I just traded what the lieutenant wanted for what I wanted. It's part of the business. And I got an exclusive for bargain prices—with a rebate." Janice gazed wistfully at the ceiling. "And what a rebate."

"You make life sound so trivial, so—meaningless."

"Life is what you make of it. I decided a long time ago that I was going to get out of it whatever I could. And Uncle Bart says you don't have to step on anyone else's toes to do it, either. I make my own way, whatever way I can. At Glassboro State I made a pact to live life to the fullest, and so far I've been pretty successful."

"What I don't understand—" Cliff paused when the waiter brushed his leg as he placed a vodka Collins in front of his wife. He pulled back, and stretched his feet under the table. "What I don't understand is why someone with a straight 4.0 average—and you were a science major at the time—didn't choose academia. Janice, you could have won the Nobel prize by now."

Black hair swung wide as she laughed it off. "Can you imagine me in a laboratory, wearing a white smock, and pouring chemicals from one test tube to another?"

Cliff smiled. "With black horn-rimmed glasses?"

"And my hair in a bun? Oh, God. What a sight." Janice laughed out loud. "Cliff, I got out of there with a BS, which is exactly what you need in this job, but I had no intention of having it Piled Higher and Deeper. I'd have made a lousy scientist, unless I was doing sex studies."

Elaine steamed quietly at the private repartee.

"I've found my place on the opposite side of intelligensia. Instead of a Ph.D, the art of knowing more and more about less and less until you know everything about nothing, I became a writer. Now I know less and less about more and more. Eventually, I'll know nothing about everything."

Cliff raised his glass. "To the educated BS, the degree that runs the world."

Janice clinked glasses. Cliff veered his upheld glass toward Elaine, but she left her hands in her lap and her drink untouched. He continued to smile as he took a sip.

"Come on, Babe. Don't be such a sourpuss." Janice touched her glass to Elaine's, where it sat making a wet circle on the napkin. "Eat, drink, and be merry, for tomorrow we die."

"Elaine. Honey. Don't be so glum." Cliff reached under the table and squeezed her leg. She jerked away. "Come on. We're only having a little fun."

"Babe, you should be the happiest woman in the world. All I get to do is flirt with this big hunk of flesh. You get to go home with him."

Elaine scowled.

Cliff retreated. "I don't think that's what she wants to hear."

"Then maybe it's about time she did hear it. You just don't know how lucky you are. When I knew this varsity champion he was as shy as a duckbilled platypus. Wouldn't even say hello to me. Am I right?"

Cliff raised his eyebrows, and looked down at his drink.

"The fastest wide receiver in the field, but the slowest mover on the sidelines. Girls hanging on him like tinsel on a Christmas tree, and he's walking around with horse blinders on. Then, in the middle of a great career, the most valuable player ups and quits the team, and heads for the land of the setting sun. It was as if Horace Greeley spoke to him one night in his sleep: 'Go West, young man.' And he did, right when the best part of the team was disabled in a car crash. What a disaster. Glassboro didn't stand a chance after that."

"Football isn't a career, it's a dream. One with a rude awakening." Cliff sipped his drink, and rolled the clear liquid around the glass. "And if I hadn't gone on to UCLA I never would have met Laine, and got my law degree—the two best things that ever happened to me. In that order."

Elaine looked at him askance, her head lowered so her vision was partially blocked by the hair framing her face.

"Cliff, you sure as hell feathered your nest with the finest down." Janice drained her glass. "Babe, you better start paying more attention to this hunk, or you might lose him."

Elaine rankled. "To you?"

"Not me, babe. Like I said, I can get through life without hurting anybody. But a lot of gals don't have my strict moral code. No, if you lose him to anybody, it'll be Elaine Inertia. She's your biggest competitor. Put on some makeup for a change and flirt with him. This handsome devil loves the shit out of you."

"How romantic," Cliff said. "Do you use such metaphors in your writing?"

"You know what I mean. And you *do*, too. I see it in your big brown eyes whenever you look at her. The last time a man looked at me like that I crawled under the covers and hid, then made sure I never saw him again."

The waiter hovered nearby, one hand on his hip and the other held delicately, limp at the wrist.

"Listen, I'd better leave you two lovebirds alone. I'll be working late tonight on this story. And I have to type up the copy on that hunter they found in the pine barrens, so—"

"What?" Elaine said shrilly. "Did Jake put you on follow-up on my story?"

"My, but you're touchy tonight. And before you get your dander up, no, he didn't. That story's deader than the buried remains, and just as old. No, this is another case, and a lot more gruesome than a lost panhandler. Some piney got himself torn to shreds by a wild animal. You should have seen him: one arm ripped right out of the socket, the face a mess, a chunk of flesh—"

"Janice . . ."

"Oh, sorry, Cliff. Anyway, they identified the body by his dentition. He had prints, of course, but not on record. Had a loaded 30.06 and never fired a shot. Anyway, the strangest thing is they found an old grave site nearby, and someone—or something—had dug up the body and desecrated it. Do you want to hear any more of this?"

"No."

"Yes!" Elaine demanded.

"Do you two always agree on everything? Well, anyhow, I broke a heel on my good shoes—the red ones—checking out the scene of the crime. The sheriff seemed to think the guy must have surprised 'crimnals,' as he put it, digging up the body. They hacked him up with a spade, then rats got to the dead body in the grave. It doesn't make any sense to me, but—"

"Who was the sheriff?"

"Big roly-poly guy, grim, with ten chins. Named Hinkle."

"That's him! That's the same one I tangled with."

"Yeah, a real sourpuss. Had no love for reporters, that's for sure. Seemed like he wanted to hush the whole thing up, but not with this lady of the press. I wangled some heavy info out of him before the day was over."

"How? Did you sleep with him?"

"Cute. Real cute. No, this was a bully job, not a blow. The pen is mightier than the sword, and the word processor is one tough son of a bitch. I smote him with my rhetoric, cut him to the quick with my sharpened wit, carved his intestitudinal fortitude with journalistic prerogative. Did everything but stroke his testicles with my nails—figured he would have liked it. Let me tell you, Babe, he's a tough cookie, and didn't crumble easily."

"What did you find out?"

Janice smiled, hiked up her décolletage, and pushed back her chair. "You'll read all about it . . . in tomorrow's headlines. Ta-ta." She stood up and left.

Elaine stared openmouthed at the petite retreating figure. *"Ooh,* how I hate that vixen."

Cliff wiped the smirk off his face. "Laine, you leave yourself open for it."

"I don't care. She pisses me off."

"And that's why she does it. Because she knows she can get your goat. She's only kidding."

"That old goat can't have kids. Unless she can spit them out."

"Laine, calm down. Why do you let her get to you that way?"

With Janice out of sight, Elaine stared down at her glass. "What am I supposed to do, let her walk all over me and not say anything about it?"

"Honey, why can't you two be friends? Stop viewing her as a competitor, or an enemy. After all, she got you your job in the first place. This isn't any way to repay her."

"You let me worry about my debts. You don't have to pay them for me."

"And what's that supposed to mean?"

"It means that you two see an awful lot of each other."

"Laine, maybe it hasn't occurred to you, but we're friends. I've known Janice a lot longer than I've known you."

"Biblical connotations aside, I just don't like her encroaching on my territory."

"Oh, so now I'm a piece of real estate."

"It just seems that she's always around. Sometimes I think she got Jake to hire me just so she'd have an excuse to be near you."

"Laine, do you know how paranoid that sounds? Honey, look at me. Are you aware you've got a problem? You see every female as a potential threat."

Elaine continued to watch her drink. "I see Janice as a conniving woman whose professional position is higher than mine, and I want to make sure that that hierarchy stays in the office. In fact, I'd like the opportunity to climb the ladder without bumping into her spiked heels."

"Honey, look at me." Cliff reached across the table and laid a firm grip on Elaine's hand. "Forget about Janice. *She's* not your problem. Stop looking for things that aren't there. Stop—"

"But Janice *is* there. And all too often."

Cliff shook his head slowly. "Honey, I meet women all the time. I work with women. I have women acquaintances and women business associates. It just so happens that half the human race is made up of women. So there's no reason to get jealous every time a woman looks at me, or talks with me, or bumps into me. It's all part of human events."

Elaine picked up her glass, ice cubes tinkling, and drained it at a gulp. She stared at Cliff with clouded eyes. "Is this all a joke to you? Don't my feelings mean anything to you?"

Cliff sighed, and scratched his hairline with an errant finger. "Laine, what's the point? Why do we always get stuck on the same merry-go-round?" When she did not answer, he went on. "I care about you very much. But why do you have to be so sensitive about a normal social occurrence?"

Icily, she said, "You know why."

"Come on, Laine. That was ten years ago. And we weren't married then."

Her smile was toothless, and hard. "Oh, yes. I forgot. The contract hadn't been signed, so that made it all right."

Cliff ground his teeth, and muscles bunched on his upper jaw. He stabbed at her with a stiffened index finger. "Stop it. Stop trying to manipulate me with guilt. I'm sick and tired of it. The least you can do is be original, and pick on something that makes sense."

"I think I need another drink. Waiter—"

He was walking by when Elaine raised her glass. He stopped short. "Ma'am?"

"Another vodka Collins."

The waiter took her empty. "Sir?"

Cliff looked down at his still-full glass. "No."

"Would you like an appetizer?" the waiter lisped with a smile, eyes glittering. He placed his free hand on Cliff's neck and indicated the menu with the other, finger extending beyond the cupped glass. "Could I recommend—"

Cliff swung his forearm hard into the waiter's shoulder. "Get your goddamn hands off me, you faggot."

The waiter was propelled backward by the blow, and twisted around. Ice flew out of the cocktail glass, hit Cliff's Botany 500, and slid into his lap. He jumped up out of his seat, knocking the chair over behind him. The general hubbub died in a flash, and in the utter silence of the moment that followed numerous eyes lay askance at the disruption.

"I'm . . . I'm sorry, sir. I was just—"

Cliff brushed the front of his trousers. "Forget it. Just get me my check."

With a hastily retrieved towel the waiter reached toward the wet spot on Cliff's pants. "Just let me—"

Cliff grabbed the waiter's wrist and applied enough pressure to make the slight man wince. With slow deliberation, and enunciating each word perfectly, he spat, "I . . . said . . . don't . . . touch . . . me." He flung the trapped hand down with venom.

The waiter backed away, cringing, and tucked his injured hand up to his chest. Startled eyes never left Cliff's.

Cliff took a leather billfold from his vest pocket and ripped off some greenbacks. He threw them down on the table. "Laine?"

Elaine nodded openmouthed, snatched up her pocket-book, and backed away from the table. Cliff was already walking toward the door. She glanced momentarily at the waiter, then hurried after her husband.

"Pardon me, sir. Is there something—"

Cliff brushed the maitre d' aside without slowing down. "No. It was my fault." Then he was outside, and the door was closing behind him.

With short, pouncing steps Elaine charged past the startled maitre d', and ignored the frenzied looks from staff and patrons. She saw Cliff walking quickly along the sidewalk, but it took her half a minute to catch up with him.

"Cliff? Cliff? Wait up. What's wrong? Why did you— Why did you do that?"

"What did you expect me to do? Stay there and be embarrassed?"

"But, the waiter— What—"

"He touched me, that's what. The goddamn analretentive was hovering around all night staring at me."

"Cliff, I'm sure he— Cliff, slow down." Elaine took hold of his arm and held him back. She felt the blood pumping in his arm. They stopped, and stared at each other. "You're really— That really bothered you, didn't it?"

"I don't like being pawed by queers."

"Oh, I'm sure he didn't mean anything by it. After all, this *is* the City of Brotherly Love."

Cliff snorted. "All right. So maybe *I'm* a little oversensitive about some things. Come on, it's a nice night. Let's walk. We'll pick up a cheese steak on South Street."

Arm in arm they sauntered along the white cement past plate glass storefronts. Stars shone down sharply on the darkened side street.

"It's not exactly beef Wellington, but it'll do."

"You said you weren't that hungry."

"I wasn't—then. Now that that hussy is out of sight I've regained my appetite. I'll show her. I'll get a story out of the pines if it kills me. And it'll be a better exposé than she ever—"

"Honey, don't—"

Elaine held up her hands in mock defense. "I'm not jealous. She has her methods and I have mine. And I have no intention of adopting hers. But I'm going to follow my lead and . . . well, it was she who said 'you don't find good stories, you make them.' And I'm damned well going to make this one."

"Laine, now, you know I've never interfered with your careers before, or tried to dissuade you from your goals. But this time I'd— You're better off writing historical pieces, nostalgia, nature articles. I'd like you to leave the murders and mayhem to Janice."

"Why, because she's better than I am?"

"No, because . . . because that's her business. She's a tough woman, and—"

"And I'm not."

Cliff glanced up at the sky. "No, you're not. You're soft. No, I don't mean it that way. You're soft to the touch. More feminine."

"Like that waiter?"

"Forget the waiter. Forget Janice. You're not a femme fatale. And that's what I like about you."

"What are you talking about? I'm a Valley girl."

"Fer sure, fer sure. But not stereotypically. You're a good, warm-hearted woman—"

"Who knows her place."

"Would you let me finish?" Elaine saw he was serious, and kept quiet. "It's just that I don't want you getting mixed up in something in which you might get hurt. If Janice wants to go questioning pineys, that's her business. I don't care about her in the same way I care about you. She's a friend—a good friend. You're my wife."

"And you want to protect me."

"Yes, as corny as it sounds. And I don't want you sneaking up on a bunch of ghouls and finding out something you shouldn't. Those pineys are crazy from years of inbreeding. They're—"

"They're people, like you and me. It's just that you believe all those childhood stories your grandfather told you. Cliff, it's because of you and your boogeyman stories that that old man scared the piss out of me. But when I got to talking with him, I found he was a sweet old soul who wouldn't harm a fly."

"He's an exception. And I'm sure there are a lot of others. I'm not saying the woods are full of imbeciles and cutthroats, but an awful lot of strange things go on there. To say nothing of the wild dogs."

"You've seen *Deliverance* too many times. Although I'll grant you the dogs. They had me so panic-stricken I forgot to try turning the doorknob."

"And you see, that's where Janice has the advantage over you. You didn't try it because you would never think of breaking into someone's house. You have that simplicity, that trust and honesty. But in a barbaric situation that kind of attitude will cause you more harm than good. Honey, I'm just afraid for you."

"I will not be frightened by a bunch of hokey stories. I'm going to continue conducting an investigation. There's something weird going on. Even Janice said it. As if that sheriff was covering up something."

"And he's another character I'm suspicious of. He's a piney, too, long before he's an officer of the law."

"Well, I'm not over fond of him myself, but I doubt if I have to worry about the impotent bastard. Except as a barrier."

"He's still a piney, and— I guess this means you're still going ahead with it? With doing this story?"

Elaine nodded. "I have to."

They stopped at an intersection. The light was green for them, but Cliff waited as cars sped by alongside. He turned to face her, and took both her hands in his.

"Well, I didn't figure I could talk you out of it. But I'll only let you do it on one condition."

Elaine jolted back. "What do you mean—"

Cliff placed a finger on her mouth, and waited for her to stop. "I know you think the pine belt is a lovely place for a Sunday stroll, and as long as you're on the nature trails that's probably true. But when you get way back in the bush, where no one ever goes except outlaws and aborigines, you're looking for trouble. Now, if you want to go traipsing through the woods interviewing a bunch of congenital eccentrics about what they think of the Jersey Devil, you wait till the weekend and I'll go with you. In the meantime you—"

"Cliff, I'm not a baby—"

He clamped his hand over her mouth. "You're not listening," he singsonged. He let her breathe, pulled her close, and put his arms around her. "In the meantime, if you want to conduct an official investigation, that's fine. But stay on paved roads and in public buildings. And, just as a precaution, I'm going to put my gun in back of the Jeep."

Elaine inhaled sharply to protest, but Cliff hugged her tightly and squeezed the air from her lungs.

"Have it visible, and it'll keep away the curious. Put a round between a dog's legs, and it'll stay off your tail."

He released her, and let her step back a pace. She looked up into his eyes, and saw the sincerity in them. She nodded slowly.

"I can think of one bitch I wouldn't mind keeping off my tail."

INTERLUDE 1

It remembered.

It saw the flames, and it remembered.

Somewhere in the pines, a long time ago, when its inner mechanism called in excess hunger, when there was not enough dead meat to sustain it, there were those who saw its plight, and who made food for it: converted living, unpalatable flesh into the decay on which it survived.

Not until it was decomposing could meat satisfy its urges, give strength to powerful muscles, sustain a soul that craved for bloodless flesh. For blood meant life, and that it could not abide. But after all motion ceased, when the red fluid was dry and cracked, when putrefaction set in, then could it siphon off the energy it needed so much.

And if the animal screamed for mercy during its conversion, cried in pain, shrieked with unconsolable horror, then the value of its flesh was intensified, and its potency enhanced.

This it had learned during its death time. This it had taught its supporters. This was passed from generation to generation, from the feather wearers to the tricornered hats, from the stick bearers to the steel pointers, from the walkers to the riders, from the painted men to the painted women, from teepee to bungalow.

They would never forget. It would not let them forget.

The fires. It liked the fires. And among the blazing pine

boughs, it liked the squirming, the internal agony, the utter helplessness of a creature about to meet its destroyer.

It crept spiderlike through the underbrush, body stiffened, arms outstretched. It scampered on fingers and toes with unbelievable strength, not moving its hands and feet, but only the gnarled knuckles. Yet it moved with lightning speed, a horizontal board surfing through the flora, soundlessly, stealthily, like a wraith.

It sensed the nearness of fire, heard the crackling of wood, felt the sparks in its bones. It could not bear to look at the light: the brightness caused its eyes to sting as if the darkened orbs were being licked by the sun. Face down, eyes clamped tightly shut, it drew close on dancing digits, feeling through its mother earth the way to salvation.

Its excitement grew. No blood flowed in its veins, nor ever could. It was not a creature of life, but a phantom of death. But it felt excitement in other ways: in the smell of charring flesh, in the hammering within its breast, in the quivering between its legs.

Soon it would feed.

It felt the heat. Its olfactories took in the exquisite stench of burning flesh on a stick. Its mind absorbed imagery from the trees, from the grass, from the very earth.

Something was wrong. The stick pierced the organs, went all the way through the body, but there was no anguish, there was no torment, there was no convulsion. This flesh was already dead.

They were trying to cheat it. They were offering flesh without agony, meat without suffering. They thought they could get away with it. But it was too old to be fooled . . . way too old. As old as the earth itself.

They had done this before . . . and paid dearly.

They would pay again for their attempted deceit.

It melted into the ground, became as one with the earth, and wormed forward: a dark mound like a wave rolling across the surface of a stormy sea. They did not see it coming—could not see it coming—until it was too late.

It erupted from the ground like black lava, a huge, roaring silhouette, rumbling and swaying, shrugging off grass and ferns and moss and dark, enriched soil, towering high like a scarlet oak, its branches reaching down, clutching, rending, shredding, its cavernous mouth spewing molten saliva.

Its anger died down. It was ashamed. It was scared. It had touched life, that which it detested. But it was necessary—to teach the others a lesson, to let them know it could not be fooled, would not be forgotten.

It slunk away, deflated and impotent, its power temporarily lost in post orgasmic release. It slid into cool water, sank below the mud, hid in the ooze and slime.

It waited.

CHAPTER 6

Sheriff Hinkle scowled as he leaned back in his swivel chair. Something creaked raucously, either unoiled hinges or overburdened bones. "Lady, I got headaches enough without havin' ta wrestle with the press."

Elaine remained adamant. "Sheriff, I'm not trying to beat you in a match. All I want is public information."

"You reporters don't seem ta unnerstan' that I gotta conduct an investigation a certain way, an' any meddlin' by outsiders is likely ta make it more difficult. Like you walkin' all over the beach takin' pixtures. Why, you coulda trampled out who knows how much evidence."

"Oh, come now. Be realistic. Those kids had been all over that stretch of sand. And there's not going to be any footprints left over from ten years ago."

"That's not the point. Maybe that time ya din't do no damage, but maybe the next time ya will. An' I tole that other lady the same thing—"

"What other lady?" Elaine did not care if her voice was too loud.

"That black-haired lady. From the *Bulletin*, too. Why can't yer paper jus' send out one leg man at a time?"

Elaine felt the hair rise off the back of her neck. "She's doing dailies. Skimming the surface for a quick column. I'm working on an in-depth article that will cover in detail the recent spate of killings and uncovered bodies."

The sheriff groaned. "Lady, we ain't got no spates o' nothin'. We got bodies buried all over these pines, from prohibition on up. An' now we got druggies comin' in here alla time from the city. They knock somebody off in the Bronx an' either sink 'im in the Hudson or cart 'im inta the barrens. Ya can lose a body better in these here swamps 'n ya kin in the ocean. Ain't no scalloper gonna dredge 'im up outa the bogs. But that don't mean we got a lotta crime here. We're jus' the dumpin' grounds."

"That hunter wasn't dumped. According to the reports he was torn to shreds."

The sheriff shrugged. "Animals, that's all. We got red fox, gray fox, black bear. You got a color, we got a animal for it. Hell, we get reports ever' so often o'people sightin' mountain lions."

"Don't mountain lions live in the mountains?"

"Naw. Wildcats, catamounts, cougers, pumas—all the same cat with different names. They're shy. That's why most people don't see 'em. But they're there. Ask the folks who live hereabouts, they'll tell ya. Get reports about cattle bein' tore up, chicken coops bein' broke inta . . . don't find nothin' in the mornin' but a bunch o' feathers. Dogs ain't no match for 'em, neither."

Elaine walked toward the window, and leaned against the sill. "I thought all that was the work of the Jersey Devil."

The sheriff let out a loud guffaw. "Now where'd you hear a silly notion like that?"

"All over. Newspapers, magazines, books, word of mouth. Everybody's heard of the Jersey Devil."

"Ever'body's heard o' Paul Bunyon, but that don't make 'im real."

"Don't you believe in the Jersey Devil?"

"I ain't a believin' man. I believe only what I kin see. An' I ain't never seen no Jersey Devil. Don't never 'spect too, neither."

"Do you believe in God?"

"Lady, what the hell's the Almighty Lord gotta do with anythin'?"

"Most people who believe in God have never seen Him. But they still believe."

"That's differ'nt. But this Jersey Devil's jus' a bunch o' stories tole ta keep the kids inna house at night. Don't mean it's gonna eat 'em up like steak an' taters."

"How about the worshipers? Are they real?"

The sheriff stiffened momentarily, then pasted back on his perennial blank expression. "Lady, we got all kindsa people in these here woods. Most of 'em simple folk. They keep their own mind, an' ta some that seems kinda strange. Almost unnatchral not ta stick yer nose inta somebody else's business. But we like it that way. An' we don't cotton to outsiders tryin' to horn in on our affairs."

Elaine allowed herself to be stared down. She gazed out the window of the small red brick building. Maple trees provided ample shade with their newly grown leaves. "Are you denying, then, that such a cult exists?"

The chair creaked as the sheriff leaned forward and planted his stubby elbows on the cluttered desk. "I ain't denyin' nuthin'. Alls I'm sayin' is we got a quiet community here, with no more crime 'n any other, an' a damn' sight less'n you got inna city. So don't make up nuthin' jus' to write headlines."

Elaine spun around and advanced to the leading edge of the desk. "If you'd stop covering up information and start divulging the facts, there wouldn't be so much uncertainty in my mind. You've dug up two bodies in the past week, found one man dead, and issued no official reports. I know. I checked with the State Police."

The sheriff worked his jaw and pursed his lips. "Lady, you rankle me to no end."

"That's my job. I'm supposed to gather the news. Do you think it's your job to suppress it?"

"My job is ta investigate the goin's on in ma district. An' I'm doin' it right now. Got deppities out doin' the leg work, got the cor'ner takin' care o' the bodies, got clerks fillin' out papers. Don't none of it happen overnight."

Elaine took a folded newspaper out of her voluminous handbag and slammed it down on the desk, front page open.

"And what about this body cut up with a chain saw. Marlton quoted you as saying you found pieces of it spread out over a house-sized area. And that hunter who stumbled over it was found with large chunks of flesh missing. Is that your idea of a quiet community?"

The sheriff ignored the tattered sheets, and sighed tiredly. "Lady, sometimes you reporters are too persistent fer yer own good. Gonna git chu in a lotta trouble some day."

"Is that a threat?"

"Just an observation. An' I din't never say nuthin' 'bout no chain saw. Your lady friend musta 'magined it."

"Did she imagine the scattered remains? Did she imagine gnawed bones? Something out there was eating dead meat."

"Lady, we all eat dead meat, ever' time we choke down a fast food burger. Hell, I swaller live oysters right outa the shell, but that don't make me no pervert. Eat the fried blood at the bottom o' the pan, too."

Elaine pounded the fiberboard desk with a rigid finger. "And what about the hunter."

"A poacher, caught in the act by some animal. Shouldn'a been there in the first place. Deer ain't in season. An' one shot ain't gonna scare no bear, or cat."

"Or the Jersey Devil. And how about that body those kids found by the embankment. What did the coroner have to say about that one?"

"Ain't said nuthin' yet. But I kin tell you it ain't related to the other two. It's just coincidence they was found near 'bouts the same time. It happened two months apart, there wouldn't be such a stir."

"What about torture?"

"What about it?"

"Was there any sign of torture on the remains?"

"Lady, I tole you the cor'ner ain't finished with his report. But it wouldn't surprise me if that fella *was* hacked apart with a chainsaw, and it was done while he was still breathin'. They got some pretty sick weirdoes in the city and I like to keep 'em outa ma district."

Elaine spoke quickly, to catch him off guard. "And what

about this Jersey Devil cult? Don't they torture their sacrificial victims?"

The sheriff was silent for a moment. He pushed up with his elbows and brought his bulk to his feet. "Yer damn near as ornery as that other lady. She's always pokin' an' proddin' fer somethin' that ain't there, an' won't take no fer a answer. But I gotta tell ya something. I don't—"

The glass door cracked open and a sweating, gasping deputy charged into the room. His hat slipped off his head, and he fumbled to catch it before it hit the white linoleum floor. "Sheriff, you gotta come quick. We got another one and— Oh, God, it's terrible."

The sheriff was taken aback. "Hopper, what the Sam Hill's gotten inta ya?"

The deputy was almost in tears. He wiped his nose with the back of his sleeve. "It's awful. Dear God, it's horrible. The blood . . . the body . . . the goddamn thing's spread all over tarnation, like it was run through a shredder. Jesus Christ, you wouldn't believe it . . ."

"I can't believe nuthin' less you tell me what the hell's goin' on. Now calm down an' git yerself tagether."

Hopper played with his hat, running it around and around by the brim. He hunched over, shaking, staring at the floor. "It was old man Rudley, he called us in. We were at the grocery store when he pulled in with his pickup—"

"Son, jus' tell me what he found."

"It's murder. Brutal murder. He took us out into the woods. We followed him. He said there was a fire. He saw the smoke. But the body—I mean, what was left of it—was hacked up all over the goddamn forest. An arm here, a foot there. Oh, Jesus Christ, it was awful. Bridger stayed there, told me to come on in and get you. I wiped out the side of the car on some trees. I couldn't stop from shaking. Dear God, it's a bloody mess."

"Why the hell din't you use the radio? What the hell you think the county spends all that money fer?"

"Bridger, he said . . . he said he didn't want to take no chances. You know, like the other day. Being overheard."

"Well, that's just wunnerful. So you come in here an'

blab the whole thing right in front o' the same busybody. That's jus' great."

For the first time the deputy looked up, and saw Elaine. Great tears dripped down from wide, bloodshot eyes, over blushed cheeks, off a quivering chin. He was nothing more than a boy, she thought.

He fought to control his breathing. "Oh, sorry, ma'am. I didn't see you. I'm sorry about the language."

Elaine swallowed hard, unable to reply. Just the sight of this young man, and what he must have seen, made her feel queasy.

"Hopper, git outa here. Go round up the cor'ner—by telephone—and have him meet us. Ya think ya can handle a car enough to git me there in one piece?"

"Y-yes, sir." He continued to wring his hat, mindless of the tears. "I can do that, sir."

The sheriff bent forward, hands on hips. "Then git on with it."

Hopper nodded epileptically, backed into the door with a crash, fumbled with the handle, and let himself out.

The sheriff took a deep breath, retrained his gaze on Elaine. "Looks like you done stepped in shit agin."

Elaine held her hand clasped tightly to her mouth. She had to tear her gaze away from the glass door, from the deputy in the next room punching frantically at the telephone, hanging up, trying to hit the correct numbers again. She forced herself to breathe.

"You'll pardon me, lady, if I hafta go out on business?"

Elaine forced her head to turn, forced her eyes to meet the sheriff's. She nodded weakly. Suddenly, realizing what she was doing, she sputtered, "*No!* Wait! I want to go with you."

The sheriff pulled a pistol belt off a hat rack and strapped it around his considerable paunch. "Lady, I'm tellin' ya right now, this is official police business. Ain't no place fer a woman."

"Forget my sex. I'm a reporter, and have the privilege of the press. You try to keep me off this case and you'll regret it. I'm here to gather material for a story, and your prohibiting me access to a crime scene will make a nice slant that won't exactly endear you with my readers."

He pulled out his .45 revolver, held it up in the light, and spun the cylinder. He jabbed the gun back into the holster. "Ya tryin' to threaten me?"

"I'm trying to tell you that you can't prevent me from following you, so you may as well cooperate."

The sheriff scowled. He glanced out the window. "Cloudin' up out there. S'pose to rain agin this afternoon. The barrens ain't no place fer a car."

Elaine smiled smugly. "I've got a Jeep."

"Yeah, I remember." He took a yellow raincoat off the hook and wriggled into it. "Lady, yer a pain in the ass. An' I'll tell ya somethin' else. Ya may think murders and killin's an' dug up bodies look good in the papers, but I got a lot o' folks gonna be scared enough as it is without ya stirrin' up their fears. The barrens is a spooky place sometimes. Things go on there we jus' don't unnerstand. But fer the sake of the people, we try to play it down."

"No sensationalizing, I promise. Just a straightforward story." Elaine broke into a halfhearted smile. "Besides, if it's too gory my editor won't print it anyway."

The sheriff ran his dark tongue over stained front teeth. "I'd rather ya din' know about it a'tall, but since ya already do I guess I got no choice. But mark my words, ya don't touch nuthin', ya don't go where I say ya don't, an'—no pixtures. Or so help me, I'll toss that cam'ra inna crick."

Elaine considered arguing, but decided she had pushed him just about as far as she could. Reluctantly, she nodded. "Okay. No pictures."

The sun had retreated behind dark clouds, and by the time they turned off the macadam onto the dirt tract a fine drizzle was coming down. The stiff suspension did not help the functioning of her kidneys, and the wind from the high speed travel along the hardtop had rattled the plastic windows with annoying racket.

She followed the four-wheel drive police Suburban containing the sheriff, the coroner, and two deputies. Hopper hugged the wheel, and Elaine could see him through the rear window, jabbering constantly. When the truck stopped at a siding behind a police car and a red pickup, the rain was coming down in sheets, and the temperature had dropped significantly.

Elaine put the camera aside, abandoning the idea of secreting it in her handbag. She buttoned the Corinthian leather jacket up to her neck, and pulled on a navy blue beret. She looked over the seat into the cargo compartment: there was a gun, but no umbrella. She turned up her collar and ran up behind the slickered policemen.

Hopper rambled continuously. "It's right down this trail, Sheriff. Just a few yards. Old man Rudley said he was 'coon hunting when he found . . . when he stumbled across the— It's in a clearing not too far— "

The sheriff rolled along like the Michelin man. "Son, it don't matter how far it is. We're goin' with ya all the way. Murdock, can you take pixtures in this rain?"

The young police photographer hunched over his single lens reflex. "I got fast film, but somebody's got to hold something over my head to keep the camera dry."

"Hopper'll do that. Benson, you got your kit with you?"

"No, I left it in the truck. The leather's waterproof, but as soon as I open it all my instruments'll get wet." The middle-aged coroner wiped rain off his mustache. "I'll check out the body first and make an examination back at the lab."

"Hey, lady. Y'all right back there?"

Mud squished out from under her new hiking boots. "Fine."

"It's not too far now. The clearing should be—hey. Bridger. It's me. Hopper."

Rain poured off the wide brim of the deputy's Smokey-the-Bear hat, and smoke from a cigarette hanging loosely in his lips billowed out like a local fog bank around his face. "Skirt around the edge of the clearing, Sheriff. And watch out for that chuck hole."

Elaine stopped on the perimeter of the clearing. Through the rain and haze she saw tiny red pennants waving in the breeze. "What are all the flags for?"

Bridger tossed the butt to the ground, and stomped on it with the heel of his boot. "Who's she?"

"That goddamn lady reporter." The sheriff shook his head. "Jus' happened to be visitin' when big mouth here came in shoutin' the news."

"Hey! Get away from there."

Elaine jumped back from the pennant just as Bridger shouted, but not because of his command. The head that stared up at her with stark eyes was not attached to anything, and muscles, ligaments, and arteries frilled the jagged neck like stained spaghetti. She promptly turned and vomited into a tangle of sheep laurel and sweet fern.

"Goddamn nosy reporter," the sheriff shouted. "Got whatcha came fer, din't ya?"

While Elaine retched, Bridger pointed out the markers in the clearing. "Near as I can figure, there's two of 'em. I haven't found all the parts, but I got three arms so I know there's more than one. That's the only head. Hell, could be three. Won't know till we take inventory."

"You check out in the brush?"

"Not yet. Waiting for reinforcements. Old Jake here says he come across a foot down the trail a piece. That's what led him in here."

Elaine spat out the last of her breakfast. She staggered uncertainly toward the group, the rain making loud pattering sounds on hat brims and plastic rain gear. She kept her eyes averted from the clearing.

Jake Rudley stood hatless, and wearing the same garb he had had on the other day, along with a denim jacket. He held the rifle barrel down, and close to his body. " 'Lo, Sheriff."

"Jake."

"Can't say I'm pleased to meet ya."

"Same here. Seems like lately ya been stumblin' inta all kindsa trouble."

"Mebbe you oughta make *me* a deppity. If I'm gonna do all yer work fer ya, leastways I oughta get paid fer it."

"Findin' trouble's one thing, fixin' it's another. I'll stake ya if ya think ya can end it."

"Never shoulda begun it."

"Din't have much choice."

"Kinda reminds ya o' seven years ago."

"Kinda does."

"Whatcha gonna do about it?"

"Same thing, I guess. Gotta protect the fokes. We'll git a posse together, comb the woods, see what we kin come up with. If there's something out here, stalkin' people, an' killin', I'll do whatever I hafta ta stop it. Somethin's hungry, an' we either gotta kill it, or feed it."

CHAPTER 7

Elaine nodded to the doorman as she walked through the tiny lobby of the Society Hill Towers, rounded the corner, and absently punched the elevator call button. The doors parted immediately, and Janice Marlton stepped out.

"Hello, babe. Fancy meeting you here."

Elaine's skin pimpled with goose bumps. "I live here, remember?"

"Not much, according to your neglected hubby. Evenings of late you've been running around south Jersey libraries, I hear tell. If you're on to something hot, it isn't Cliff."

Elaine nodded sternly. "Just got back from the office. I filed a story for tomorrow's edition, although I'm not really happy with the way it turned out. I brought home a photocopy so I can retype it."

Janice stepped away from the closing elevator cage, smoothing her print skirt around her flat abdomen. "Babe, I keep telling you, typing is an automatic routine, writing is a cognitive invention. The only relationship between the two is that the purely mechanical process depletes the energy stores available to the cognitive method, and cripples your creativity. Get Jake to buy you a home terminal and a modem, so you can lock into the mainframe by telephone and go over your work without all that useless key punching. Revisions are so much easier, and will leave you that much more time for other things. Like that man up there waiting patiently and breathlessly."

"I'm sure you were willing and able to help him wile away the time."

Janice smirked. "I can only do it for so long. Babe, you know I like you, but he's been talking about you for two hours. It gets boring after a while."

"I'm sure," Elaine said icily.

"Anyway, as long as you're here, let me show you something." Janice fumbled with her briefcase as she clicked across the slate floor on spiked heels and sat in a red lounge chair. "Something I came up with in the archives. Ah, here it is." She pulled out several sheets of paper. "I copied this from the microfilm files. Listen. 'The Jersey Devil can hide in the mud and pull in animals that chance to step on it. It then devours them on the spot, turning the water from a muddy brown to a bloody red froth.' Pretty heady stuff, isn't it?"

"Well, I—"

"I left copies of everything with Cliff, so you can go over it when you have time." Janice snapped her briefcase shut. She swept straight black hair out of her face with a sudden jerk of her head. "I left some pix for you, too. Got some good close-ups of that hunter, but Jake didn't have the balls to print them. Said it was too gory. Well, hell, that's the way life is sometimes."

Elaine softened slightly. "Did you get any of the grave?"

"Couple of shots, nothing spectacular. Funny thing, though. This guy—or gal—there wasn't enough left to tell—not me, anyway—maybe the coroner looked between the legs. Anyway, this guy was wrapped in some kind of robe. A satin material, with strange markings on it like hieroglyphics. Now get this, he had no clothes, but they buried him with a cane—and a broken one, at that. How kooky can you get. Like the guy was going to need it in the afterlife. Well, maybe he wasn't angel material. Anyway, I heard you had a little trouble with the dogs. Maybe you should change your after-shave."

Elaine switched feet, and continued to look down at her nemesis. "Did Cliff tell you about the old geezer?"

"No. He didn't go into much detail. Said it was your biggest story and didn't want to blab any of it away. Don't blame you, babe. But don't think I'm not going to follow it up myself. You take the Jersey Devil angle. I'm covering the hunter death. So, what did you find out from Mr. Big Belly?"

"Plenty." Elaine could not repress a smile as she returned to the elevator lobby and pushed the call button. The cage was still there, and the door opened immediately. "You can read all about it . . . tomorrow."

As soon as the doors closed she burst into gales of laughter. The image of Janice sitting there openmouthed kept her in stitches all the way to the twentieth floor and along the hallway. Still giggling, she fitted her keys first into one lock then into the other, and let herself in.

"Don't tell me. It's the one about the man from Nantucket." Cliff shuffled across the carpet on stockinged feet, and gave Elaine a peck on the forehead. "Did you see Janice? She just left."

"She was hustling, as usual."

Smiling, Cliff took Elaine's jacket and hung it up in the closet. "She's a real workaholic. Said she got wind of some new kind of festival and was off for some infrared film so she could catch the act."

Elaine wiped the smile off her face. "She certainly keeps her little tail in motion, doesn't she?"

"I told her she could stay for steak, but she said she'd get one on the road. She didn't want to hang around waiting for you. Left some material for your article, though."

Elaine plopped down in an overstuffed Victorian chair. "She read me something from an old newspaper clipping."

"*The Public Ledger*. She was rooting for some statistics on pine barrens fatalities and came across it by accident. I reminded her about the seven year cycle of the Jersey Devil, and she said that was curious because she came across something about an increased incidence of fires in the pines that coincided with the death toll. Pineys dying from fires is quite common, apparently, mostly because of poor house construction and lack of electrical inspections."

"What is she, feeling guilty? The other night she taunts me about that hunter's death, now she comes across with all these hot tips. Hey, wait a minute. I'll bet she's throwing me a red herring. She wants me to keep on the Jersey Devil's tail because she's stumbled onto some conspiracy or something. That's it, isn't it?"

Cliff sat opposite her, and spread his hands. "Laine, she didn't say anything like that to me. Why can't you just give her the benefit of the doubt and assume she might be a good person doing it out of friendship?"

"Because I know her motivations are a lot baser. I do *not* like her up here with you. And why is there only one lamp on? What were you two doing in the dark?"

Cliff sighed. "We were enjoying the view. Something you and I don't seem to get around to doing any more. Look out there. Look at all the lights. The river, Penn's Landing, the Ben Franklin bridge, the Moshulu lit up like a Christmas tree, the cruiser *Olympia*, Admiral Dewey's flagship from the Spanish-American War. And there's a full moon, shining down like a white beacon in the sky. What ever happened to the times when we used to make love by moonlight, and talk into the wee hours of the morning? What's happened to our intimacy. God, Laine, sometimes I think I'm sleeping with a stranger."

"Cliff, all that was great when we were kids in college. But we're adults now, with adult jobs and adult responsibilities. And I work so hard and so long I'm not always in the mood."

"Working for what? So you can scoop an old schoolmate of mine?"

"Stop it, Cliff. I don't want to talk about Janice any more. Can you understand that? I'm on to something. I'm really on to something. Something very strange is going on in the pine barrens. Something nobody understands, not even the locals."

Cliff rolled his eyes, and said tiredly, "Don't tell me you've found the Jersey Devil?"

"Cliff, listen to me. This is important."

"It always is. But go ahead."

"I happened to be right in the sheriff's office when his deputy ran in with news of another murder—a double murder. Cliff, this poor boy was scared out of his mind, and still shaking. I soon found out why. I've never seen such carnage. Even in war photos, with soldiers blown up by bombs and booby traps. This was incredible. The bodies were totally dismembered, joint from joint, like they'd been ripped apart by some—I don't know—and scattered over a half acre clearing."

Cliff sat up straight, his muscles tautening. "Jesus Christ, Laine. What the hell did it?"

She shrugged. "Nobody knows. And Cliff, those men were *scared*. I don't mean shocked, by the savagery, by the outrage. I mean terrified right down to the depths of their souls. And they started talking nonsense, saying crazy things I didn't understand. Not the deputies, but the sheriff, and the coroner, and the hermit Jake. As if they'd seen it all before. They—the fear in their faces— And it wasn't just the bodies. It was something supernatural. As if the ground had seethed into those bodies and exploded them to pieces."

"Laine, slow down. You're not making any sense. Was there any sign of a bomb? Shrapnel in the trees, or a crater?"

Elaine shook her head violently, blond curls whipping wildly. "No, nothing like that. It was just— Cliff, the ground was burned. Not the trees, or the grass, but the sand. It was blackened, like coal. Jake pulled up some pogonias, and the roots were singed, and covered with carbon soot. And a groundhog was fried in its hole, to a crisp. It was as if the earth itself didn't want those people there, so it tore them asunder like . . . the wrath of God."

Cliff relaxed, and eased back in his chair. "Sounds like a lightning strike."

"What?" Elaine melted slightly, and some of the fear left her face.

"Sure. Lightning can do that. I suppose." He shrugged. "You see, lightning's caused by positively charged clouds floating over the ground and dragging electrons—which are negative—through the earth until so much potential is built up that the electrons leap into the sky. Usually it discharges from a point, like a tree, or a lightning rod—"

"Oh, my God. There were splinters of wood all over the place. But I just thought—"

"Sure, they could have run for the tree to get out of the rain, and . . . zappo. No more tree, no more people. That's why they tell you to stay away from trees in a thunder storm; in case it gets struck and falls on you. Don't they have lightning in California?"

"It can't get through the smog. Cliff, that all sounds so logical."

He spread his hands. "Sorry."

"I can't believe what I saw today was a natural phenomenon." Elaine shook her head. "It still doesn't add up. There's something going on that doesn't make sense. For one thing, I caught the sheriff in a lie, although I didn't know it at the time. You remember he told Janice in the article that that hunter hadn't fired a shot? Well, today he said that one shot wouldn't have scared off a mountain lion. I think he slipped up, but the only way to be sure is to inspect the gun."

"Did you ask him to?"

"Are you kidding? He doesn't want any part of me. It was only through Janice's intimidation lessons I managed to convince him to take me along today. He told me all the personal effects are locked up at the coroner's office."

"So? Go to the coroner. Maybe he's not so ornery."

She shook her head again. "No, I spoke with him, too. He was there at the scene. I tried to catch him off guard and pump him about the body *we* saw, but he was too smart for me. It was almost as if, well, he knew I was going to ask about it. As if he had a story already prepared."

"Did he say whether or not he was through with the autopsy?"

"You know, he talked in such roundabout circles, I'm not sure. My impression is that either the autopsy results are not in yet, or he hasn't gotten around to doing it. I asked him about torture, and he just laughed. He's a queer duck."

"Laine, he's a piney."

She humphed. "Yes, I guess you're right. None of them respond the way normal people do. They're so *different*."

"Here, take a look at this." Cliff got up and brought a thick manila folder from the dining room table. "We had a board meeting today and, when it was over, I slipped out of the office early. I went to the library and did a little research. I photocopied everything I could find about the good old JD."

"Cliff," she said, taking the package. "There's enough material here to write a book."

"Maybe you should. You're spending enough time on this project, why not expand the article into a best-seller."

"But why did you do this? It must have taken hours."

Cliff scrunched his jaw. "I don't know. Haven't I always been interested in your projects? When you were running that dance school, didn't I work as a stagehand for recitals? And when you were teaching the blind for the school district, didn't I take you and the kids to the zoo, and for walks in the park, and feeling sessions in the woods? And then when you became the director of that aphasia program, didn't I always support you when you had to stay overnight so you could be with those poor people who had no way of communicating with the world except through you? Honey, I may be a big shot lawyer for a multinational corporation, but you've always done *good* things. And never for money. For humanitarian reasons. I've always respected that. I've always loved that quality in you. I guess, it's a capacity I just don't have, and the only way I can ever be a part of this great gestalt we call humanity is through you, through your sensitivity." Cliff shrugged, and reclaimed his seat, legs outstretched. "In effect, I'm buying my way in. But it's the only way I know how."

Elaine squeezed her jaw tight, and pursed her lips. She stretched her legs until they entangled with Cliff's. "I'm sorry I'm so short with you sometimes. It's just that I see you as a success, well-respected in your field. And I want some of that. On my own. I guess I've always been afraid of being bogged down with motherhood and not being able to really accomplish anything, or to be somebody. Somebody important."

"Mothers are very important people to their children. You've got a captive audience. No matter how wrong you are, or how much you screw up, they always look up to you."

Elaine tilted her head. "You know what I mean. I've always been influenced by peer pressure. I want people to look up to me, put me on a pedestal, throw wreaths at my feet."

"I can look up at you if I get on my knees."

She waved her hand at him. "I know. Maybe I just expect too much out of life. I'm racing along thinking I'm going somewhere, when all I'm really doing is keeping up with traffic. I just can't seem to slow down without crashing. And I'm afraid of changing lanes to get to the exit." Her face clouded over. "Maybe I should remind myself of that more often, so the next time I see an exit ramp I have time to put on my turn signals."

Cliff smiled. "You burn up an awful lot of fuel in the race, and it doesn't help your engine any, either. And when you think you're way out in front, all you're really doing is rounding the track and starting over the same route."

Elaine nodded. "Big wheels just travel in bigger circles. Oh, well, analyzing it doesn't really change the way I feel about it." She picked up the sheaf of papers, and flipped through them idly. "Maybe what I really need to do is concentrate on one objective, instead of changing jobs every time it gets too tough for me. Maybe this book idea of yours isn't so farfetched. With all this background—" She swept her hand across the reams of documents. "And I enjoy the fieldwork, even though it's a little frightening at times."

"The most important thing is that you have to define your goals. If they're too hazy, or not well thought out, you'll never accomplish them because you'll never know what they are."

"Cliff, don't you know by now that nebulosity is the focal point of my life?"

He squinted one eye. "Laine, I don't think I quite understand that statement."

Elaine laughed. "That's the point. You're not supposed to. So, I hereby set my goal to cover this Jersey Devil story as thoroughly as possible, all the way to the end, no matter what. Now, where's the stuff Janice left for me?"

Cliff pointed to the marble-topped end table. "Right there next to you."

She reached for the pile. "The pictures, too?"

"Underneath." Cliff slid off the chair and sat on the floor in the narrow cone of light. "I just hope you don't mind her clinical approach. Her pictures are quite graphic."

Elaine slid down next to him, leaning her body up against his. "Yes, I see what you mean. God, this is disgusting. I can't believe she used a macro lens to get close-ups of these remains. Poor Sam must have puked into the developer."

"At least in black-and-white you can't see the blood. But forget the tattered flesh. That probably *was* done by a hungry wolf or—"

"There aren't any wolves in the pine barrens."

"All right, then, a ferret. Or maybe those wild dogs that run around in packs. They're in the barrens, aren't they?"

"Don't be funny."

"Anyway, Janice was pointing out the bones. See the nicks? See the white indentations?"

"So?"

"Well, Janice said that if those are old . . . that is, if they happened when the person died, an autopsy would show it."

"Like if it was a chain saw tooth."

"Right. Exactly. But, if it's recent, like, if they were the result of some animal gnawing on the bones, they would be whiter in appearance, untarnished by chemicals in the soil. Not only that, if you get a good forensic doctor, or maybe a veterinarian, he could tell what kind of tooth made the marks. So, there's a way of finding out whether it's a wolf, or a dog, or a bobcat, or—"

"The Jersey Devil."

Cliff nodded slowly, and looked deeply into Elaine's cobalt blue eyes, so alive with excitement. "Or human."

CHAPTER 8

"Ma'am, I'm telling you I don't know. He's the boss. He can take off whenever he wants."

"But doesn't he leave word where he's going, a forwarding number where he can be reached?"

"Sometimes he does, sometimes he don't. Tonight he didn't." Deputy Bridger held out his hands and shook his head. "He don't tell me all his business."

"All right, all right. Wait a minute." Janice perched her backside on the desk. She leaned forward and fluttered her carefully stroked eyelashes at the policeman. She placed her hand on his, and delicately raked her long nails over his flesh. She felt the goose bumps rise. "When I was here yesterday, I overheard him say something about a feast, a cookout. With costumes. Tonight. Now, what does that mean to you?"

Bridger pulled his hand away and shoved back his chair. Baby blue eyes stared down at the pile of police forms as he loosened his black necktie. "Ma'am, I-I'm not tryin'— I'm not tryin' to keep anything from you. It's just I don't know. *He* makes up the work schedule. I just come in when he tells me." He pushed his hands absently through the pile of paperwork. "Look, I can give you his home phone—"

"I already called. The babysitter said they left at ten o'clock. Now where would they go that late at night?"

Bridger still did not look at her. He shook his head

slowly. "I don't know. He's got lots of friends. Sometimes they go to Atlantic City to catch a show, do a little gambling. You know. Maybe they went to a beach party. Or a masquerade ball. I don't know. There ain't much to do around here."

"I can see that." Janice pulled one leg higher up on the desk, made sure her tight fitting skirt slid up and exposed her thigh right to the bend of her hip. "But, maybe you and I can find something to do. Of course, I'm on assignment at the moment. But after I get my story—"

The blond-haired man gulped audibly. "Look, ma'am, I gotta be at this desk all night. If I get caught foolin' around on duty, the sheriff'd have my ass in a sling. On night shift there's only two of us holding down the fort, and—"

Janice picked up the deputy's hand and placed it on her leg. She pushed it up and down her clear pantyhose. Despite her purpose, she felt a tingling in her groin that was not part of her professional act. "I like men in uniform . . . or out of them. And that phone hasn't rung since I've been here. This isn't exactly the busiest county in the state."

"But Hopper's out on patrol, and due to check in any— "

"Hopper's a boy. You're a man. Aren't you?"

"Ma'am, I—"

"And single? I don't see any ring on your finger." Janice bent down and nibbled on his ear.

Bridger recoiled as if he had been branded with a hot iron. His face was flushed, but the front of his trousers bulged ominously. A dark stain, little more than a drop, soaked through the beige material. He placed his hands strategically on his lap.

"Now, that's no way to treat a lady of the press. Why, I'd almost think you weren't as sophisticated as you appear. You've done this before, haven't you?"

The deputy jumped to his feet and backed against the filing cabinet. He held one hand out in front of him. "Ma'am, I'm on *duty*."

"Is that your only excuse?"

He gulped. His eyes darted from side to side like a caged

animal. "Ma'am, it just ain't right for you to come in here an' tease me—"

"I'm not teasing. I always deliver what I promise." Janice slid off the desk top. She swung around in one easy motion and sidled up in front of him. "Now, you think back and tell me what you remember hearing from old Captain Corpulent."

"Who?"

"Mr. Obesity. The mirthful girth. The man with more chins than a Chinese phone book." She cocked an eye at him. "Sheriff Hinkle?"

"Oh . . ."

She flattened her body against him, felt his hardness against her firm abdomen. His elbows slammed back against metal, but there was no place for him to go.

Janice looked up into his face. "He must have said something. Yesterday he mentioned a carnival, and something with an open fire, like a barbecue. He was in the other room, and didn't know I was listening through the glass. Some of the words were muffled, but the gist of it was some kind of nighttime party."

Bridger licked his lips with quick, darting motions of his tongue. "They have revival meetin's at the church. Sing songs, an' all that. I don't belong. It's a pretty small congregation, an' they don't let in no outsiders. Not even me, 'cause I was born two counties away. Maybe it's a christening, or a baptism, or whatever they call it in their—"

"Where's the church?"

"Ma'am, you don't want to go out there."

Janice stopped rotating her hips against his, and backed away. She ran her hand up his leg and into his crotch, rubbed his organ along its length. "Where is it?"

Bridger closed his eyes tightly. Janice had made it impossible for him to retreat. "It's not a church, really, not like—"

She squeezed hard. "Where?"

His words came in gasps. "In the pines. Past the Nature

Center. The dirt road . . . with the red can . . . on the oak tree."

Janice smiled. She was enjoying this. She wanted to take his penis inside her, to feel his hardness, to luxuriate in the fulfilling sensations, to share his orgasm. But despite her longings, first and foremost she was a reporter. And her job always came before she did.

Beads of perspiration formed on Bridger's wrinkled brow, on his quivering upper lip. His eyeballs bounced back and forth behind clenched lids. She gripped him with her fingers, worked her hand up and down. He took a sudden deep breath, held it interminably, then let it out in short, staccato bursts. Janice did not let go until she felt him go soft.

"You don't know how much I hate to leave, but I've got bigger things in the wind." She scooped her purse off the desk and slung it over her shoulder. "But I want something long and hard between my legs, so if nothing better turns up maybe I'll stop by later."

Janice sauntered out of the dimly lit building, along the cement path to the parking lot, and climbed into a fire-engine red Corvette. Gravel spit out from behind broad racing slicks as she laid rubber and spun smoothly out onto the road.

It was several miles to the Nature Center, but speeding along at seventy-five shortened the trip to only a few minutes. The huge Wharton Tract on her left was a dark, forboding forest which was tenanted only by pineys under a grandfather clause. No one could move in there. When she passed the entrance to the Nature Center, she slowed down to fifty. In the cone of light from the headlamps, every void between the thickly needled pine trees looked like a driveway. She turned the sports car from side to side, illuminating each dark corner. She saw nothing but brush.

It was nearly midnight, and the back country road was completely deserted and devoid of light. Even the widely spaced clapboard houses along the way were darkened. *People must turn in early around here.*

A strobelike flash sparkled momentarily. Janice cut the

wheel and swept the front of the car toward the gleam of light. A metallic glint reflected back. The stout oak tree towered above the stunted pines. A flattened coffee can was nailed to the craggy, bumpy bark. She cruised past the dirt trail and kept going until she located a siding large enough to hide the radiant red Corvette from passersby.

The night air was crisp, with just enough bite to make her breath condense into quickly dispersed white puffs. Janice knew she would warm up with any amount of exercise, so she shrugged off her pink sweater and tossed it in the backseat.

"Oh, no, I'm not breaking another heel." She removed her shoes as well, then her pantyhose with the damp crotch pad. "Ah, maybe later."

She carried only her camera, an extra roll of infrared film tucked into the middle of her brassiere, and a penlight clipped to her blouse. She walked back along the sandy shoulder; the tiny granules felt cool under her feet.

As she turned into the unpaved road she noticed the deep ruts and high center scraped clean of grass. The sports car's low suspension could never have made it through unless she straddled the ruts with her wheels. She was glad she had come on foot.

Fine, damp sand squirted through her toes. It was like a walk on the beach, without sharpened seashells to contend with. Needled branches arched overhead with a tunnellike effect, making the road even darker than the overcast sky allowed. Oddly, there were no insect noises, just a preternatural silence that echoed the crunching of her footsteps.

Her ears perked up. At first, the droning ahead sounded like the wind whistling through the trees. It was soft and sibilant. But as she got deeper into the woods she detected a cadence, and the deeper, basser pitch of male voices. The cold forgotten, she hurried along full of anticipation.

The road opened out into a broad clearing. Trucks and cars of various descriptions, most of them old, were parked haphazardly in front of a decrepit building that was not a church, but a ramshackle, two-story wooden barn. The loft had two doors, both open, out of which poured a suffused yellow glow that wavered strangely. Light seeped from under the eaves, like a fringe of blond hair, and trickled through loose, vertical joints.

The tall double doors creaked open.

Janice slunk back out of sight. She cringed in the brush with only her face and lens poking through the broad leaves. She offset the focus to adjust for the bent rays of infrared. The barn now looked like a gargantuan jack-o'-lantern: the upper doors were the eyes, the main entrance a huge, gaping maw. Melted pumpkin oozed out the opening like a bloody tongue.

Janice had to blink twice before she could make sense out of what she was seeing. A procession of red-robed people walking in pairs, and holding aloft seven armed candelabras shaped like tapered pitchforks, streamed out of the barn with the slow deliberation of their chanting. Excitedly, she steadied the camera against a branch and snapped off several frames with the special, low light film. The photographic effect would be even more garish than the way it appeared.

Four robed men marched solemnly out of the barn, carrying a rough-hewn freight pallet by the corners. On the sacrificial bier lay a bulky effigy covered in red satin. Janice clicked away coolly, the motor drive advancing the film, until she noticed movement and heard the whimpering. Whoever, or whatever, was strapped to the wooden stretcher was still alive.

This was no funeral, nor baptism either. The symbolic candelabras, the sweeping robes with their calligraphic adornment, the ritualistic requiem, the sacrificial offering, reminded Janice more of a heretical inquisition, or a witch burning. The shiver that ran along her spine did not prevent her from carefully recording the event on the heat sensitive film.

At least two scores of torch bearers attended the pageant, the dancing flames leaping several feet into the air. Janice smiled kerosene. Then came the drummers, beating their tom-toms with a harsh staccato rhythm.

Slowly, the men and women filed onto the trail. They

marched deeper into the forest, singing their canticles to the trees with upraised chins and lilting voices. The lower limbs of the pines were illuminated by the undulating, golden flames.

When the last of the robed pagans entered the tree-lined road, Janice climbed from her bushy cubbyhole and dashed across the clearing to the barn entrance. The inside was black as pitch, still as death. She cupped her hand around the penlight and played its narrow beam around the straw filled room. It might have been abandoned in the last century.

Rotted traces hung on the walls, rusted farm tools leaned against a stack of pallets, a cracked leather saddle lay on the hardened dirt floor. The half loft had broken away, and boards and splinters covered one side of the interior. A partially opened trunk, mildewed with age, sat in a corner. Janice played her light under the peeling lid.

More robes were inside, half a dozen at least. Janice raised the lid and pulled one out. It was not the least bit soiled, almost as if it had been wrapped in plastic to keep off the sawdust. She studied the strange symbols embroidered across the back. They meant nothing to her, but she knew someone who might be able to decipher them. She wrapped the material around her waist, knotted in front.

What a story!

As she eased the lid closed she caught a glimpse of cigar boxes in the corner. She took one out, and studied it under the fine light. The paper label was faded, the cardboard warped, the tape holding on the lid cracked and split. It held an array of cosmetic sundries, mostly tiny jars containing pigmented makeup. She tucked the box under her arm while she unscrewed one of the metal tops and held the open jar to her upturned nose. The odor was strangely familiar, and oddly euphoric. She stuck several different colors into the pocket of her skirt for later analysis. She put back the cigar box and closed the trunk lid.

She flicked off the light and ran outside. She thought she had lost the mystic coven, for the rhythmic psalms had been swallowed up by the forest, and the torch light by bends in the trail. Janice ran after them.

She yelped once or twice as her bare feet stepped on barbed twigs or broken pinecones. But before long she heard them again, ahead and to her right. She stayed on the trail until it came to a T, and followed the chanting. Soon she saw the whole group gathered in a broad, grass-filled meadow. Flickering lights reflected down from the low cloud cover.

Mumbling repetitive vespers, the congregation set down their torches and candelabras and went about a series of prearranged tasks. Seven small fires were started in a circle around a log held up by two A-frames. The pallet was placed in the center of the ring, next to one of the crossed uprights. Robes were opened in front to expose breasts and genitals. One woman walked round and round, scattering sacrificial powder in the flames. The people took up stations around the perimeter of fires, facing outward, bending over to expose their rears to the middle of the field, as if praying in reverse. They got down on their hands and knees, chanting.

As the outer ring faced her, Janice saw that all of them, men and women alike, had smeared their faces with bold, variegated colors, like war paint. Blue smears ran down from the eyes, across the cheeks, and over the jaws onto yellowed necks. Green splotches alternated with the blue streaks. The bridge of each nose was rouged; the deep crimson vaulted upward between purplish, spear-pointed eyebrows, then fanned into a pitchfork shape on the forehead.

The smoke filling the air possessed an exotically pungent odor, enough to blur Janice's vision—or was it blurring her mind? The entire episode thrilled her more than she could understand. And any fear she had, dissolved when she heard a bark and discovered that the living shape on the pallet was a large Saint Bernard. Several women pulled the robe off its hairy body and went through an exaggerated petting motion. A smoking pillow held under its nose had a calming effect, and it soon stopped whimpering.

Something was happening. The air seemed to be thrumming, not so much with sound but with a hammering against her eardrums: a low, vibrant, ululation. The clouds whipped around in a slow, anticyclonic motion. Taunting, misty, miasmic tendrils rose from the ground, a vaporous heat that flushed over her like a soporific. Had her senses gone awry?

As Janice crouched on the ground she felt something caress her buttocks, massage her inner thigh. The unappeased tingling she had felt for Deputy Bridger returned with a vengeance. She craved more than the coarse stump she was rubbing against. Her body was bathed in sweat.

She could stand the searing fervor no more. She threw down the camera, unknotted the robe, and wriggled out of her blouse, bra, and skirt. She luxuriated in the cool breeze that played over her, that palpated her skin like delicate feathers. Without knowing why, she slipped on the robe. The silky touch was like the embrace of a man's skin.

Now the men rose from the circle. They approached the posturing women and knelt behind them like dogs in heat, pumping their hips. They stayed only a moment, then moved on in an adult version of musical chairs. Janice could not watch the sybaritic ceremony without feeling pangs of emptiness in her loins. Her passion throbbed for release, but she was unable to achieve it. She was jealous of those women, some of them *old* women. She could imagine what they were enjoying with their men kneading them from behind with stiffened members invading so sweetly.

Hastily, she retrieved the cosmetic jars from the pockets of her discarded skirt. She rubbed on enough paint to cover her face. Then she crawled into the open on hands and knees, breasts swinging like bloated pendulums. None of the cabal seemed to be aware of her: they were all caught up in the reverie of their ritual. The chanting droned on, the petting of the dog continued. The smoke continued to rise and drift, distorting her consciousness. The earth trembled more than ever, and the air beat against her with the thundering force of the backwash of a jet engine.

Janice backed into the circle of crouching women. She

bared her buttocks. A moment later someone stooped
behind her, grabbed her hips crudely, and pressed against
her. *My God, he's soft!* After a minute of ritualistic
stroking, he moved on, and another took his place. *Please
be young and virile.*

He was as limp as the first. Worse, his skin was rough
and coarse. He merely chanted in some foreign, unrecognizable tongue, then got up and replaced the man to his
right. The third man did not even touch her. He genuflected
and repeated the liturgy, and moved on with the tide.

Janice glanced from side to side. She noticed that women
periodically got up and passed through the fires to take over
the job of petting the Saint Bernard. After the fourth
impotent male barely brushed up behind her, she got up to
join the women in the inner circle.

As she knelt down by the dog another woman got up and
retreated to the outer perimeter. Janice slid into her place
and mimicked the actions of the others, taking handfuls of
scented oil from a brass urn and coating the dog's shaggy
hair. As she did, she got a better whiff of the smoking
pillow: the white powder being squeezed out of it was more
than stuffing.

Images flashed through her mind as in an accelerated
movie montage. Disconnected erotic visions heightened her
state of arousal. She was swept up by the charade. This dog
was here as a sacrificial scapegoat for a bunch of pseu-
dosexual satanists with delusions of seduction, and there
was not a functioning gonad among them.

Janice was dripping with excitement. She took some of
the oil and spread it over her own body, over her breasts,
between her legs.

"Hey, doncha know the words?"

She woke up as if from a dream. The other women
looked at her with glazed eyes, and kept repeating the
foreign litany.

"Hey, who *are* you?"

A man stood over her, a tall man wearing a doctor's mask
over his mouth and nose. Dark, pinched eyes peered down.

"I'm . . . I'm . . . I'm . . . " If she knew what she

had to say, her mind was too muddled to transmit the message. She saw nothing but the man's sagging genitals through the untied front of his robe. She saw despair. "Can't anybody here satisfy me?"

"What the hell's *she* doin' here?"

Janice thought she recognized the second voice, but could not force an image from her memory. She had never felt such intense arousal. "Isn't there a single hard-on in this bunch?"

The fatter man bent over, face masked with white cloth. He looked as fuzzy as the other. "Lady, you want a hard-on, I got one here like you ain't never had before. Git that robe off her."

The old woman to her left carefully removed the satin garb. The young girl to her right placed an arm over Janice's shoulder and rolled her sideways. The ground vibrated against her back, tingling her skin ecstatically. The sky was filled with rushing, swirling clouds, spinning around like a gigantic, inverted oil slick.

Nails raked along her body: not hard enough to hurt, but more than enough to please. She tingled all over with excitement. She felt the coolness of scented oil being poured on her skin. She pitied the poor Saint Bernard, whose place she had taken. But she was going to enjoy this to the fullest.

The pillow puffed in her face. She seemed to float right off the ground, to be moving through the air. As she hovered, nails continued to rake, strong hands rubbed and massaged her muscles. She whimpered in anticipation.

Something hard pressed against her pubis. Her eyes fluttered open. A giant, misty face grimaced down at her, seemingly from the sky. It had no features, it had no substance. But it was real. She could smell the hot breath of lust. She could feel the cool, clammy body against hers.

It nudged her, teasing, and retreated. She rocked her hips to find it, to capture it. It came back, touching, exploring, entering. It felt so good, so delicious. She worked it in with her muscles. She could not believe the hardness, the size, the length. It was too good to be true. It came in deeper than anything she had ever felt before. It brought with it waves of passion that went on endlessly.

Then it was hurting her, coming in too far. She could not stop it. She forced her legs together, she clamped tight. But it kept coming in. What at first was exquisite pleasure slowly became horrible, searing pain. It threatened to tear her apart.

"Stop. Oh, stop."

But it did not stop. It kept coming . . . and coming.

And coming.

INTERLUDE 2

It was attracted like a moth to the flames.

It remembered the night before, the rabbit on a stick, the two people by the camp fire, the paltry offering, the sacrifice that was already dead, the suffering it had to inflict, the lesson it had to teach.

If they thought they could cheat again, to change the ritual, it was prepared to make them pay. Anger built up inside its calcareous breast, pumped its muscles with power, flushed its thwarted brain with tormented images, filled its groin with impotent lust.

It returned once again to the sacred spot—to watch, to feel, to enjoy, to feed on the psychic energy released by fear, by pain, by the ultimate transformation from life to unlife.

They were there. Not just two lonely campers, but the whole tribe. Red, cryptic robes billowed over naked bodies; multicolored splashes covered aged, timeworn faces; half-lidded eyes gazed in somnambulant dread; torches were held aloft in upthrust hands; cracked, unsure voices chanted the ancient songs in somber cadence.

The sacrifice was ready. It heard the screams. It drank in the fear, the anticipated terror. This was what it needed before it could feed, the aperitif to whet its appetite. Now it would not have to kill. Now it could luxuriate in the ritualistic fervor, its inner being fueled, intoxicated, by fanatic turmoil.

Aroused, it drifted close.

Its body flowed through the soil, through the grass and brush and trees. Each blade was a sensor, each leaf an observer. The earth sucked in emotion like a sponge absorbing water. The shrieks of torture were music to its ears, animation for its heart; wanton, voluptuous release.

Still living, still throbbing, they lashed down the offering, boomed incantations, swung the flaming torches. The creature was pierced, slowly, gently, so as to keep the body intact and unruptured, to make last the draining of the life-force. Greedily, it spread phantasmal tendrils, to absorb the vital spark like a flower collects the rays of the sun.

They swung the sacrificial creature high into the air on a shaved sapling that only recently had been part of the forest. The animal writhed like a puppet gone crazy, screeching madly.

It consumed the agony with passion, it devoured every vestige of life with frenzied zeal. It sucked the creature dry until nothing of its spirit was left but an inner shell, an empty husk. And in return it released its own passion, felt its groin burst, left a track of liquid waste that covered the shrubbery, that filtered through the soil like paste.

The creature danced above the flames, weaker now, and weaker, slipping closer to the earth, until it sagged like a limp, broken doll, unmoving. It had nothing more to offer, its body and soul were sucked dry. The incantations faded, the torches lit the base of the brand, let the flames lick upward, scorching the flesh just enough to char it black. The pole snapped, the creature fell to the earth, inert.

It had had its fill. It pulled back from the ground, the grass, the brush, the trees. It reformed slimy ectoplasm into a hulking shape, out of sight of the fires, away from the scene of anguish.

It slunk off into the pines, sated with the gore of death.

CHAPTER 9

"Yer a pretty brave gal ta come out here agin, after them dogs chased ya down."

Elaine downshifted as they neared a water-filled washout in the middle of the trail. She laughed. "This time I'm armed. At my husband's insistence. Not that it'll do me much good. The last time I fired this cannon it almost tore my shoulder off."

Jake cradled his own weapon in the crook of his arm, with the barrel pointing out the open window. "I don't never walk in the pines less I got ma piece with me. Never know what chu might run inta."

"The Jersey Devil, perhaps?"

Jake humphed. "Ain't no man-made weapon gonna bother the likes o' it. Nor incantations, neither."

"You mean, like from the worshipers?"

Jake rubbed a gnarly finger along his bulbous, veined nose. "Blasted fools think singin' hallelujahs is gonna chase away evil spirits, like the Dark Ages. This here's modern times, an' the Jersey Devil ain't nobody's fool. Besides that, it ain't no spirit."

Water splashed under the floorboards, and the Jeep slewed sideways until it bounded up the other side of the puddle. Elaine spun the wheel and centered the vehicle on the narrow dirt tract. "Then what is it?"

Jake swiped at a dragonfly and shooed it out the window.
"It's the earth."

Elaine glanced away from the road for a moment. "What
do you mean by that?"

"I mean its mother is the soil, its father is the pines. Oh,
it was human once, born o' man an' woman. But that was
a long time ago, 'fore there was settlers in this here land.
Back when this was a real wilderness, an' the critters ruled
the barrens. It was what you call a mut . . . a mute . . ."

"Mutant?"

"Yeah, a mutant. I don't know much 'bout genes, 'cept
the kind ya wear, but somethin' sure went wrong in its
mama or papa. Maybe both. Slow down a mite, miss."

Elaine took her foot off the gas pedal and touched the
brake. "You think it was a mutation, then?"

"Well, it sure as hell ain't normal. Near as I kin figger—
Here it is. Turn onta this ole wagon trail. An' keep it down,
or you'll tear the springs right outa the brackets. Anyhow,
I been hearin' 'bout the Jersey Devil all ma life: facts an'
figgers an sightin's. Even tracked the blasted thing ma own
self. Ten mile it went, right through the swamp, inta the
cranberry bogs. I'd pick out a straight line, go ta the other
side o' the bog, an' sure 'nough there was its trail comin'
out agin. Don't know if it swum, or walked across the
bottom."

The Jeep pitched and yawed on the hardened, uneven
trail. Elaine put the transmission into low gear and crept
along at a snail's pace. "Was there ooze in the tracks, that
it might have brought up from the bottom of the bogs?"

"I been trackin' critters in these here woods since I was
a boy, so I know whatcher gettin' at. But there ain't nothin'
ever clung to the Jersey Devil's feet. Like it floats over the
ground, never crackin' no sticks or breakin' no twigs. But
it leaves a funny print jus' the same, almos' like it was burnt
inta the ground. Kinda clubbed in the sole, but splayed like
a wild turkey. An' heavy enough to come from a elephant."

"Where'd it lead you?"

Jake humphed. "Not to its lair. Usu'lly, I had to give up
'cause o' dark. Mosta the time it jus' disappeared in the

bullbriars where I couldn't git through, or was swallered up by spragnum. Moss jus' jumps back up like a coil spring. Once, I picked up the trail fust thin' in the mornin'. Follered it all day till jus' before sundown, when ever'thin' started lookin' familiar. Turns out it was leadin' me in a big circle. Never did see where it got off."

"Do you think it knew?"

"Course it knew. It knows ever'thin' that goes on in the pines. It *is* the pines."

"Think it knows we're looking for it?"

"I reckon it knows. It jus' don't care. Got more important things on its mind."

"Like?"

"Food. It's gotta eat. That's why it comes out ever' seven years, to quench its thirst for blood an' fill its empty craw. I ain't never writ anythin' down, but I remember ever' word that's ever been said 'bout the Jersey Devil." The old man tapped his temple with a bent forefinger. "I done put all the pieces together, like in a jigsaw puzzle. Some o' the stories come handed down from ole Injun legends. Got translated inta English 'long the way, like our fokes invented the Jersey Devil. But it goes way back.

"The way I figger, it come from normal parents, but was disfiggered when it fust stuck its ugly head inta the world. Instead o' cryin', like normal babies, it let out a squeal that scared its mama inta catatonia. The little devil natchrally started suckin' its mama's breast. Got milk, but no response. No holdin', or cuddlin', or cooin'. Well, its mama din't never recover, an' jus' laid there till she was sucked dry.

"The kid had powers. It was different, an' could do things no human bein' could do. It crawled away, like a caterpillar, over the ground. An' it learned to survive. It learned things 'bout the earth no mortal never did learn. The pine barrens become its foster parents, an' it drew its strength right from the soil. Eventually, it *became* the earth. Now, it lives in the ground—all aroun' us an' under our feet an' in the bark o' the trees. Like the bushes are its ears, the trees its eyes, the ground its nose. It's only the stomach that wanders, only the soul, lookin' for food, lookin' for death, lookin' for the mama it never had."

Elaine fought the wheels out of a rut. "And you say it can only get its energy, its sustenance, from meat that's already dead and decayed?"

"It ain't alive, so it can't digest what is. No, ma'am, it's on a diff'rent plane. It ain't animal or vegetable. It's somethin' all its own. A mindless wanderin' hunger that thrives on the once livin'. It ain't ta blame, it jus' don't know no better. It's a poor, deranged soul lookin' for salvation . . . an' findin' an eternity o' deathless animation."

Jake fell silent, and Elaine sensed a reverence which her propriety would not allow her to break. With deep significance she took the tape recorder off the dashboard, switched it off, and slipped it into her jacket pocket. She kept the Jeep moving at an easy five-miles-per-hour pace over the pot-holed path, and drove on for another mile in awkward silence.

This was not a dense swamp, but an open swath of pine trees with sandy soil and great stretches of visibility. The trees were spaced airily, and the scent of pine filled the air as thickly as the needles covered the ground. White clouds fluffed the gray sky like cotton balls, not reducing brightness but alleviating harsh shadow. With a practiced eye Elaine estimated she could still shoot ASA 64 at F8 or F11.

"Why'n chu park here an' we'll walk the rest o' the way?"

Elaine eased the Jeep into the weeds, switched off the engine, put on the parking brake. She reached over the backseat for her gadget bag and stuck her hand into a mangled mess of sinew and stiff hair. She jumped sharply with a sudden intake of air. Still bugeyed, she glanced at Jake. "Sorry. I forgot about the dogs."

"What's left of 'em, ya mean." He handed her the camera and gadget bag, and readjusted the worn plaid blanket. "Better keep 'em covered or they'll be full o' maggots 'fore you get 'em home. Or wherever you're takin' em."

Elaine turned the recorder back on, and slung the various equipment straps over her head. "I don't know that, myself. All I know is the coroner is being very secretive about the autopsy reports, and won't let me have an outside, independent examination performed. I think I'm going to have to pay his office a sneak visit, catch him off guard. I want to know what kind of animal was feasting on these mongrels."

"Prob'ly jus' rats or field mice. Could be a coon or cat. They'll eat carrion if they git hungry enough."

"I wonder if the Jersey Devil eats road kill." Elaine slid out from behind the wheel and readjusted the array of gear hanging from her neck.

Jake got out of the passenger seat, clutching his rifle. "Don't pay ta joke about it. The trees got ears."

"I thought the bushes were the ears, and the trees the eyes."

Jake tugged his dirty coveralls, his heavily lined face reflecting his consternation. He lowered his voice an octave, coming across like an Evangelist preacher. "Don't treat its name in vain. It'll hear, an' it'll come. An' you'll beg forgiveness at the sight o' it."

Elaine realized she had offended the dour hermit. "Jake, I'm sorry. It's just that . . . well, I guess I'm a little uneasy, and the humor helps take the chill off. My, but it's beautiful here." She strolled through the pine barrens understory, camera clicking.

Jake followed her like a faithful dog, rifle poised. "Got some juniper trees yonder. An' scarlet oaks." His experienced eyes picked out flora better than any trained botanist. "That's a yellow-crested orchid; that's Loesel's twayblade; an' that's helleborine. Now that, that's candy root." He plucked the tiny plant and shook off the dirt. "Tastes like peppermint candy."

Elaine took the proffered piece, and sucked on it gently. "Hey, you're right. And, don't tell me, that's dogbane."

"And right next to it's foxtail moss."

"And goldcrest. Did you know that its nearest relative is clear around the world, in Australia?"

"Right smart gal, ain'tchu? What's this little feller?"

"Hmmn." Elaine studied it though her macro lens, moved Jake's hand so she could get a better shot of it. "Rattlesnake fern?"

"Close. Ebony spleenwort. Don't grow in the barrens of its own accord. Too much acid in the soil. Butcha find it 'round old buildin's an' town sites."

"Was there an outpost here?"

"Usta be, 'bout a hunert years ago. T'was a stagecoach stop, the only place ta ford the crick for ten miles in either direction."

"Oh, yes, I've read about the old wagon routes. I've done a lot of research on south Jersey. Oh, look. Indian shoe-string." Elaine was quickly out of film, and changed rolls with professional speed as she walked. "Did you know that eighty-four kinds of birds breed in the pine barrens? Look, there's a white-breasted nuthatch. And a cedar waxwing. I can hear a warbler, but I don't know what kind. And I think— "

She stopped short, for Jake had raised his rifle with one long arm, and held it at half-mast. She saw the cleared area, the pile of cinders, the thick log stripped of its bark and held horizontally off the ground by two lashed A-frames. Viscous, milky puddles filled in shallow depressions.

"Jake, what's this goo in the water?"

He thrust out his left arm, and stopped her in mid stride as if she were a play doll. "Wait." He spoke calmly, but with absolute authority.

Elaine's skin tingled where it touched the old man's flaky epidermis. The tingling was contagious, and spread to every part of her body. She felt her scalp rise, and the hair move. Her eyes darted over several fire pits, but she detected nothing out of the ordinary. "What is it?" Her voice was a hoarse whisper.

Jake's eyes moved with robotic intensity, scanning the site. "It's been here. *They've* been here."

Some of the strain passed from Elaine's taut muscles. "Isn't that why we came? Didn't you want to show me—"

"I mean lately." Slowly, so slowly it hurt Elaine to

watch, Jake bent his knees, aged cartilage creaking, and stretched out a hand that was rock steady. A long time later he was crouching, extended fingers touching the charred logs. He placed his hand flat over the remnants of a fire. His broad chest barely moved inside his faded flannel shirt. "Last night."

"You mean, you can tell?"

"Last night. They were here last night. These coals're still warm."

"Now, wait just a minute. *Who* was here last night?"

"*They* were. The cult. They made another sacrifice."

Elaine was haughty. "You can tell all that by a few old cinders?"

Jake maintained his half crouch. "I seen it before." His hand came away with a splinter of wood. He gave it to Elaine. "See the red?"

She took it, and held it up high as she viewed the sliver from all angles. "Blood?"

Jake nodded seriously.

"You know, there's probably a logical explanation for everything." She wrapped the specimen in a sheet of lens tissue and tucked it in her gadget bag. "Cliff told me how lightning could have caused that . . . that tragedy . . . yesterday. A freakish accident."

"Weren't no accident. Neither's this. That was the work o' the Jersey Devil. This's the work o' the cult. Don't know which one's worse."

"Well, even if they did slaughter another sheep, it's nothing worse than a pig roast, or a clambake."

"The victims are sacrificed alive."

"So are lobsters and sushi. Look, how do you know it wasn't just some backpackers barbecuing a couple of burgers?"

Jake rose and stepped back from the fire pit in one fluid motion. "We gotta get outa here."

"Jake," she whined. "Stop being mysterious. I don't see anything here out of the ordinary. My God, this is a splendid spot for a campsite, surrounded by fresh green trees and blossoming flowers. There are plenty of pine needles for ground cover, an open view of the stars, running water nearby. What more could a camper want?"

Jake cocked his rifle and walked away, toward the Jeep. "I seen it all before."

Elaine ran after him, pleading. "Jake, you're not being reasonable."

"I'm leavin'. You comin' or ain'tchu?"

"Jake . . ."

"It ain't safe here. They might be comin' back to bury the body, after they done their ritualizin'."

"Who are *they*? Who belongs to this Jersey Devil cult?"

The old hermit quickened his pace. "Don't know. Don't wanna know."

"So what are they trying to do? Kill the Jersey Devil?"

"It can't die. It ain't never *gonna* die. They're only kiddin' themselves by feedin' its depravity." Jake tramped right on past the parked Jeep, and continued on down the narrow trail. "Oughta jus' leave it the hell alone. It kin fend for itself."

"Jake . . ."

He never turned around. "Leave here 'fore dark. Mark ma word."

"But I wanted to climb the fire tower. Get an aerial view."

He was almost out of earshot. "Ya got the map."

"I thought you weren't afraid of them?" She slammed her fist on the fender of the Jeep, and watched him go out of sight. Then she shouted, *"Coward!"*

The soft, sibilant rustle of wind through the trees was the only reply.

"Damn."

Elaine grabbed the topographic map from between the seats and unfolded it on the still-warm hood, ripping the paper in the process. She found the road they had come in on, and highlighted it with a yellow marker that stood out boldly on the green overlay. The turnoff was drawn as a dashed line, denoting a four-wheel drive trail. Then she took her red pen and made a big *X* where the map showed her to be standing. It was approximately equidistant from the other three *X*s marking the sites of the recent atrocities.

A shadow suddenly fell across the map. It was her own, and she saw that the clouds were breaking up and the sun coming out. Now the glade was even more charming than before. She stuffed the map through the window and walked about with her camera, taking pictures, keeping her new boots out of the puddles of white slime scattered throughout the clearing.

Golden shafts of light beamed through the pines, back-lighting the needles like a starburst. She put a cross-screen filter on the fifty millimeter to get a diagonal four-point effect from the sun. Then she ambled about shooting flowers with the macro. Bright yellow honeybees buzzed around the orchids, landing on the delicate petals while they lapped up nectar with extended, hairlike tongues. Flies darted past incessantly and large beetles droned by like B-52s. She captured all the sounds on her hand-sized tape recorder.

The western horizon melted into streaks of red as the sun dodged behind dissipating clouds. It was going to be a clear night. Elaine took several pictures of the glade with the wide-angle lens, then sat down with her back against a pine, to enjoy the spectacle of sunset. She placed her equipment next to her and every couple minutes picked up the camera for a shot with the sun in a different position.

She sat perfectly still, except when she had to swat a mosquito. Bluejays cawed raucously in the treetops. A robin strutted across the ground in its eternal search for worms. A nighthawk swooped through the clearing on an errant mission, and somewhere distant Elaine heard the tapping of a woodpecker.

Venus appeared, bright and twinkling. Elaine shivered with a slight chill, not just from the cold. In the gathering darkness what had appeared scenic by day was quickly becoming portentous. She tried to shrug it off as the result of suggestion, of Jake's renunciation of justified reality for his backwoods precepts. But she could not.

From far off she heard a strange caterwauling, like

battling demons: It ranged up and down the musical scale like a lost violinist.

The woods seemed alive, as if the trees were humming and the ground vibrating. Her skin crawled. Each tiny hair on her body rose with the excitement of static electricity. She heard nothing, yet sensed a deep bass throbbing through her legs and thighs where they touched the cool ground. She had never felt such stillness, had never heard such awesome tranquility. There were two opposing forces vying for control. Her heart fluttered like a leaf in a gale, her blood raced.

Then he was there, among the trees, rifle poised. She had not heard a sound of his approach, but was as glad to see him as she had been that day he had saved her from the dogs. "Jake."

She left her gear on the ground, and got up running. The giant figure slid out into the glade, soundlessly, as if on rollers. She stopped. Her lungs froze. It was not the old hermit.

It was bigger, like a small tank on trunklike stilts. Its head was massive and knobby, with large lumps that stuck out as if overlapping basketballs had been cut in half and the halves glued on top of each other. Its eyes were small and dark, but glowed with an inner light that made them leap out of the deformed skull.

Its body was mountainous but formless, covered with a scaly skin that reminded Elaine of crusts of mud from a dry river bottom. The arms were bulky, and fatter than her thighs. There was no anatomical definition between the legs, just a cancerous growthlike egg-shaped bubble of gray plastic. The legs were enormous pylons, truncated in clublike appendages that sprouted thick, prehensile digits.

Out of necessity she started breathing again, shallowly. Neither moved. Elaine could not take her eyes off that awful spectacle. And though it might crush her to a pulp in the next second, she could not help but pity its hideousness. As the first horror wore off, she fought down her repulsion and looked upon the creature as she had looked upon those blind, misshapen, retarded children she had worked with for so long.

The feelings of guilt returned. That she should be so pretty, so attractive, and they—and *it*—so ugly, affected her sense of righteousness. Tears rolled down her cheeks.

Here was one whom no one had ever loved, whom no one ever *would* love. It had known loneliness with unfathomable intensity. It had suffered pain of incredible proportions. And it went on knowing and suffering and enduring. Worse than being hated by others, it hated itself.

Waves of compassion rippled across the vastness of space between them. Elaine saw not a repugnant distortion of humanity, but an infant pleading to be held, a sensitive child seeking attention and acceptance.

Elaine overcame the physical barrier, and peered through those trusting eyes into the thing's inner being. Mentally, telepathically, she petted its fragile ego, stroked its psyche, lamented the cruel twist of fate that had buried so decent a heart in so loathsome a body.

She held out her hands. She knew she could not touch it, that it was beyond even her sense of empathy. But she could offer. She could show this grotesque monster that it was not alone, that she held feelings for it, that she understood its plight. If only it were possible to share some of her own beauty. She wished so much that she could mother it.

Her hair was lifted off her shoulders by a sudden, blasting wind. The trees shook like blades of grass. The ground trembled. The stars spun across the sky.

It was gone.

Elaine was alone in the clearing, alone with her thoughts, her perceptions, her . . . dreams? She lay flat on her back, staring up. The sky was a deep purple, the stars were out in full panoply. She ached all over. Her muscles were stiff, as if she had just completed a rigorous set of isometrics. Her thighs throbbed, cramped. She felt so . . . full.

She stumbled back to the pine tree, bent with a groan, grabbed the loose equipment straps, and carried everything back to the Jeep. She stowed the camera and gadget bag on

the passenger seat. Her head was filled with fading hallu-
cinations.

The recorder was still on, but it had run to the end of its
tape. Numbly, dreamily, she brought it up to her lips and
thumbed the stop button. "Beam me aboard, Scotty."

INTERLUDE 3

It crawled up out of the earth as soon as the red, tearful ball of the sun dropped below the horizon.

It felt good. They had treated it like a pagan god, and filled it with the effluvium of sacrifice. Last night it had gratefully taken the soul of their offering, tonight it would take the body.

Its jowls drooled with the thoughts of charred, decayed meat, the taste so much better than what it could scrounge from the forest, from the graves. The nourishment that came from devouring the total entity of a creature was pure nirvana, the harmony of absolution, the sweet richness and assimilation of inner forces.

It glided through the barrens like an apparition, neither stirring the brush and low-slung branches, nor frightening the four-footed denizens it chanced to pass. None were aware of its presence, of its comings and goings. It was ubiquitous, and not there at all.

Rapidly it strode toward the pine-shrouded altar, the sacrificial pit, to await the oblation it had witnessed last night, to taste at long last the flavor of flesh that had been slaughtered in its namesake.

So eager was it, so quickly did it move, that it did not notice the creature waiting in the clearing. She did not wear red; her robes did not flow about her feet, but clung to her legs like an extra layer of skin. She held no torch, sang no chants; her face was devoid of paint. She was a stranger to the woods.

She was also . . . different. At first she exhibited no fear, no doubt. The emotions that flowed from her brain were full of brightness, expectancy, naiveté, trust. He sensed those feelings cloud as his presence metamorphosed into corporeality. Then came . . . not fear, not dread, but timidity tainted with lack of comprehension. She was shocked, but constrained.

It had never encountered this before, had never observed this reaction to its appearance. It was itself stymied motionless. It felt a tingling in its body . . . not in its genitals, but in some indecipherable place that lay within its breast. It sensed a fullness, a completeness, a throbbing that was reminiscent of pain, but the result of which was good and fullfilling and . . . desirable.

It looked deep within its core, fumbling for ancient thoughts, for forgotten feelings, for repressed emotions. It was uncomfortable, and for the moment was without power, without hatred, without hunger. It tasted a satisfaction that came from something other than death and destruction, something it did not recognize, something out of a dream, a fantasy.

The creature's sight organs leaked, her upper appendages reached out . . . not to attack, but to hold, to caress, to cuddle.

Its chest heaved. The throbbing within threatened to burst its torso. What kind of power did she have over him? How could she, a weak creature like the one on the altar, command such control over his body, his mind? She exhibited some force it had never encountered, a force that could destroy its very being, and all it stood for.

Yet, it was a destruction it had long sought, a release it knew not how to effect. Somehow, it knew it was facing the savior of its soul. Her eyes closed, and her mind went numb. It sought to return her embrace the only way it knew how: not just with its repulsive physical anatomy, but with its innermost self. It gathered up its elemental forces and entered this strangely silent female, melded with her that it might understand her incredible faculties.

It sensed that her body was receptive, that her mind was open, that her response was not inconceivable, but rare. It touched her, as one touches a holy relic. And when it did, it lost some of itself inside her.

Then it cringed away. It retreated into the forest, under the ground, through the granules of sand, to lie hidden among the roots.

It had to think. Something new was awakening within, and it needed time to ponder. Perhaps this was the secret desire it had denied all these years, all these centuries. Perhaps this was the way toward the consummation of its purpose on earth.

And perhaps this was the path to salvation.

CHAPTER 10

Elaine parked the Jeep down an abandoned driveway about half a mile from the coroner's office. It was well hidden behind a stand of oaks.

She left her purse and gadget bag under the seat, but made sure she had her recorder, camera (with a small strobe clamped in the hot shoe), and a flashlight. Under the cover of darkness she slipped through the trees only a few yards away from the road. She kept on a parallel course, ducking each time headlights warned of an approaching vehicle.

Branches grappled with her blond tresses, and foliage stung her face. But at least no one could possibly see her moving through the tree line. Her only concern was the crunching of leaves and twigs underfoot. She was thankful that the coroner's office was not in the middle of a crowded community, but set apart in a typical south Jersey pinelands setting.

It was nearly midnight by the time she reached the white picket fence that surrounded the brick building. She slung her equipment under her arms, jammed the flashlight into a tight-fitting back pocket, and used the limbs of a pitch pine to help her over the sharpened pickets. She was careful not to slip and impale herself on the wooden stakes.

She landed sharply on her feet, lost her balance, and stumbled across the newly mown grass for several feet before catching herself. She dropped to her knees, and looked around for any sign of movement her noisy entrance might have aroused. No dogs barked, no lights went on, no doors opened.

In the full light of the moon she scampered across the lawn to the back door. Her breathing came hard, not from exertion but from sheer excitement of what she was doing—and about to do. She was going to show that ass wiggling hussy that she was not the only reporter who could make a story.

Her visit to the coroner that morning had been more ruse than interview. The scant information Benson had parted with was only enough to pique her curiosity, and to sound the alert that he was withholding much more. But she had learned what she wanted: the layout of the office, the location of the files, the absence of a burglar alarm system. She had even stood unnoticed by the rear window, on the pretext of observing the hearse in the driveway, and unlatched the lower casement. Now she pushed gently upward, and the window creaked open with all the raucous squeaking of an ancient crypt.

With camera and recorder clattering, she climbed over the sill and let herself into the eerie, evil smelling darkness. She quickly closed the window behind her.

The flashlight revealed a laboratory full of test tubes and surgical instruments, X-ray and diagnostic equipment, chemical baths, specimen jars, microscopes, and racks of tinctures and powders. She went through the only door into a utility room. With the flashlight shining down on the floor, the dim glow depicted a closet to her left, and a long counter top to the right. The coffee maker, a small refrigerator, and boxes of cereal and cookies and other foodstuffs were crowded together with a sink full of stained cups and dirty dishes.

She hurriedly passed through into the main office. No night-lights were on, and thick, purple velvet curtains prevented outside floodlights from lending illumination. The flashlight flickered, and went dim. Elaine banged it against her thigh. It came back on to full brightness.

The first filing cabinet came into view. She pulled open

a drawer and rifled through the manila file folders: receipts, state forms, legal documents, miscellaneous papers. She eased it shut, pulled out another on smooth roller bearings: more of the same.

This is ridiculous, she thought. Anything pertaining to recent events would not yet have been stored. She went through the desk drawers, and found named dossiers, address lists and the like, but nothing pertaining to fatalities in the pines, or bodies recovered from graves.

The flashlight dimmed again, and stayed that way. She banged it, and the bulb brightened momentarily, then returned to its dull yellow glow. She had to hold it inches away from the desk top to see anything. And that was how she noticed the cremation reports lying right in plain view.

The individuals were identified only by numbers, but the dates coincided with the recent casualties. On one form someone had scrawled in pencil, "parts of both."

So that's how they dispose of the evidence, Elaine said to herself. She rotated the focus ring to minimum distance, 1.5 feet for the 50 millimeter lens, and switched on the strobe. When the ready light came on she bent over the documents and approximated the focal length with her outstretched fingers, and pressed the shutter release. In the confined darkness, the flash of light seemed like the explosion of a miniature sun. The strobe whined as it recycled. She exchanged papers and fired again.

Underneath was a leather bound address book with a list of names, but no phone numbers or addresses, just dates—dates that went back years, decades. The print was small, some of the lettering faint. She pressed the recorder button and read into the machine, spelling out names that were illegible or difficult to pronounce. She still had one page to go when she heard a car pull up in front of the building.

Elaine sucked in her breath, her pulse rate doubling instantly. She scooped up the flashlight, now almost dead, thumbed off the switch, and backed through the office with her eyes glued to the front door. She hit the wall, knocking a hanging picture askew, turned and straightened it, and kept slithering along the white sheetrock until the doorknob goosed her. She fumbled for the brass handle, twisted, and backed into the utility room just as the blinds on the front door rattled.

She heard muffled voices. She continued to slide along the wall until she felt the door handle. She turned it and slipped into the darkness.

She expected to see the glow of light from the window, smell the chemical odors of the laboratory. Instead, the pitch-blackness carried with it the strong scent of formaldehyde. She thumbed on the flashlight. The barely visible glow was enough to show that she was not in the lab.

She could make out a counter top full of displayed instruments and clear plastic gloves, a stainless steel table whose perimeter was a shallow channel, a glistening red cloth covering a human form with twin bulges on the chest. Then the light faded completely, leaving her staring into the darkness with the latent image of the preparation room impinged on her optic nerves.

An outer door opened, the voices grew louder.

With one hand clamping her recorder and camera gear to her breast, Elaine played blindman by feeling across the open space until she bumped into the examination table. Gruesomely, her fingers wrapped around a satin covered foot. She jerked her hand back as if she had been stung.

Footsteps in the utility room forced her into action. She reoriented herself on the very edge of the steel table, worked her fingers around it, bumped over a protruding wooden lever, and turned the corner to the side opposite the door.

A latch creaked, a shaft of light appeared, and Elaine gasped as she ducked below the edge of the table and crawled under the frame.

"Whaddaya expect her ta do, git up an' walk away?"

"I'm just checking."

"Kinda difficult to walk attached to a pogo stick, doncha think?"

"I said, I'm just checking."

Elaine suddenly realized that the strobe ready light was a giant red beacon. She eased the dead flashlight to the white tiled floor to free her hand, and ran a finger over the rippled slider that switched off the power circuit. Now it became apparent that her wristwatch was sending out a phosphorescent glow that could have been a flashing neon sign. She pressed it hard against her slacks.

Only when the fluorescent lights came on did she appreciate how exposed her hiding place was.

"She still there?"

A pair of dusty black shoes came into view, and two legs of dark brown woolen trousers. "The robe's a little off. This stuff is slippery as ice."

Elaine crouched only inches away from the striding pants. Her heart pounded like a kettle drum, and she shook so hard she could barely keep from collapsing into a puddle. Couldn't they hear her bones rattling? She clutched the camera tighter. Material flapped over her head.

"Hey, stop lookin' at her pube. Din'tcha git enough o' that last night?"

"Cut it out. I'm just checking the flow of blood. It wouldn't like it if she was all dried up."

"I thought dead bodies din't bleed."

"No, when the heart stops pumping you don't get leakage through open wounds, but the blood doesn't coagulate until it's oxygenated. How the hell do you think we get it out of the veins when we have to pump in the embalming fluid?"

"Guess that's why you're a cor'ner an' I'm jus' a sheriff. How soon before they git here with the hearse?"

"As soon as they get it filled up. It wouldn't pay to run out of gas in the middle of the barrens, not tonight, and not with this cargo. It'll be hungry, and I don't plan to be around when it comes to feed."

"I'm with ya on that. I'll be glad when this week's over. Got deppities out lockin' up speeders. Nex' time I'll be retired."

The shoes pointed toward the door. "Doesn't mean you won't be called in. We need somebody with your contacts." The legs moved away. "Let me just write down the name and date, and we'll get out of here. The boys can pick up the chum and meet us at the crossroads."

The lights went off, the door slammed shut, the voices retreated.

Elaine waited as long as she could, then she let herself go and caved in on the cold floor like a puppet with the strings cut. She did not care at all about her camera chipping the grout. She huddled on the floor, sobbing uncontrollably, too weak to do anything other than lie curled up against the stanchion of the adjacent examination table.

Five minutes passed while she had her cry, and recouped her strength. Slowly, she got up on hands and knees. Using the table leg for support she pushed herself upright. Her legs were still a little weak, but she managed to stay on her feet. The blackness was now a welcome cloak.

She fought down her panic, forced herself to think coolly. She switched on the strobe, heard the whine of recycling nicads, saw the ready light, aimed blindly in front of her, closed her eyes, and pressed the shutter release. The strobe fired. But when she tried to recock the shutter, the lever would not advance. Elaine knew her equipment by feel. She checked the main switch, the battery chamber cover, the film rewind knob, the aperture lock pin, even the mode selector. In desperation, she disengaged the lens and re-mounted it, in case the bayonet had jumped its sleeve: to no avail. Some internal mechanism had broken, or become misaligned by the sudden jar. For the moment, she was out of the picture taking business.

When she pressed the manual firing button on the strobe, the burst of high energy light almost blinded her. Without the automatic sensor to cut off the power, the capacitor discharged at full output. Seconds later, she still retained a retinal image of the sterile room, of a shapeless body under a red satin robe, of some weird stenciled calligraphy, of the glint of a diamond ring, of gleaming red nail polish.

Elaine swallowed. Hard.

She took a step closer, and flashed the strobe again. She kept her finger jammed on the bottom. The powerful battery pack recycled in two seconds, and went off as soon as the ready light glowed red. She took another step, and another. The strobe flooded the preparation room every two seconds, like the dance floor of a discotheque.

Bold images leaped out at her, moving like isolated frames of a motion picture showing only every thirtieth frame. She avoided touching the exposed hand, and moved along the table to the foot. Sticking out was the wooden pole she had accidentally touched earlier. It was not part of the table mechanics; the end was burned, and broken off.

Elaine touched the robe, felt the cool, satiny finish. Once moved, it slid easily away from the body, on its own. The bottoms of the toes were burned right through to the bones, and the nail polish blistered. The soles of the feet were singed black, with the skin peeled off in long, disgusting strips, like overcooked bacon. The lower legs, and the wooden staff between them, were charred.

She shook her head slowly from side to side, muttered "no, no, no" under her breath, could not stop the tears from dripping down her cheeks. She already knew what was coming, but was mesmerized by the stroboscopic effect, each flash revealing more of the contorted body.

The flaxen thighs came into view, then the groin. The pole disappeared into the body cavity, below the curly tuft of hair. Prominent hip bones protruded above a flat belly, the ribs showed through soft, delicate skin, the enlarged breasts sagged sideways like two empty sacks.

The robe fell to the floor. Tongue protruding grotesquely, Janice Marlton stared up at the ceiling through sightless eyes.

Elaine could not stifle a scream. She backed into the tiled wall, engulfed by darkness, overcome with fear. She felt her heart pounding, the blood racing through her eardrums. Her legs would hardly support her. For one brief moment she stooped helplessly, cringing, mouthing silent words, almost too weak to run.

The she bolted, through one door, then another. She fumbled with the window, got it open in time to retch over the sill. She climbed out and fell into the mess, scrambled to her feet, ran headlong into the picket fence, tore her clothes and skin getting over it, snatched goggle-eyed glances over her shoulder as she ran through the darkened woods to the Jeep, to the macadam road, to the river, and to home and the comfort that only Cliff could give her.

INTERLUDE 4

It waited for the feast.

It was confused by the earlier meeting, with the woman, but that confusion was put aside in mouth-watering anticipation.

Tonight it would have meat. Freshly killed, just for it. Last night it had savored the scent of sacrifice, tonight it would taste the flesh. No more rats, no more field mice, no more dogs, but actual, tantalizing, human flesh: the gift of everlasting existence, the stimulus for its seven year resurgence, the energy source that was its deathlihood.

It drew power from the pines, strength from the earth, vigor from the atmosphere, but it needed that vitality, that spark, that came only from the life-force of creatures that could metabolize without supernatural catalysis. It maintained its animation through a chemistry that was beyond the pale of biology, more than divine intervention: a satanic debt that was paid off in morbid expiration.

The malady of death could be slowed down, but not cured.

It did not lose strength, it only increased pain. Strength meant pleasure, strength meant gratification, strength meant the exercise of power, the calm, deliberate control over the environment, over the flora and fauna, over the earth, over the moon and the stars. All these things it gained from its voluptuous excesses.

And if it did not seek to increase its strength, the pain and torture of weakness became intolerable. Then it had to kill, then it could not wait for sacrifices.

But tonight it would feed.

It crept through the ground, it climbed through the trees, it flew through the air. Tonight, on the energy of sacrifice, it could do anything it desired. Tonight, it did not just live in the pine barrens, it was the pine barrens.

But it was a long way from satiation.

They came. Bearing torches in front of them, torches that carved tunnels in the darkness. They paraded through the woods, bringing with them the prepared sacrifice, the offering of flesh. It was everywhere, and it watched, like a bird in the treetops watching a procession of earthworms on the ground struggling through deep puddles after a rainstorm.

It kept all its senses alert, following them. The iron pageant halted, the offering was removed from its noisy, smoke-belching coffin, and carried on a wooden pier along the narrow pathways it created for them, to the prepared clearing where the rites would take place, where the banquet would be held.

The sacrament was raised. The fires were lit. The red robed figures began their saturnalia, whooping around the glade in their painted faces, pounding the ground with naked feet, chanting in drug-crazed voices.

The flesh was not yet decayed, but that did not matter. This was not carrion, this was not an abandoned cadaver, but an oblation, a true glorification of the power it held over them. They respected it, they feared it, they supplicated to its awesome, unrelenting force.

And if they demonstrated such devotion, it would let them keep this weak, useless condition they called life.

CHAPTER 11

If Elaine wore mascara, it would long since have run down her face like blackened rivers. As it was, tear trails plowed through dirt-covered cheeks, showing white skin through the brown.

"Hey, I just saw him walk into the office."

"All right, pal. Give the guy a chance to sit down, will ya?"

Cliff blocked the police sergeant's path. He raised his voice over the sound of clattering typewriters, telephone bells, talking and shouting, and rushing, uniformed pandemonium. "Either you announce us, or I'm walking right the hell in there."

"You do, an' you'll—"

"Don't threaten me, Sergeant. And don't try to intimidate me. We're going in." He turned and stooped by his wife, and ran a wadded tissue under her puffy eyes. "It's all right, honey. Everything'll be all right."

She shook her head, and mouthed unintelligible words with a quivering jaw. "I can't . . . go through . . ."

"Sure, you can. You can do it. I know you can. You just tell the lieutenant what you told me." Cliff stood up, pulling her gently by the elbow. He gave the burly sergeant a defiant look.

The sergeant scowled, turned, opened the door, and

stepped inside. "Lieutenant, this guy out here's got a bug up his ass. Insists on seeing you pronto."

"What the hell, Burke, I haven't even had my coffee yet. Take a report."

"He won't talk to anybody but the head of the department. He says—"

Cliff pushed past him and into the office, with Elaine in tow. "I don't deal with underlings. It would just mean repeating the story ten times. And Laine's in no condition to go through a police grilling. Call off your dogs, Lieutenant."

The officer sidled around his desk wearing a hard-nosed expression on his grisled face. "Now, just who the hell do you think you—"

Elaine sank into a chair.

"Cliff Adams. And this is my wife, Elaine. We've got a homicide to report, and this big oaf thinks he can solve everything with police forms and carbon paper."

"Well, maybe you'd just better learn something right from the beginning, mister. I run this office, not you, and Sergeant Burke has full authority to act, with or without my presence." The old, three-piece suit fit him shabbily, as if he had weighed more when it was purchased. His hair was permanently disheveled. "And, as department chief, I don't engage in personal investigations. I'm in charge of operations and procedure. If it's important, in his mind—" He jerked a thumb at the sergeant's ample waist. "He'll bring it to my attention. Now, go on back outside and use the chain of command. And leave me the hell alone."

Cliff approached the lieutenant and stood nose to nose with him. In a lowered voice, he said, "It's about Janice. Janice Marlton."

The lieutenant's eyes pinched. "Did she send you?"

Cliff jerked his head. "Can we be alone?"

The lieutenant stared for a moment, then looked at the sergeant and raised his brows. The sergeant left the room, shaking his head, and closed the door behind him.

The lieutenant sipped black coffee from his mug, picked up a smoking cigarette from a nearly full ashtray, and stabbed it between dry, colorless lips. "You better be on the up and up, Mr.—"

"Adams." Cliff stepped back, and placed a hand on Elaine's shoulder.

"Wakeley. Bartholomew Wakeley." The police officer retreated behind his desk, puffing furiously on the butt. "Now, what's this have to do with Janice Marlton? Why didn't she come here with you?"

"She's dead."

The police officer stood stock-still for several seconds, frozen like a block of ice. Then he sagged. His face melted like a snowman in the sun, his shoulders drooped. He plumped down in the swivel chair, the cigarette hanging limply from the corner of his mouth. "Well, I'm sorry to— How did it— I mean, I'm sorry."

Elaine bent over in the wooden chair, sobbing hysterically.

Cliff stooped to one knee, and held her head against his shoulder. "Honey. Honey. Take it easy. It'll be okay."

She shook her head slowly. "No . . . it . . . won't . . . Janice . . . isn't . . . coming back . . ."

"Okay, honey. Just take it easy. Lieutenant, do you have any water?"

Wakeley's eyes came back into focus. "Uh, sure. In fact, I've got something better." He pulled open a desk drawer, pulled out a hip flask and a shot glass, and filled it with scotch.

"Thanks." Cliff took it and forced the glass between Elaine's quivering lips. She gagged at the first sip, but he kept tilting the glass until she swallowed at least half the liquid.

Still standing, the lieutenant pulled out another glass. "You want a shot?" When Cliff shook his head, Wakeley poured a good measure into his coffee, stirred it with a plastic swizzle stick, and took a large gulp. He left the capped bottle on the desk. "You know, this comes as quite a— I mean, Janice and I were very close and— Well, I guess you know all about that, or you wouldn't be here. Uh, it's not common knowledge. How *did* you know?"

Cliff swung around into the seat adjacent to Elaine, and looked up. "I had the keys to her apartment. We— When I found out we went over there. Elaine and I. There was a picture of you and your wife—"

"Late wife."

Cliff nodded dumbly. "We went through her effects, found her address book with your name—"

"So why come to the office? You could have called me at home."

"Because she was murdered."

"Oh, dear God." Lieutenant Wakeley leaned forward, chair creaking, and took another huge gulp of coffee. He scowled, poured another finger of Scotch into the mug, and drank it down. Bushy eyebrows shot up, adding to the lines in the already wrinkled forehead. "Not in Philly. Not in my jurisdiction?"

"New Jersey."

The lieutenant let out a long breath. "No, of course not. I would have heard about it already." He poured another cup of coffee from a thermos, and added a healthy portion of alcohol. "I usually have my work load advertised on the radio. Damn reporters are blabbing the lowdown before I get to the office. Well, I certainly do appreciate you letting me know. I mean, it's better coming from friends. How long have you known her?"

"Since college. We lost touch for a few years when I went to the West Coast."

"I never heard her mention you."

"Janice was a very private person. She never mixed her crowds."

Lieutenant Wakeley nodded slightly. "Yeah. Always was a mixed-up kid. Hey, can I get you some coffee?"

Elaine stopped sobbing but remained hunched over and staring at the worn wooden floor.

Cliff shook his head. "No. Thanks. But we didn't come here just to break the news. I got the feeling you were— from the picture, and the letters— Well, I thought you must have been close to her."

Lieutenant Wakeley stared out the window, lit another cigarette. "Yeah, we were close."

"And being in homicide, I figured you'd be the best one to handle the investigation."

The lieutenant took another drag, let out smoke, swilled the spiked coffee in his mouth. "Even if I could, I wouldn't. One thing you learn in this business is never get personally involved. I wouldn't be able to conduct a thorough and impartial investigation."

Cliff fidgeted in his seat, got up, and paced the room. "Lieutenant, you're already personally involved by your relationship with Janice."

"Exactly. And no matter what I thought of the girl, even if the case took place within city limits, I'd have to hand it over to a subordinate. No, it just wouldn't work. Besides, the local authorities have jurisdiction. I couldn't just butt in—"

"You can if there's reason to believe the local authorities may be implicated in either the crime or a cover-up."

Wakeley looked up sharply. "That's a pretty strong accusation. Do you have any evidence to back it up?"

Cliff grabbed Elaine's shoulder bag and dumped it on the desk. "Plenty. And there's more in the Jeep."

The lieutenant's eyes widened at the pile of pictures, tapes, maps, and photocopies. "When did you say she died?"

"Night before last."

Deft hands sorted through the overabundance of material. "That's an impressive amount of work for only a little more than twenty-four hours. You've been busy."

"It doesn't all have to do with the murder. Elaine's been doing research for an article, for the *Bulletin*. She's been involved right from the beginning with those bodies exhumed in the pine barrens."

"Oh, yeah. I've been reading about it. Was that you?"

Elaine managed a weak nod.

"What's all that crap about the Jersey Devil? Newspaper hype? Hell, we got enough ghouls running around without adding junk about werewolves and vampires. Christ. So,

what's all this"— he spread his hands, palms up—"got to
do with Janice? She was working on a wild animal killing.
Hey, that was in the pine barrens, too, wasn't it?"

Cliff stopped in front of the desk, nodding. "Yes, a hell
of a lot's been taking place in the barrens lately. Most of it's
been buried—and I mean that literally. The sheriff's doing
his best to keep it underground."

"Well, there's no reason to panic the public. They got
enough to worry about."

"Lieutenant, keeping news out of the papers is one thing,
but hiding it from your higher-ups is another."

"What makes you think—"

"I called the State Police this morning. Okay, so they
didn't have their computer on line. But I talked with several
troopers in the office, and none of them knew a thing about
what's been going on in the barrens except what they've
read in the papers. Apparently they've been led to believe
that everything's under control."

"Yeah? Who by?"

"The sheriff. He's been giving us a hard time ever since
that first corpse was dug up last weekend. Strange things are
going on, and he's part of it."

"Well, again I'll have to say that's a pretty strong
accusation. All right, give me a quick rundown."

Cliff looked around at his wife. "Laine, do you feel up to
talking about it yet?"

She met his eyes, and took a deep breath. "No. But I
guess I'll have to." Her voice throbbed, as if her throat was
full of phlegm. Elaine told the story haltingly, with tears,
sobs, and a great deal of help from Cliff. Half an hour later,
she completely broke down. "And . . . and . . . and
the . . . stake . . . I thought . . . it was . . . a control rod . . . or something—it wasn't . . . it was . . .
it was . . . stuck . . . up her . . . you know . . . it
was . . . up her . . ."

"Okay, Laine. Okay, honey. It's okay. Nobody's going
to get you now." Cliff cradled the hysterical woman in his
arms, kissed the top of her head, held her tight, ran his

hands over her face and back. "I won't let them get you. You're all right. It's all over now."

"No . . . no it's . . . it's not. They're still . . . out there . . . She's still . . . out there . . . they're going to . . . feed her . . ."

The lieutenant was riveted to his chair, staring madly. "Oh, Christ. Oh, Jesus Christ." His desk phone rang, startling him. He grabbed it for an instant, shouting. "Shut up. No calls." He slammed the receiver down so hard the desk rattled. "Oh, Jesus fucking Christ. How the hell do you expect me to believe—"

"My wife doesn't lie!" Cliff shouted. "I know she's emotional, but if she said that's what happened, then it happened."

The lieutenant had already bit off all his nails, and was now chewing them down to the quick. "Poor Janice. My poor, sweet Janice." Someone knocked at the door, the sergeant pushed his way into the room. Lieutenant Wakeley jumped up, and roughly shoved him out. "I said no calls, dammit."

"But, sir, the Inspector—"

"Later!" He slammed the door, ran back across the floor and unplugged the phone. The ashtray was overflowing, and butts lay strewn about the desk. He lit another, and took another jolt of scotch, straight from the bottle. "Oh, dear God. I wish I didn't believe you."

"Here, listen to this. In the ruckus Laine forgot to stop the tape." Cliff switched on the recorder and turned up the volume. The coroner and the sheriff repeated their conversation with the nasal intonation of the cheap, miniature speaker. "Is that proof enough for you?"

"All right. I believe you. I just wish to hell it wasn't true. Christ, I've been on a lot of weirdo cases: chain saw murders, penis dismemberments, ritual rapes and gang bangs, a skin collector, a nipple slicer. But this, this is unfuckingbelievable. That some cult of devil worshipers could actually think they could—" He threw his hands up into the air, sputtering. He dropped into his chair, put his elbows on the desk, and lay his head in his hands. "Janice.

Hell, she's no older than my own daughter would have been. Disappeared after high school. Never heard from her again."

"Lieutenant, can we come back to the present?" Cliff leaned on his knuckles. "I know it's a shock. But it's been a lot worse for Laine. If she had gotten caught . . . if they knew she was there—You've got to do something without letting on what you know. You've got to catch those bastards before they get to somebody else."

"All right!" Lieutenant Wakeley sat up, hands thrust out in front of him. "All right. I know. But I need some time to think. You've dropped all this information on me, and by rights I should be assigning a whole pack of investigators, going through channels, alerting the State Police, the FBI, asking for cooperative jurisdiction. But legally—and this is just between you and me—legally, I can't just take somebody's word for it that this devil worship cult really exists. I have to have a corpus delecti. I mean, I have to have more concrete evidence, not just tape recordings and pictures. I also can't handle it alone. There's too much to do."

"So farm out what you can: the preliminaries, the background work, the checkups on the sheriff and the coroner. Have it done discreetly. But do the field examination yourself." Cliff thrust out his arm, index finger extended. "Her body's out there somewhere in the pines. And they must have done something with her car. Put out a stolen car bulletin with the Stateys—"

"Adams, I know how to do my job. I've been here long enough. Too long. Fourteen goddamn years." The lieutenant ran his hands through tousled hair. "I don't care if we do have a suspect, or suspects. I've got to have evidence of a crime before I can throw half the police force into the woods tracking down some goddamned Jersey Devil. Oh, that would look great on my records. They'd think I went completely bananas and have been peeling for years. I started this job with a case I was emotionally involved in, I don't want to end it that way."

"All right, I'm not pressuring you. Janice is dead, and nothing's going to bring her back. But if what Laine says is true, if what she picked up from this old man makes sense, they're not going to stop now. Whatever kind of fantasy world they live in, we haven't seen the end of it yet. And one thing you don't want to do is tip your hand. Obviously you can't assign Philly's finest to go traipsing through the pines looking for sacrificial remains—they might get dirty. And the Jersey Stateys are too busy giving out speeding tickets on the parkway to do anything important."

Wakeley rolled his eyes and looked up at the ceiling. "So, Adams, what is it *you* want me to do?"

"Let's go over there. Just the three of us. We can—"

Elaine gripped the arms of her chair until her knuckles were white. "I'm not going back into the pine barrens. Ever."

"Honey, it's all right. We'll—"

She kept shaking her head. "Never."

"—go in broad daylight. We'll have—"

"No."

"—a police escort. He'll be right by our side. You won't— "

"*No!* I'm not going back."

"Laine."

"And that's final."

"But, how else are we going to find Jake's cabin? How else can we locate that makeshift altar? How else can we avenge Janice's murder? Laine, we're going beyond personal considerations, here. We're not just researching another article. We're citizens, fulfilling an obligation. The one thing they impressed upon us in law school was that a citizen, any citizen, and especially an attorney, moral justifications aside, has a duty to see that the law is upheld."

"Cliff, save the civic responsibility speech for the boy scouts and the Kiwanis Club. You're not doing one of your weekend lecture tours."

"All right, then think about Janice. Honey, I know you're scared. But, hell, you saw her . . . afterward. You, of all people, know how she suffered. You know—"

Elaine buried her face in her hands and cried uncontrollably. "Cliff, I'm scared. Please hold me."

Cliff ran to her, hugged her, petted and kissed her. "Honey, I'm sorry. I didn't mean to badger you. It's just—"

"If you don't mind my butting in—" Lieutenant Wakeley walked around his chipped, wooden desk. "I know you two have been through a lot lately. Especially you, Mrs. Adams. So I'll tell you what. Why don't you go home, get some rest—you've been up all night, haven't you?—and let me start culling this mountain of stuff and see if I can make any sense out of it. I'll start some preliminary action, get the ball rolling, and I'll call you this afternoon.

"I'm going to handle this personally—by myself—until I know what the hell's going on. Janice was a very special person to me, and I'm going to see to it that whoever did this obscene thing to her pays, and pays dearly. Because now, now that she's gone, I haven't got a goddamned thing to lose."

CHAPTER 12

The Italian market was crowded with throngs of people bustling about the street in frenzied haste. Hawkers shouted the freshness of their fruits, vegetables, fish, and meats, amid the wild mixture of aromas that swirled through the bright sunlight.

"Thanks for bringing me here. I really needed to . . . be with people. In a crowd. To hear voices. With smiling faces and an air of . . . normalcy."

Cliff dodged through the jostling horde, acting as running block for Elaine. "I don't mind getting in touch with the ordinary world myself. Dealing with bankers, lawyers, and politicians all the time, I'm likely to forget that real, honest, straightforward people still exist. I'm fed up with conniving and manipulation, deals and super deals, the total disregard for human values, the intolerable lack of feeling. It's an environment that's utterly hostile to homo sapiens, with enough pollutants to drown the hardiest survival types. If OSHA ever knew what it was like in big business, they'd enact regulations against it: psychiatric evaluations for all participants, mandatory sensitivity training, automatic retirement for convictions of power pilfering and corporate acts of aggression. Of course, if they put all the crazies away, there'd be nobody left to run the world."

"Maybe we could find some people who just wanted to *walk* the world, like a dog on a leash."

"And maybe we could repeal the law of gravity. Laine, ever since man climbed down from the trees he's kept his course of travel. The bulk of humanity are slowing this downward progress, but complete reversal is still in the future. But if we each give it a nudge in the proper direction, eventually it'll happen."

Elaine detected a warm, sweet scent wafting through the stalls. "Cliff, let's get some croissants. They smell delicious."

"Your wish is my command." Cliff pulled some bills out of his pants pocket as they entered the bakery. They bought half a dozen of the homemade flaky pastries. He waved off the change, and added the wrapped package to the carton of eggs in the shopping bag he cradled in his arm. "Why don't we get some fresh scrapple while we're at it?"

"And bacon. I'm ravenous."

"Ravishing, too." Cliff led the way along the sidewalk, smiling and nodding to shopkeepers and store owners, some of whom called him by name. He returned the compliment.

"Do you know all these people?"

"Only on a first name basis. I shop here all the time, remember?"

"Do all attorneys buy their own food? And do the cooking?"

"They do when they're married to runabout writers instead of stay-at-home housewives and mothers of ten."

Elaine plucked a purple grape off a display crate when the proprietor was not looking, and caught up with Cliff at the intersection. "And which would you rather have?"

The light changed, and Cliff stepped off the curb. "A little of both, I guess. When we're ready, I'd like to have some kids."

"When *I'm* ready, you mean."

Cliff shrugged. "Well, I wouldn't want you stifled by an occupation you didn't find fulfilling. There's still time."

"I'm past the magic age."

Cliff shrugged again. "Laine, I certainly know what a hardship it would be for me to get off the train in the middle of a career. Once you get the ball rolling, it keeps gathering snow. But if you lay back to sit in the sun, the snow starts melting. So, I can easily understand why you don't want to suddenly stop and have babies."

Elaine grabbed his jacket sleeve. "But you would like me to?"

He met her gaze. "Of course. But when you're ready. I wouldn't want you to change. I wouldn't want you to stop being a runabout, stop having your fingers in so many pies, stop your zest for life and your inclination for involvement. I like a woman who gets around, too."

"Yes, like Janice." Ice hung on the statement.

"Now what's that supposed to mean?"

Elaine averted his gaze. "I'm not sure. Except that my competition has dropped out of the race."

"Laine, have some respect for her. She's dead."

"That doesn't make her any better. She still— Oh, God, what am I saying? I saw her . . . like that . . . less than twelve hours ago."

"And were crying over her less than two."

Elaine clutched his sleeve, pulled him out of the human treadmill and into the aisle of a closed storefront. "All right, don't get me wrong. I'm sorry she's dead. I'm sorry she had to suffer. I—I wouldn't wish it on my worst enemy, even if it was her. But, dammit, Cliff, dead or alive, I still don't have to like her. That two-timing nymphomaniac."

Cliff bolted back as if struck. He glanced around at the passersby, all ignorant of their argument, or unconcerned. "Laine, you have no right to say that."

"Why not? Truth doesn't end with death. She was screwing everything with pants on. Maybe slacks, too, for all I know. And she didn't care whether they were married, or old enough to be her father."

"Look, if she brought some pleasure to a lonely lieutenant—"

"I don't give a damn about the lieutenant. But I do care about her messing around with married men. Especially *my* married man."

"Oh, come on, Laine. Don't start this again. You know we're nothing but good friends. Were."

"I know she was meeting you in restaurants. I know she was visiting you in our house. I know you had a key to her apartment. I'm not a complete idiot, you know. I may not have a degree in calculus, but I can still add two and two."

"Laine, you know me better than that."

"Like I knew the ex-football hero in college."

"Come on," Cliff whined. "It was a fraternity party. I was drunk. I don't even remember it. And there were no feelings involved. No emotions. No—love. It was just an act. And I'm not even sure it really happened. I only know what I was told afterward. It could have been a bluff, a college prank."

"Well, *I* know. Just like I know what was going on between you and Janice."

"Don't do this, Laine."

"Feeling guilty?"

"You're jumping to conclusions."

"Like you jumping into bed with your little fucking playmate."

Pain washed over Cliff's face, and anger soon followed. "You have no right to say that."

"Don't you talk to me about rights. I've got *my* rights, too, you know, supposedly guaranteed in a marriage contract. Now, I'm sure that somewhere in that legal mind of yours you've found a loophole that fits neatly around your zipper, but I don't buy it, I don't like it, and I'm not going to stand for it."

"And I'm not going to stand for your silly accusations. Where's your evidence? Where's your proof?"

"Don't give me that legal mumbo jumbo. This isn't a courtroom. And I've just told you what I've seen going on between you two."

"That's purely circumstantial. Laine, why do we have to have this same argument every couple—"

"Because I'm acting on my feelings, that's why. You just can't understand, in your manly world of tangibility, that some things don't have to be seen, they can be felt. Don't you think I've been aware of how you respond to me?"

Cliff's voice was loud, but controlled. "How the hell can

I respond to you when you're never around? Why don't you try staying at home for a change, instead of running off following another lead, or writing another story, or taking pictures of sunsets and pitcher plants? You think I like spending my free time in front of a VCR? You know what the problem with you is? You just don't take the time to sit down and figure things out. You just don't—"

"I figured out what you and Janice have been doing."

"You only think you did. You don't know what's going on in the real world. Only that tiny microcosm inside your head."

"I know enough to know what's happening between us."

Cliff clutched the shopping bag tightly. The other hand was balled into a fist, clinging to his side. "Do you? Do you really? Then tell me what's going to happen between us in a few months. Go ahead. Think about it. What event is about to occur? Ah, you're at a loss. Your head's so far up in the clouds your mind's blanking out from lack of oxygen. All right, I'll tell you. Anniversary number ten."

Elaine worked her jaw for a moment.

"And you want to know what's been going on between Janice and me? All right, I'll tell you. We've been planning a big anniversary party. The Venus Lounge. Everybody's invited. Friends, family, co-workers. Your folks are flying in from L.A. I was going to take you out for a quiet, candlelit dinner, and surprise you. I've got the entire place rented for the evening. Now, are you happy? You see where your jealousy and your suspicions and your lack of trust got you?"

"Cliff, I—"

"You don't believe me? Go to work. Ask your friends. Ask Sam, in the photo lab. Ask your boss. Jake was *there*, at Janice's apartment, when we made up the invitation list. Janice made the arrangements for the Lounge in her name, just so word wouldn't get out accidentally."

"Cliff, I—"

"Oh, yes, you're sorry, I'm sure. Sorry you spoiled it all. Well, stop feeling sorry for yourself for a change, and think about the people around you. The people who care about you. Maybe they deserve a little consideration just for putting up with you. Maybe they—"

Cliff took the paper bag in both hands and shoved it so hard at Elaine that it knocked her back a step. He dug the key ring out of his pocket and slammed it down on top of the eggs. He turned and marched off.

"Cliff, I— Wait a minute."

He merged with the rushing mob, and used his dodging skills to forge ahead. Elaine could still see his tousled brown hair above the others, but was unable to catch up with him. By the time she reached the intersection, he was half a block away, down a side street.

"Cliff!"

He did not turn around.

Elaine wiped away tears as she sped across the street, past the throng. The sidewalks were too crowded for fast travel, so she ran along the narrow, one-car lane, past the wheeled carts, past the blazing, fifty-five gallon drums, past the fish smells and hanging bananas and plastic toys, past the merchants and corner peddlers, past the shoppers and tourists.

The BMW was parked in a side lot. She hastened past the parking attendant without a glance. The keys jingled in her free hand as she tried for several moments to find the right one, then fought to get it into the lock. She tossed the groceries across the seat and leaped in. The engine roared to life, and in seconds she backed out and charged onto the street.

She waited impatiently for the light to change at 9th and Washington, then sped off in the direction she had last seen her husband. She cruised all the main thoroughfares, and stopped and stared down every side street. Cliff walked to and from the Italian market often, and there was no telling which itinerant route he would take home—if, indeed, that was where he was headed.

But she knew him. He was not likely to stop off at a corner taproom. He had no drinking buddies and, except for cocktails and an occasional beer, was not alcoholically inclined. He had no place to go *but* home. Despite midday traffic, she could beat him there.

She parked in their spot in the underground garage, and took the elevator up to their condo. The lights were all off, the drapes were still pulled, and no one answered her call. She set the shopping bag on the counter and inspected the rooms.

Then, she sat down to wait, wondering what she would say to him.

It was not until she heard the locks rattling that she realized she had fallen asleep on the love seat. A glance at her watch proved that only twenty minutes had passed. She sat up quietly, blinking her eyes. When she cleared them she saw Cliff leaning against the door frame staring at her.

"Cliff."

He bunched his lips and shook his head. He unzipped his jacket and sat down in the chair opposite her. "Well."

Elaine exaggerated her motions, rubbing sleep out of her eyes, rolling her shoulders, kicking off her shoes. "Guess I was pretty tired. Passed out like a log as soon as I sat down."

Cliff looked at her intently.

"Stop it."

"Stop what?"

"Stop staring at me like that."

"Well, what the hell do you expect me—"

"Cliff, don't yell at me. Don't . . . yell at me. I'm sorry. I know I've made a mess of things, and I'm sorry. But please don't yell at me."

Sarcastically he said, "Oh, you expect me to have a calm, reasonable discussion with a totally irrational woman."

"Cliff, I said I'm sorry. I don't know what else to do."

"Try."

Elaine waited expectantly, waited for Cliff to give in and come to her side. He always had before. But now he just sat there, staring with those chocolate brown eyes, pinched and piercing. She was immobile. She did not know how to go on. She had gotten so used to Cliff taking the lead that she did not remember how to act otherwise.

Slowly, and haltingly, she slid off the sofa onto her knees and waded through the deep pile carpet. She put her hands on Cliff's knees, pushed them apart, and crawled in between his legs. She looked up at him, horrified at his bland expression, his seeming indifference. She ran her hands along his outer thighs, gripped his limp hands.

"Cliff, I know I've been difficult lately. I've been under a lot of strain. All right, maybe it *has* been self-imposed. I know that. But, that's the way I work best—under pressure. I need that incentive. I pit myself up against an obstacle, then fight to overcome it. I write myself into a corner, then take a picture of a window to climb out of."

His face was a mask, cold and defiant. "If you want to start saving this marriage you'd better get a motor drive. I've quit making excuses for your behavior."

Elaine pressed up against him, placed the side of her face against his chest. A shirt button stabbed her, and she wriggled her head to find a comfortable resting spot. "Cliff, please give me a chance."

"You've had ten years. You want another decade?"

"No, I just want . . . well, I'm not sure what I want."

"I've known that longer than you have."

"Then why didn't you say something?"

"Because I've been trying to help you. I've been trying to share the discovery of this dream, this quest of yours. But, I don't know what it is anymore. You get deeply involved in something, work like the devil at it, and get burned out after a few years. And that just can't happen in a family situation. Once you've got the ball you've got to go for the score. You can't give up at the fifty-yard line."

Elaine ran her hands up his sides, squirmed her fingers behind his back. He was placid and unyielding. "Cliff, I'm confused. I need you. I want you to hold me. But a part of me doesn't want that . . . dependency. That's what it is. I don't like being dependent. I want to stand up on my own two feet and face the world on my own terms."

"And you do."

"But it's not the same thing. I've always had someone to

fall back on. When I was growing up, I had my parents. Now, I have you."

"You're no different from anyone else in the world. Everyone needs a steadying influence. Why do you think I married you?"

"Do . . . do you mean that?"

"Have I ever lied to you?"

Elaine shut her eyes tightly, fighting back the tears. "No. You've never lied to me. But I've—I haven't always believed you."

Cliff made no movement, no acknowledgment.

"I guess I haven't really been fair to you, have I? I mean, I guess I've gotten used to you. I guess I've taken you for granted." She rubbed her eyes on the flannel, and pulled her hands together and worked open a shirt button. Last night (was it only last night?), when she had come home hysterical, he had dressed hastily. Lightly, she kissed the thick mat of hair on his chest. "I guess I've taken a lot of things for granted."

She flipped open another button, a lower one, and another. Cliff did not resist; he continued to breathe at a slow, steady rate. She moved her lips up his chest, opened the last button, and continued on to the tender side of his neck. She pressed her body close, rubbing.

"Laine—"

She placed a finger on his lips, silenced him, then added a kiss. She worked her fingers into his temples, then up into his hair, squeezing the skin at first, then scratching it.

"If you want to go into the—"

"No. Right here. On the rug." She backed away, pulling him by the belt, undoing it as she did, feeling the tautness in his trousers. With a snap and a zip his shorts were exposed. Unyielding, he lay down and let her finish the task of undressing him. She continued to rub his body, to drag her lips along his skin, to keep up the mood, as she slipped out of her own clothes. She gently squeezed his firmness, ran her fingernails over his skin and scrotum.

His eyes were closed. He breathed heavier, and faster. Once she was free of her underthings she slid overtop of him, gently setting herself down so their genitals touched. She took his hands from his sides, stretched them over his head, and leaned against his palms—a ritual of submission. Then she searched for his penis with her vulva, soaking him, teasing him, until he slipped inside her. She brought her knees close to his side and gently rocked him, watching the fluttering of his eyelids, listening to the quickening of his breath.

It did not take long. She saw his face contort, felt his hips arch forward, heard a long, drawn out gasp, smelled the sweet scent of perspiration on his body. Then she lost all sensation in her own wave of orgasm, lost all sense of reality, was swept up in her own world of tingling pleasure and passionate satisfaction. When she opened her eyes the world was still there—*her* world was still there, lying childlike and vulnerable, so alive behind his eyelids, so trusting.

She let his hands go, drew her arms over his chest, and let her weight down on his muscular body. She was still gasping, and had to turn her head in order to get enough air. She felt his body calming down along with her own, felt him soften and slip out of her. Then she relaxed and very casually, very tenderly, joined him in sleep.

When Elaine awoke, the sun had set and the nearly full moon was tossing beams over Camden and the Delaware River right into the living room. Sometime during the afternoon she must have rolled off Cliff, for she found herself lying next to him with one leg thrust over his and her head tucked into his armpit. Cliff stirred at her movement, and in the light of the moon she saw his lids flutter.

She pecked him on the cheek. "Hello there. Enjoy your nap?"

Cliff struggled with his eyes, squinting and rolling them in their sockets. "What time is it?"

"Who cares?"

He managed a wan smile. He drew his arm tightly around Elaine and pulled her close. "Time is but a measure of quantity, but quality is timeless."

She snuggled up against the warmth of his body, thrilling

to his strength for the first time in ages. "That's very profound. Who said it?"

"I did." Cliff made an exaggerated motion of looking about the room, then at Elaine. "Honey, don't you know we're alone?"

She swiped at his chest. "Silly. You know what I mean."

"Silly? You haven't called me that for a while."

"I guess there's a lot I haven't done in a while." She pursed her lips, and glanced away. "Cliff, have I really been that unattentive?"

"The word is 'inattentive,' and the answer is yes."

She pounded him playfully with her fist. "All right, but you don't have to answer so fast. At least make the pretense of thinking about it."

"I'm only teasing."

"No, you're not. I mean, I know you mean to tease, but there's truth in what you say. I just . . . I just didn't . . . I've been moving so fast I haven't been able to enjoy the scenery. Like I'm in a high speed train passing through the most beautiful park, full of trees and cliffs and waterfalls, and I'm reading a magazine while it all goes by. That's what I've gotten myself into. And I don't even *know* it. That's what hurts. If you hadn't pointed it out—"

"Stop knocking yourself out. It's easy to get caught up in the suction of the train, and carried along against your will."

"Ooooh, but not this gal. She knew where she was going all the time. She was just too stupid to get off at the next station. And that's one of the things I like about you. You always know what's coming, and where to get off. As if you read the schedule."

"Well, I didn't *always* know."

"Okay, but you learned it a long time ago. Like, when you made the decision to quit football and go for a degree."

"Part of that decision was made for me. I just used the impetus to point myself in the right direction."

"Really? What part?"

Cliff shrugged, and his grip tightened. "Oh, just that I didn't fit in. I wasn't made out to be a football player."

"Oh, come on, now. You were the best they had, and they knew it. Even Jan—" Elaine gulped, then went on with only a slight bump. "And you obviously wanted to play football or you never would have gotten on the team."

"Oh, yes. I wanted it at the time. But you know, times change and situations change and people change. The things that are very important at one time or in one situation, lose their importance after a while. And sometimes you just don't get what you want in life."

"But you wanted football. Then. What made you change?"

"Just . . . things."

Elaine rested on one elbow, so she could see his face better. "What kind of things?"

"Situations. People. I guess I just didn't get along with all the team members."

"Cliff! You get along with everybody! You're so . . . mellow."

He shrugged.

Elaine felt an awful power in his grip. She touched his chest and he cringed. She felt his legs tense up, nearly crushing hers. "Cliff, what is it? What made you quit the team when you could have been an all-star? A pro?"

He stared up at the ceiling, his eyes glistening in the soft white light. His Adam's apple bobbed up and down silently. "I was— It was some of the players. I don't remember their names. Don't want to remember. They— I was always shy around girls. It's not that I didn't like them, or anything, I just—I don't know—I guess I was afraid of them. I guess because in high school the games they would play . . . Teasing and taunting, saying one thing and meaning another, or just doing things to attract attention but never following up. I guess teenage girls, at least, poorly bred girls, get a kick out of seeing how many boys they can wrap around their finger. They'll do anything to get you interested, then drop you once they figure they've won. It's a game, a cruel game, just to bolster their own warped egos. And I always got hurt by it. My feelings . . .

"Anyway, after a while, I stopped playing their stupid

games. I just didn't listen to them anymore. I ignored them. And some of the guys on the team, well, they thought maybe, since I didn't like girls, maybe I was gay. And some of them were. Oh, some of them definitely were. Here are your big college heros, your macho tough guys, wearing panties under their uniforms. I thought it was just a gag at first. You know, I was naive. I figured, this is more locker room levity. Drawing attention to themselves.

"There were four of them. Big guys. Bigger than me. And they were strong. Well, they . . . were friendly. Asked me to stay after the game, maybe go to the shore with them. One of them had a place in Wildwood—or his parents did—and they were all going there for the weekend. They asked me if I wanted to come along. The place had a fire pit, and a whirlpool, sauna, a small gym. Sounded like a resort so I said fine, I'd love to.

"We drove down together. There was lots of small talk, ass grabbing, that kind of stuff. I know now what they meant, but at the time it just passed right over my head. They kept saying how good a time we were going to have, and I just agreed. When I asked if there would be any girls, they all laughed. It seems so obvious now, but then . . .

"When we got there, the guy who owned the place took me for a tour. We wound up in the gym, and I started working out. He tried to get me to go to the sauna, but I said no, I liked it there. Pretty soon they all came into the gym, and pretty soon things started to happen. I don't remember how it started, but it got pretty rough. Only they were too powerful for me. Before I knew it, they had me pinned down on the press bench, facedown, one holding each leg, another holding both arms. Then . . . then . . . then . . . they . . . raped me."

Cliff's voice was flat and unemotional, almost as if he were describing a scene from a movie. But tears poured from his eyes and rolled across his temples and into his ears.

Elaine gulped so hard it sounded like a burp. She was blinded by tears, and her chest ached with a deep, abysmal pressure that threatened to seize up her heart. "Cliff, I didn't . . . I didn't know. You never said anything . . ."

He sniffed. "Well, it's not the kind of thing you go bragging about."

She wiped away his tears, kissed the near temple, and cradled his head as she would a child. "Oh, Cliff, I'm so sorry for you. I don't— I can't even imagine how it must have been, how you must have felt." Tears kept streaming out, and Elaine kept wiping them away. She rolled over and grabbed a box of tissues from the end table, and handed one to Cliff. "So much pain."

He sat up, and blew his nose. "There's more."

"Oh, no."

He wadded up the soggy tissue and placed it in an ashtray. He was smiling. "As soon as they let me up, I beat the living shit out of those guys."

"What?"

He nodded merrily. "I started swinging an empty weight bar. Before they knew it they were dodging cold steel. They were a sorry looking bunch when I left: broken noses, broken arms, broken collar bones, broken jaws. They looked like four skydivers who had forgotten to pull their chutes. Then I went out and smashed the car to smithereens. A brand new Thunderbird. At the hospital, they told the police they'd been in a crash, hit a deer and rolled the car over, and had it towed to the house. None of them played ball for the rest of the season. Two of them never played again."

"Oh, Cliff, that is unbelievable. I never knew . . ."

"No one ever knew. You're the first, unless one of them let it out of the bag. But I doubt it."

"Cliff, I just can't believe— I mean I've never seen you act violent before."

"Violent times call for violent measures. You do remember that old lecher at the party, don't you."

"Oh, my God, yes. The one who stuck his hand up my dress in front of all those people. You cold-cocked him on the spot. That was right after we first met."

Cliff crossed his legs and leaned back against the love seat, facing Elaine. "Yes, and I was so enamored with you,

I just couldn't stand having anyone touch you, especially
like that, and especially in public."

Now Elaine laughed. "It was weeks before you touched
me like that yourself. I'd never slept with a man before, and
just slept. Let me tell you, it was frustrating."

Cliff tilted his head, smiling whimsically. "Well, it
wasn't easy on me either, it's just that I was still suffering
from the aftereffects of—you know. Besides, I never was
one to talk with my hands. I like to discuss things first, see
where I'm going, make sure it's the right decision. I wasn't
used to you Valley girls, jumping into bed at the *thought* of
a drop of a hat. I mean, not that there's anything wrong with
it. Sex is great, on its own. But, it's just that I've never been
able to separate making love from being in love. For me,
they complement each other, and the lonely, sexual gratification is one I'd rather avoid, because it's too likely to make
me lose my sense of detachment. I don't like being out of
control."

Elaine shook her mussed up curls. "Well, you sure had
me out of control. I thought there was something wrong
with me, because you stayed on the other side of the bed."

Cliff shrugged, smiling. "Laine, that first night, lying
next to me, you looked so delicate, so fragile, I was afraid
if I touched you, you'd turn into a puff of smoke and vanish
like a dream. I never slept a wink that night, I just lay there
thinking about you and stealing glances, wanting to reach
out and put my arm around you, to draw you close, to
cuddle up with you, but afraid that you weren't real, or that
you'd give me an elbow in the ribs or a slap in the face. I
guess I just didn't have enough confidence in myself. I
never could read body language; I've always relied on
English. And I'd had my full of playing games, like the
let's-see-how-far-I-can-go-before-she-stops-me game. That
doesn't even work for kids, I certainly wasn't going to play
it as an adult. Of course, in your case, I didn't have the
shadow of a chance of being rejected sexually."

"Cliff!" She playfully slapped his leg, then stretched her
feet under his thigh and tickled him with her toes.

Cliff grabbed her foot and pinned it to the floor, then

worked his hands up along her calf until he was on top of her. He kissed her on the lips, then rolled over next to her, one hand absently caressing her breast. "You know, I still feel that way about you."

"What, that you don't have to worry about being turned down sexually?"

"No, that you're still a delicate flower with soft, fragile petals."

"Yes, like a rose. I guess I've been pretty thorny lately, haven't I?"

Cliff shrugged, and pursed his lips. "Well, you have been a bit preoccupied."

"Ah, the master of diplomacy strikes me with a feather."

"Okay, then distant is a better word. I mean, we haven't really been communicating for the past several—"

"Years?"

He huffed. "It seems like a long time. Either I've become dyslexic, or we're talking different languages. Or maybe the signals are just getting crossed. But we don't seem to be *sharing* as much as we used to. It's like, we're sitting here watching television, and you suddenly announce you're going to bed. Just a flat statement. And it doesn't leave me much of an opening. You don't seem to think that I might like to go to bed with you."

Elaine fidgeted uncomfortably. "I don't think I want to hear this, but go ahead."

"Laine, I don't mean to hurt your feelings, but—"

"No, it's about time you hit the mule over the head with a baseball bat, before he makes an ass out of himself."

"I think it's the other way around: you make a mule out of an ass."

"Never mind! Don't drag out the pain. Just get it over with."

"Well, maybe I shouldn't—"

"No, I need to hear it."

He kissed her cheek, and ran his hand over her face. He leaned up and looked deeply into her eyes, rubbing her all the time. "Laine, sometimes it's difficult to . . . I mean, when we're in bed . . . I can't get your attention. You're propped up on your pillows reading a book, and you never notice when I crawl under the covers with you. I have to yank it out of your hands, or pull the plug, just to get you to lie down with me. And then it's no good because I have to force you. It seems like *I* always have to make love to *you*, you don't take the initiative any more. This was the first time in— And when we do make love, there's no . . . no response. No emotional response. And I need that. I need that feeling that you still love me like . . . like I love you."

Elaine grabbed a handful of tissues and ground them into her eyes. They came away soaked. "Have I—Have I really been that callous?"

"Well, I don't know. But that's how I perceive it. Maybe it's just me."

Elaine rolled over onto her side, facing him, pondering his questioning, childlike eyes. "No, it isn't just you. I'm to blame. You're always there for me, always attentive, always there when I need you. And sometimes I forget that I'm supposed to be there when you need me. I forget that love isn't a one way street. It's give and take, and I've been on the take too long. I'm sorry you had to hit me over the head with it. I'm sorry I put you in that position. I'm sorry I've shut you out. I do love you, Cliff. It's just that sometimes I forget. Your love is so constant that I take it for granted. And for that, I'm sorry. Just do me a favor. Every once in a while, if I act remote, give me a swift kick in the pants as a reminder. You mean too much to me for me to lose you now. You're irreplaceable. And I do love you dearly."

INTERLUDE 5

Flesh.

It smelled flesh.

The people were gone, the fires were damped, the flesh hung on its pole. The body was limp, held upright only by the thick wooden shaft that worked as a vertical spit. The head careened to one side with the tongue hanging out—forced out by the end of the rounded post. Long black hair cascaded over marble shoulders, framing sagging breasts.

The scent was strong, so strong it had almost attacked the flesh before its worshipers left. But somehow through extreme will, it managed to wait until their departure so they would not see its form. It enjoyed their fear, but not their fright.

It moved, and the earth moved with it. The trees waved. The air hummed. It summoned all its powers as it swept through the barrens, enveloped the sacrificial glade, plunged down upon the makeshift altar.

Then it tasted the flesh.

It tasted the sweet, decomposing meat. It nibbled on the skin, tearing chunks out with pointed, razor-sharp teeth. Its thick black tongue savored each morsel, masticating slowly, stretching out the pleasure of the foul human flesh.

It dug into the muscle, ripping out meat, sucking in tendons and ligaments like strands of spaghetti. It gnawed on the bones of the limbs until they were stripped clean of all vestiges of meat, and gleamed silently in the moonlight like white candy canes.

Already the internal organs were swollen with putrefaction. It pulled down on the legs, jamming the stake upward, tearing through the inner fabric, draining the blood with ritual satisfaction. It flowed red down the smooth sides of the pole, out of the bowels, leaving behind just the meat: the tasty, bloodless meat.

It ripped open the stomach, gorged itself on the contents, pulled out the viscera with clawed hands, stuffed the torn scraps into its mouth: chewing, drooling, groaning with ecstasy.

Last night it had watched this body transformed from the domain of the living to the realm of the dead. Now it was consuming the nectar of death-force, making itself stronger, reinforcing its deathhood, so it could go on forever in deathless continuance.

It plucked out the heart like a plum off a tree, squeezed the blood out of it as one would squeeze water out of a sponge. Then it filled its cavernous mouth with the potent organ, sucked out its raw being. The vital force that once pumped life through a living body would now pump death through the essence of the pines.

It pulled the head close by the thick black strands. It tore into the face with a savagery that was the destructive force of its existence. It wanted to take that pretty face and make it ugly, make it repent, make it unrecognizable, make it more like . . . itself.

It put its great mouth up to the eye, inhaled deeply and sucked the organ of sight out of its socket. It kept sucking, compressing the gray matter like a sausage and drawing it through the hole, slurping, chomping, swallowing, until the skull was an empty husk.

When it was satiated, when there was no more to consume, it wallowed off into the woods, its power at last restored.

But its desire for more only whetted.

CHAPTER 13

He heard it howling.

In the dark, still of the night, he heard it howling.

Jake Rudley shifted uncomfortably on his surplus army cot. One wizened hand extended out from under the torn, patched covers and felt the air of the cabin. It had suddenly become icy. But the chills that coursed along his spine were not from the cold.

He had felt them before, and remembered them vividly.

Quietly he slipped out from beneath the woolen blanket. The cot's wooden legs creaked sonorously. The floor groaned under his weight as bare feet touched the dirt-covered surface. In the stygian blackness he threaded his way across the room, deftly avoiding bumping into his meager furnishings. He knew exactly where everything was located—including his rifle.

Strong fingers curled around the long smooth barrel. He picked it up and pulled it tight against his chest. His other hand ran down its length, thumbed off the safety, and gripped the trigger. His eyes never left the cabin door.

The howling was not continuous, but discordant and intermittent. As it grew louder, the wind rustled through the surrounding trees. Branches scraped against the shingled roof. Jake felt completely naked in only his underwear. The door rattled with the uneven gusts. Jake retreated a step.

Something was out there. A presence.

Flashes of light darted around the edges of the door frame like sparks from a grinding wheel. Jake took another step back. He gulped. He lowered the long barrel until it pointed at the door's central crossmember. Sweat poured off his beetled brow.

The howling crescendoed, then ceased abruptly. The door burst open and a wild zephyr charged into the tiny cabin. Dirt, loose papers, and miscellaneous debris spiraled around the interior as if in the clutches of a tornado. Outside, a bold white light hung like a halo around an amorphous, nebulous shape that hovered beyond the reaches of the porch. From the top of the silhouette shone two red splotches, like glowing embers. They stared with horrifying intensity.

Jake did not move. Nor did he attempt to fire his gun. He was caught somewhere between fear and mesmerization.

The apparition expanded and contracted noiselessly. The eyes were two parallel lasers, burning into Jake's skull. The door slowed its banging against the wall, the churning maelstrom abated. Scraps of paper fluttered to the floor. The dust settled.

Jake gaped at his nemesis. It glared back.

The red embers dimmed, became black coals. The evanescent light sputtered behind the dark figure and went out. The blackness left behind was palpable. The howling, now a stridulating screech, languished in the distance.

Jake was alone in the frightful silence.

On its own, the crudely made door swung shut and latched itself.

For a while he just stood and stared. When his muscles began to cramp from his tensed position, he forced himself to ease off. He turned around. He became disoriented and stumbled into the rocker, then banged his shin against the stove. The fire had gone out. He felt his way to the counter, located the matchbox and lantern, pressurized the fuel bowl, and, leaning the rifle against his body, lifted the glass port and ignited the mantle. The soft yellow glow that suffused the room was wonderful and soothing.

He carried the paraphernalia to the center of the cabin.

Using the rifle barrel as a staff, Jake eased his weary, aged body into his favorite chair. He lay the rifle across his lap as he stuffed newspapers and kindling into the stove. He was in no mood to build the fire meticulously, so he squirted gasoline from a plastic squeeze bottle onto the shaved wood, and tossed in a match. The blaze flared out of the opening. As soon as it died down he threw in some split oak logs, peeling bark down. He closed the stove door.

He sat on the edge of his seat, the rifle clenched tightly in both hands. He watched the crackling flames seep around the edges of the circular grates. When the fire had been roaring for several minutes he picked up the copper kettle that lived on the stove top and poured lukewarm water into his cup. He dropped in a teabag and let it steep.

For the rest of the night he sipped his brew. Eventually, he let himself slide to the back of the rocker. But he did not rock. He just sat, and stared, and thought. The rifle lay athwart the armrests like a safety bar, offering security. First light was a long time coming.

At dawn, Jake began to move about. He rinsed his face and hands in the washbasin and dried off on a tattered towel. He opened the flour can and perfunctorily checked it for bugs. He scooped out a cupful of flour and dumped it into a tin mixing bowl. The bucket still contained water, so he ladled out half a cup and poured it on the flour. After adding a pinch of salt and a teaspoon of baking powder, he stirred the concoction until it had a doughy consistency. A little bacon fat greased the iron frying pan. With a spatula he scraped the bannock mix into the bubbling grease. He let it cook slowly.

He donned his faded coveralls and threw on a denim jacket. He fixed his socks so his hard-nailed toes did not protrude through the holes. He laced his boots with exaggerated slowness, double knotted so they would not come untied.

He cooked the bannock to a golden brown. After he plopped it on a chipped china plate to cool, he mixed another. He sat in his chair, munching the first bannock while the second one cooked. Another cup of tea completed the simple breakfast.

As the bannock cooled he took his knapsack off the shelf. The shoulder straps were frayed, the buckles rusted, the grommets missing. He made room on the counter by pushing aside a box of rat poison. A large jar contained chunks of meat soaking in a milky solution. He picked them out one by one with a long-handled fork, and deposited them in the olive drab pack. The water soaked through the canvas, but not enough to drip.

He crammed the bannock and extra shells into his jacket pockets. He slung one pack strap over his left shoulder, picked up his rifle with his right hand, used the tip of the barrel to jiggle the door latch, stepped outside, and pulled the door shut behind him.

The sun was just crowning the treetops. Golden beams, highlighted with dust, knifed through the upper boughs. The air was crisp and clear. Jake's thoughts were unmuddled by the events of darkness. He knew what he was about.

The tracks began at the edge of the porch: huge, tricornered prints that could have been made by a grossly deformed, oversized turkey, or an extinct dinosaur. They were sunk deep into the sandy soil. The three down-pointed toes dug furrows like plowshares. They did not lead off in a straight line, but meandered along haphazardly. They might have been the ramblings of a playful child.

Twice around the pump, halfway around the pickup, then along the side of the road they went. The stride was half again as long as Jake's. He stalked the creature the same way he had in the past, slowly and carefully, always observing his surroundings as he followed the oddly shaped spoor. He watched the ground, the trees, even the sky. He kept a sharp lookout far ahead, and periodically turned around to check his rear guard.

The pine barrens appeared normal, like any other spring morning. Birds chirped and flitted about, warning trespassers off their territory. Rabbits darted through the underbrush. Frogs croaked from their hiding places along the muddy banks of numerous rivulets. Bees hovered over newly opened petals, seeking honey for their hives. The woods were fresh and alive.

Jake fished a chunk of meat from the knapsack, and dropped it on the ground where the devil tracks had flattened out the grass. There may have been a reason for its behavior, and it might return to that spot. Jake did not want it to go hungry. The Jersey Devil did not like hunger.

The tracks faded over the hard ground of a clearing. Jake walked straight ahead, directly to the opposite side, and there the three-toed indentations began again at the tree line. He ducked under the low limbs. How a creature of any size could have gone through there without changing its gait was incomprehensible—unless one knew that the Jersey Devil was without limitations. Jake had to get down on hands and knees, crawling over wet, mossy earth, yet the imprints were as evenly spaced as if no obstructions existed. When he was able to climb to his feet, he rubbed the ache in the small of his back. But he did not slow down. He had several hours to make up, and the only way he could possibly catch up to the maker of the tracks was to keep a steady pace, and hope that the creature he was tracking would stop for a rest.

The first creek was only six feet across, and ankle deep. A couple of fallen trees spread their branches from bank to bank, but Jake did not even consider crossing on the pine boughs. *It* would not be slowed down by such petty inconveniences, and he could not afford to be. He splashed across the cold water and climbed up the shallow bank where the prints began again.

The tracks went around and around the base of a giant oak so many times that they trampled the ground into a muddy pulp. But only one set of prints led away from the tree. Jake dropped another chunk of meat and kept going.

The next creek was broad and deep. Jake held his rifle up high as he slid down the mud and waded into waist-deep water. He shivered as the cold reached his crotch. Despite its looks, the bottom was hard sand: large granules that offered excellent footing. The current was negligible. The water was dark, the color of weak tea: cedar water. But when he scooped some out with his hand, it appeared gin clear. And it tasted as sweet as if it had only recently gurgled from a deep spring. He climbed up the opposite bank by clutching handfuls of green reeds and pulling himself up. He relocated the tracks twenty feet upstream.

Jake noticed the change in direction. At first, the general trend was east, toward the ocean. Now it was north. He left more meat along the bank where the tracks seemed to mill. The prints traversed several four-wheel drive roads.

By noon the sun was hot and the woods became an oven. Jake wiped sweat off his brow with a red-checked handkerchief. His whole body was bathed in perspiration, but he did not bother to unbutton his jacket. His trousers had long since dried, and become damp again. He took the bannock out of his pocket and nibbled around its crispy edges. But he did not stop walking.

At the next stream he halted halfway across, knee-deep in clear cedar water, and took a long drink from his cupped hand. It took several minutes. That was the only rest he allowed himself. As soon as he had his fill he trudged on. Shortly after that, the trail ended.

Not abruptly, for the prints gradually got shallower, as if the creature making them was losing weight, or substance. The soil was just as sandy, and Jake's own shoes sank in the same amount. Over the course of a hundred feet the prints faded into nothingness.

Jake stood in the grove of cedars that bordered another nameless tributary to the Batsto or the Wading. In the marshland it was difficult to tell where a course of water would eventually lead. Jake reached upward, but could not touch the lowest limbs with his rifle outstretched. He carefully studied the vegetation for signs of disturbance: broken twigs, pulled leaves, or grass that was slowly springing upright. His eyes were the eyes of a tracker with seven decades of experience; he saw no indication that anything, not even a rodent, had passed this way.

He went ahead in a straight line for a hundred feet, then started sweeping. Intuitively, he veered first to the left, and soon came across the distinctive prints he had been following for half a day. They headed in the direction of the westering sun. He took out his bannock again, always transferring the rifle to his left hand so he could eat with his right. He handled the meat with his left. He wiped his brow on the back of his wrist, and took up the trail.

He was led into a nearly impenetrable thicket, so dense that he had to hack and push through clinging vines and sharp needled thorn bushes. Yet the prints did not change in any way; they might have been trampling across a rolling meadow. He held his Winchester out in front of him as a shield. Briars tore at his skin and clothing, ripping both to shreds. When he emerged into a more open area, his face and hands were bleeding and his denims were pulled and full of thorns.

The footprints—or pawprints—ambled across a muddy marsh, appearing only on clumps of grass that stood up out of the water. In between, where connecting prints should have been visible in the shallow, muddy bottom, there was nothing. Jake trudged through the morass, his shoes slurping at every step. Sweat trickled down under his arms. Back on high ground, he looked down at his own feet. He saw the wet spot they left when he took the next step. Yet *its* tracks might never have touched water. Upon closer inspection Jake also noticed that twigs and leaves lay across the devilish prints as if the creature had stepped *under* them or as if the tracks had been pulled down into the ground from underneath.

Again they disappeared. One print was there, the next was fainter, the next barely visible. Where the next one should have been was soft sand all around, and no trees overhead. He lost a half hour scouring the countryside before he found a line of faint impressions headed south. They appeared fresh, the sides of the holes not caved in.

It was getting dark, and he knew he had to hurry.

Then he heard the howling.

It lasted but a brief moment. The short whine was swallowed up by the forest. Jake gulped, frozen in place. Very slowly, very deliberately, he raised his gun, though he knew it was useless against whatever he was stalking, and put one foot in front of the other.

The high-pitched whine started again, went on for several seconds, and died out. Jake's breath halted, his heart palpitated. The howling beckoned, running up and down the musical scale, grating to the ears. Jake responded to the awful call.

He treaded through the dense understory of the pine forest, able to see only a few feet ahead. Thick pine boughs blocked his vision. He held his Winchester out in front like a spear. He released the safety and ran his finger over the trigger. He licked his lips.

Jake heard a loud scraping sound, like two sheets of sandpaper being rubbed together. The air was split with a loud crash, and dust belched up into the air. The howling died out. Silence, deafening silence—a warning—ensued. Jake did not take heed. He was this close. He wanted to see it in the daylight, even if it cost him his life.

He took a step forward, and the howling began again. It was a cry of pain, as if the forest resented human intrusion. Jake stopped involuntarily. He had a sudden urge to urinate. He held it in, glanced from side to side, licked his lips, tightened his grip on the rifle. He took another step forward.

The screeching resumed in earnest. Jake's resolve faltered. His steps became shorter, more unsure. Now that he was so close he was afraid of what he might see. But more, he was afraid of being seen. Still, the curiosity of decades drew him on. He had tracked this beast for more than half a century, and if it cost him his last breath he wanted to have even the merest glimpse of it before his time was up.

The howling. It was an animal untamed, a lion wounded, a gorilla insane, a herd of stampeding bison, a flock of raging gulls. It was reaching out with all its might, with all the forces it could muster. The scent of tortured pine filled the air. The cacophony of terror shrieked down from swirling clouds. The ground shook beneath his feet.

Then he heard the scream of a man.

The howling continued for several seconds, then stopped abruptly. Deathly silence filled the dusky sky like a pall.

Jake smelled the odor of death. His knees were weak. He let himself down to his knees, and advanced ever so slowly.

The brush parted before him. He knelt at the edge of a clearing. On the far side, a dark blue four-wheel drive pickup was parked half off a dirt road. The tailgate was down, and the bed was piled with freshly cut timber.

A bleeding torso lay on the ground. The head was still attached, but horribly hacked apart. The limbs were stacked in front of it like pickup sticks. Blood and gore spattered the ground.

Jake was shaking so hard he feared he would crumble to pieces. His bladder winced with pain. He unbuttoned his trousers and relieved himself. Then he leaned back against a moss-covered stump, never taking his eyes off the awful carnage. When he felt as if his legs could support him, he pulled himself up with his rifle. He worked sideways through the brush until he reached the road, then turned and loped off as fast as his aged body could carry him.

He did not know where he was going, only what he was getting away from. His elongated shadow was about to fade with the sunset, and he desperately did not want to be caught out in the woods at night. It was not until he saw his own familiar cabin that he realized he had spent the day being led in an enormous circle, that the road he was chugging along was his driveway, that the dismemberment had taken place only a few hundred yards from his own front door.

He dropped the Winchester on the ground. The well head offered a place to lean while he caught his breath. His throat was like dry parchment. He flung a weary arm over the handle and started pumping when—

—He was jolted out of his skin by a loud, resonating blast of sound. His whole body shuddered as he looked up. Coming out of the shadows was a lighted, flashing phantasm. He was blinded by white beams that pierced his skull. Red and blue lightning bolts stabbed through his cornea like sharpened spikes. His body quivered in abject terror.

The sound stopped. The lights died out.

"Hello there, Mr. Rudley. The sheriff sent me out here to— Hey, are you all right?"

Jake's heart started beating again. He stood as high as his

stooped shoulders would allow, and breathed deeply. He tried to control his voice. "You like to give a body a heart attack, you come in blastin' your siren that way."

Deputy Hopper jumped out of the police car, stumbled in the soft sand, and hurried toward the old hermit. "Gee, I'm sorry if I scared you, Mr. Rudley. I was just playing a joke. I didn't mean anything by it. I guess, I just wasn't thinking."

Jake brushed him off. He was too relieved at the deputy's presence to chastise him. "It's okay. You just startled me, is all."

Hopper glanced around uncomfortably. "Uh, here, you need a hand with that pump?" He took over Jake's position and pumped furiously. "Looks like you've been out tramping around."

Jake jerked his stubbled chin over his shoulder. "Seen something down the road a piece you might be interested in."

"Yeah, well, before I forget, the sheriff's got a couple of confiscated vehicles he thought you might be interested in. One's a nice new Corvette with the front all smashed in. I never knew they were made out of fiberglass." Water bubbled out of the spout and hit the ground with a sudden spurt, splashing wet sand over Hopper's spit-shined shoes and creased uniform trousers. He vaulted back. "Damn. Hey, you got a bucket or something?"

Jake cupped his hands under the stream and splashed the cool ground water over his head and onto his leathery face. "Keep that handle goin'." Hopper leaned close enough to grab the handle and resumed pumping, while Jake held his knapsack in the flow and rinsed out the meat stains. He turned the canvas pouch inside out, and tossed it up on the porch. "That's enough."

Hopper stepped back, smiling. "You really like this wilderness life, don't you, Mr. Rudley?"

"Not sure any more."

"My grandmother used to have a well just like this, outside of Smyrna. We used to say Delaware was just a state of mind. My dad built his own house on the farm, so I grew up with plumbing. Pumping these contraptions isn't as much fun as it used to be when I was a kid. I guess it's not a bad life, is it? No mortgages, no taxes, no bills to pay. You don't have any credit cards, do you?"

Jake let the young deputy ramble on while he dried his face and neck with his sweaty handkerchief. "Got other problems."

Hopper laughed. "Hey, you haven't come across any more bodies, have you?"

"Just one. Leastways, most of it."

Hopper's smile faded. Then he snickered. "What? An animal."

"The way it's chopped up you'd a thought it's a vegetable."

The deputy put his hands up in front of him, palms out. "Hey, Mr. Rudley, don't kid around. I can't take any more of this killing and maiming." He grimaced. "Oh, I get it. You're getting even with me for scaring you with the siren. Aren't you? Aren't you, Mr. Rudley?"

Jake pursed his lips. He bent down and picked up his rifle, held it in front of him like the pitchfork in *American Gothic*. "I wisht I was, boy. I wisht I was."

INTERLUDE 6

This one was different.

It was old, and it was a friend.

Many times in the past they had frolicked along together, romping through the pines, flitting through the brush, soaring over streams and swamp. It tagged along as it moved under the earth, out of sight of the awful sun.

It would not come out at night. It was afraid. And it liked the fear of others. As long as this one did not see it, it enjoyed leading the chase. Now that it was not so hungry, now that its stomach and groin did not growl and distract it with pain, it wanted to play.

It rose up from the ground in front of the artificial cave in which the old one lived. It gathered its forces from the sky, from the trees. The wind churned through the pine needles, its limbs tapped on the top of the wooden abode. It let the old one know that it wanted it to come out and play. It whispered through the air, its air, Come chase me. Come follow me through the woods.

I demand it.

It opened the door and breathed into the old one's face. It was poised with its stick, peering out, numbed, afraid. It let the creature know that it was an old playmate ready for fun. It made sure the old one understood, then it pranced off through the trees, to hide, to wait, to play as they had played in the past.

At dawn it melted into the earth, watching. Soon the old one emerged. Here I am, I'm over here. *And the chase was on. It cavorted through the woods at a pace just slightly quicker than it could go. It concealed itself under rocks, dashed into the brush, climbed to the tops of tall trees—but stayed under the bark, in the dark, out of the sun's rays. It skittered easily through the water, always making sure it remained below the surface.*

It stayed ahead, always ahead, but not out of touch. It made sure the old one was still following. The sun rose high, peaked, and started to lower. Soon it would be able to come out, to prowl ghostlike without being blinded, to cross above the water without being scared by the awful apparitions that hid in still pools: the things that looked out with such ugly, frightening countenances. It did not like those terrible monsters called "reflections."

They neared the beginning. It let the old one catch up. It kept an eye out to make sure it was right behind. It moved slowly backward, keeping just out of sight, just out of view. Then it came to an emptiness. The trees, its trees, its senses and members, had been removed. Something was there. One of them. *And it was removing a tree that did not just belong to it, but was part of it. And the remover, the profaner, was in the act of amputating one of its body parts.*

It felt the pain as steel teeth sliced into its skin, as its wood was gouged in two, as its sap bled from the wound. It recoiled in anguish, but could not escape the biting blades. Then it was gone. The tree was still there, but it was no longer a part of its body. The trunk had been severed, and nothing was left alive but a horrible, throbbing stump. It watched in torment as the creature furthered its sacrilege by chopping up the fallen timber into smaller pieces.

As it recovered from the shock it gathered its forces. It would not let the creature escape punishment. With all its wrath it struck out blindly, unrelentingly: swinging, clubbing, carving. It screamed in agony, the same agony it had felt when its limbs had been separated from its body. It wanted to teach the defiler what it was like to be disjoined. It dissected the thing that had hurt it. It hacked away until it stopped screaming, ceased moving, until it could learn no more.

Then it slunk away because once again it had been forced to touch that which it despised, that which lived.

It wanted death. It wanted that which did not move, or think, or feel the anguish of going on.

Please, give it death.

CHAPTER 14

Lieutenant Wakeley stepped out of the battered Mercury, wearing a blue suit that was just as wrinkled and loose-fitting as the gray. "This sure the hell is an out of the way place."

"You expect them to make human sacrifices in the City Hall Annex?"

"That's what I like about you, Adams: always with a sense of humor."

"If I *had* any sense, I wouldn't have let you drag Laine out here." Cliff glanced at the pitch pines surrounding the clearing.

Elaine loaded a fresh roll of film before climbing out of the back seat. "If *I* had any cents, I'd save them up till I had a quarter, and call my analyst."

The lieutenant hiked up his pants as he strolled across the glade. "Can we cut the comedy act? We're supposed to be investigating a murder."

Elaine clicked off a couple pictures. "Sorry, but it all looks so peaceful in the bright sunshine, and with a couple of big strong men around."

Wakeley flicked a cigarette butt into a puddle, and immediately reached into his jacket pocket for another. "I'm glad you kids changed your mind and decided to come with me. I'd have never found this place on my own, even *with* the map. Hell, I get lost on an elevator."

Cliff bent down to inspect the brownish water. "How did you ever get to be a police officer?"

"Let someone else push the buttons. Hey, is that gook in the water what you were talking about?" Wakeley bent down beside Cliff, found a stick, and poked it into the thick, clear mass of jelly.

Elaine took a picture. "Yes, I noticed it after Jake ran off the other day."

"What do you think it is? Ectoplasm?"

"Well, from the sensations I was getting, the sexual connotations, I was thinking more in terms of sperm. *Don't touch it!*"

Cliff took a wad of goo off the stick, and held it up in his hand, against the sun. "I don't see any black dots in it, but my guess is it's a gelatinous mass of frog eggs. This is the season for it."

The lieutenant tossed the stick into the puddle, and stood up, looking around. "So, tell me, Mrs. Adams, what did this man look like? Describe him for me."

"Lieutenant, I didn't say it was a man. If it was, it was the most horribly deformed human specimen I've ever seen. It was just *pitiful*."

"Can you be a little more specific?"

"I don't know his hat size."

"How tall was he? How much did he weigh? What kind of clothes was he wearing? Jesus, tell me something. I don't want to hear about how he floated over the ground without leaving footprints. Did he have any distinguishing characteristics?"

"I told you, it's hard to describe. His body was just huge, immense, like a mountain. And his skin—he wasn't wearing any clothes that I could tell—was covered with these big bumps, like bubbles, or pustules, or slimy pimple balls. Only larger. He was gross."

"Or diseased. I've seen some pretty sad cases in my day. But those deformed bodies usually cover the mind of a prince or a moron." The lieutenant wandered over to where the thick log lay between the lashed A-frames. The bark had been meticulously scraped off, and the finish was smooth, almost polished. With a rigid forefinger he touched a red spot spread along the grain. "Hmmn. Appears to be a speck of—"

"Hey, Lieutenant. Take a look at this." Cliff knelt on the ground where chunks of burnt wood lay scattered over bare earth. "It looks like pieces of flesh."

"Oh, *Cliff*."

"No, I mean, like chicken skin. It's all over the place."

"Wild dogs probably had a feast around here. Caught a grouse, or a pheasant." Wakeley picked up a handful of sand, and let it filter through his fingers. "Doesn't it seem a little . . . reddish?"

"That's what I was thinking. Like blood was spilled all over it."

Elaine shuddered. "Would you two cut it out."

Imitating Lamonte Cranston, Cliff intoned, "The Jersey Devil knows."

"Cliff!"

"All right, honey. I'm sorry." He stood up and put his arms around her. She shrugged back at first, then snuggled close. "I didn't mean it."

"Where did you wipe your hand?"

"On the back of your blouse. No, only kidding. I think you're right. With the sun out and all, it just seems like a pleasant spot for a picnic. That's probably what was going on here."

Elaine snickered. "That's exactly what I said to Jake. But after that . . . experience. Cliff, I never felt any malevolence. Just a-an impression of loss. Or of being lost. And there was no smell, no odor."

The lieutenant ran practiced fingers over the ground, picking up scraps of meat and storing them in the palm of his hand. "A guy with that kind of disease would stink to high heaven."

Elaine shook her head. "No, there was nothing. Nothing but a preternatural silence, as if time had suddenly stopped. As if the barrens were frozen, stuck in an instantaneous moment. I felt as if I were seeing a single frame of a movie, on and on. And then, then came the sound. Like a wild animal howling. Not in pain, but in heat."

Cliff pointed his chin in the lieutenant's direction. "She played the tape for me last night. It sounded like a screech owl."

"No. No, it was something else. Then, it was there, and the silence was back, and the frame frozen. Only this time this . . . thing, this . . . creature, was in it. Floating. Watching."

"Laine, it was probably some lunatic piney, feeble minded after generations of incest. You're lucky he didn't kill you."

"Or worse." Lieutenant Wakeley scrambled around a clump of grass.

"No, it wasn't like that at all. I wasn't picking up hostile vibrations. It was just— It was as if this creature wanted to be held, to be mothered. And I felt like I did when I used to work with blind and retarded children. I felt sorry for them in a way, and guilty, and full of love and caring. And they can pick that up. They have an increased awareness of other sensations, some of which we don't even understand. And this thing, this man or woman, was able to detect those feelings in me. He was even responding to them."

"How? How could you tell just from—"

"Take a look at this." The plug of grass came up in the lieutenant's hand, revealing a hole in the ground. "Looks like a cast-iron drainpipe. Now what the hell is something like *that* doing out here in the woods?"

"Jake said there used to be a town here, a stage stop. Can we go now?" Elaine detached herself from Cliff and edged back toward the rust-eaten car. "Maybe Jake'll be home by now."

Cliff was persistent. "Wait a minute, what about this response mechanism you were talking about?"

Elaine took another picture. "In the car?"

Cliff nodded, and followed. "Have you seen everything you need to see, Lieutenant?"

"I guess so." Wakeley ambled back across the clearing, wrenched open the car door on sprung hinges, and slipped behind the wheel. "Get me a plastic bag out of the glove compartment." Cliff obliged him, and the lieutenant shook the scraps out of his hand and sealed the rim of the bag. "I'll have them analyzed. And hand me that bottle, too."

Cliff obliged him again, and exchanged the plastic bag for the hip flask. "Do you do this all the time?"

"Sure. In this business you take every scrap of evidence, go over it ten times, and maybe then discover something you missed the first nine. It's like putting together the pieces of a puz—"

"No, I'm talking about liquor."

"Lick her? I don't even know her. Oops, sorry, ma'am."

"That's all right."

"Do you always booze it up like this?"

"Ever since I lost my little girl." Lieutenant Wakeley started up the engine and turned the car around. Slowly, he bumped over the rutted dirt trail. "I had just become head of the department. It meant a little more money, a little more prestige. I could buy things I couldn't afford before. Bought a new car—this one, always loved Mercs—and gave the old one to Sharon. Betsy and I, we were going to send her off to college. She wanted to be an archaeologist. You know, digging up bones and all that. Was interested in ancient man. Dated one, too. Older than me. Couldn't ever figure it out."

"Maybe it runs in the family."

"Naw, Betsy and I were the same age. Couple of months apart. Knew each other since grade school. Anyway, Sharon went to the shore with this old fossil, and she just never came back. We never heard from her again. Him either. It was as if they vanished off the face of the earth. No letters. No phone calls. I checked every lead, called all the hospitals and police stations. Never found a trace of her. Damn near ruined my career. And it killed the missus. Died a year later of a broken heart. But I keep hoping that one day . . ."

"I'm sorry, Lieutenant. I didn't mean to criticize."

"That's all right, son. I understand. You see an old geezer like me pickling himself, and you think you ought to help out. Well, I appreciate it. I really do. Most people just don't give a flying—" He glanced over his shoulder at Elaine in the rear seat. "They don't give a damn. Sometimes *I* don't give a damn, either. I'll always wonder whether they ran off to some foreign country and got married, or made a suicide pact and walked into the ocean. I guess I'll just never know."

They rode on in silence for a while, leading a trail of dust that sparkled in the rays of the sun. Turkey vultures graced the skies with their black, swept-back carriages, cruising like lost kites. The woods were alive with sounds: blue jays, hummingbirds, thrashers, and meadowlarks; bees and beetles; deerflies and tree frogs.

"Laine, what were you saying about picking up feelings, or sensations?"

"Oh, yes. Well, when I worked with severely retarded children afflicted with sensory blockages, they had no way to communicate with the world. They may not have even known a real world existed. They actually live inside their own heads, and any perception of the world, any physical awareness, is wildly distorted from our view of reality."

Cliff raised a finger to intervene. "Isn't it true that any individual's perception of reality is purely subjective? That there's no way of proving any form of objective reality? That we each sense reality through our own eyes, and our own senses, and that beings with different senses would perceive reality differently?"

"Well, that's being simplistic. Solipsism, in the sense that the individual, or the self, is the only provable point of reference, is a philosophical argument. You have to take as a given that there is a fixed, objectively verifiable truth based on consistent natural laws. Sure, our perception of that reality may be different from person to person, but those perceptions won't change the basic structure of the universe."

"Kind of like the old branch-falling-in-the-middle-of-the-woods argument. If no one is around to hear it, did it really make a sound?"

"Exactly. Logical, rational deduction tells us the molecules vibrated, whether or not there was an ear, or a receptor, to detect it."

"And radiation existed before man invented the Geiger counter."

"So, here I was, working with autistic kids, and it was my job to break them free of their abnormal subjectivity, to counterbalance their fantasy world with a better concept of the real one, to coordinate their spacial relationships within a framework they could understand. I can't say that I always succeeded. And in fact, it's impossible to discern the amount of achievement, if any.

"But the important thing that came out of the experience—for me, that is—was an understanding of the true meaning of perception. You see, we suffer from chronic sensory overload: sights, sounds, smells, tastes, surfaces we touch, or come in contact with. And this shackles our subjectivity. We're so in touch with substance, with physical objects, that we lose our sensitivity to the ethereal. We come to believe that if something isn't tangible, if we can't see it or touch it, it doesn't exist."

Cliff interrupted. "Are you following this, Lieutenant?"

"She lost me when she started moving her lips."

"Shut up when I'm on a roll. Anyway, these kids had the uncanny ability to pick up emotions without a word being said. You know, when you talk to a cat, you can call it every name in the book as long as you say it in a soft, cooing voice. It'll still purr. But these kids could tell what you were feeling without a word being spoken, without any form of recognition, just by your presence in the room. They knew when I was happy, or sad, or frustrated—"

"Not my fault," Cliff said.

"—or elated—"

"Guilty as charged."

"—or expectant—"

"I'll take the fifth."

"—or tired, or fidgety—"

The lieutenant tilted the bottle to his lips. "Most of it's gone, but you can have a swig."

Elaine slapped the seat. "Oh, *you*. You men are impossible. Will you listen to what I'm saying?"

Cliff waved the bottle aside, and stifled a grin. "I'm sorry, honey. Go on."

"With no interruptions."

"Promise."

"Well, this . . . this woods person . . . was like that. He was like a vacuum cleaner, sucking up every emotion, every emanation. It was as if he had no feelings of his own, and was so thirsty for mine that he just soaked them all in by osmosis. I could feel . . . the drain. I could feel my soul being absorbed. And more than that, I was able to sense, just as I could with those kids, what it wanted, what it needed, what I had to offer. It was such a *powerful* experience. I'll never forget it as long as I live."

"Here's to bright memories." Lieutenant Wakeley held up the flask, took a long draft, gurgling, and set the bottle on the seat beside him. "May they be forever dimmed."

"You're disgusting." Elaine glared at him through the rearview mirror.

"Nah, I'm just not hip at all that college-type mind expansion jargon. You ever take drugs? No, you better not answer or I may have to lock you up. But you sure sound as if you've had some kind of loco weed in your life. You didn't get that description out of a book."

"Lieutenant, that description came from within. It's a picture of emotions. It's what I was feeling when that . . . creature . . . came upon me, when he caught me unawares."

"Just don't let him catch you with your pants down again. You never know what these retards are going to do. I've come across enough of them to know."

"Oh, Lieutenant, you're insufferable."

"One of my strongest qualities. Cliff, you got quite a wildcat on your hands here. Don't let anybody take her away from you."

"I don't intend to." Cliff pointed through the windshield. "Hey, there's an old man tinkering around in that junkyard. Is that Jake, honey?"

Elaine leaned forward, between the two in the front seat. "Yes, that's him. He's not as scary as he looks." Wakeley stopped the car, and Elaine got out waving, taking pictures through the telephoto lens. "Jake, it's Elaine. Elaine Adams."

The men followed her to the backyard. He stood expressionlessly, hands at his sides, a pipe wrench clutched in one great fist.

"From the *Bulletin*."

"I know who you are."

"Well, we thought you might be able to help us. My girl friend— Oh, I'm sorry. This is my husband, Cliff. And this is Lieutenant Wakeley. Philadelphia Police Department. My girl friend is missing, and the lieutenant would like to ask you a few questions about the Jersey—"

Elaine saw movement out of the corner of her eye. She gasped when she recognized the man in the white uniform.

"You a little bit outa your bailiwick, ain'tchu?" The sheriff stepped around the back of a green Impala, screwdriver in one hand and license plate in the other.

"I'll handle this," Wakeley said under his breath as he passed by Elaine. He took a leather folder from his jacket pocket and flipped it open so his badge was visible to the sheriff. "Lieutenant Wakeley. Homicide. I'm doing a little investigating on a gal who might've . . . well, might've got lost . . . in the woods. May be hurt."

The sheriff ignored the badge. He stared straight into the lieutenant's eyes. "An' you don't think us hick cops kin handle the job?"

Wakeley flashed a mouthful of tobacco-stained teeth. "No. No, that's not it at all, Sheriff. It's just that this gal is a special friend of mine. My investigation is completely unofficial, and—"

"Then you ain't got no authority to work my beat. You got something you want done, you send a request through proper channels."

"No, Sheriff, you don't understand." Lieutenant Wakeley replaced the folder in his pocket. "We don't even know

if the girl is even here. But this is where she was, uh, last
seen, so I thought—"

"You thought you'd do a little snoopin'." Sheriff Hinkle
stopped in front of the lieutenant, hands on hips, his nose
only inches from the thin man. "An' you stop takin'
pixtures."

Elaine jumped as if the sheriff had struck her, and let the
camera drop to the end of its neck strap.

"Is this the kind of cooperation I would have gotten by
going through official channels?"

"I got ma own way o' doin' things an'—"

"Then let me tell *you* something, mister. I've got *my* way
of doing things, too. I operate a department that's bigger
than your whole township. And I got to be in charge of it by
not taking any lip from any big-mouthed fatsoes playing
John Wayne. You think slinging that forty-five low on your
hip makes you a bad ass? You better think again, mister.
'Cause if I don't get all the cooperation I ask for, I'll have
the State Troopers blow you right out of office. You get the
message?"

Sheriff Hinkle was silent, but did not back down. He
wagged a finger at the lieutenant, but was interrupted before
he could speak.

"Now, I can get what I want the easy way, or the hard
way. But I guarantee you, if I have to get it the hard way,
you'll go down. And you'll be begging for mercy."

"Stop takin' them pixtures!"

The camera never left her midriff, but Elaine was
swinging around and snapping off shots from waist level.

Cliff jumped forward and shook a fist in front of the
sheriff's face. "And you stop yelling at my wife, you
ignorant bastard."

"Shove it up your ass—"

Lieutenant Wakeley pulled the gun out of his shoulder
holster so fast it seemed to Elaine as if it had sprouted right
from his hand. He grabbed the sheriff's necktie, and
rammed the barrel up against his pudgy neck. "And you
watch your fucking language, you big gorilla, or I'll ream
you a new asshole. You ain't fooling with any small-time

hood. I'd love nothing better than to blow your fucking guts out all over the woods."

Sheriff Hinkle stared with bulging, beady eyes. He gulped, but said nothing. A county car pulled up in front of the driveway, dragging behind it a cloud of dust. A deputy reached across the seat and rolled down the window.

"Sheriff— Hey, what the hell—"

Lieutenant Wakeley shoved the sheriff away. "You better call him off, if you know what's good for you."

The sheriff stared for a long moment, then glanced over at the deputy climbing out the opposite door with his gun in both hands, aiming over the roof. "It's okay, Hopper. The situation's under control."

"Not until he drops it."

The lieutenant slowly reholstered his gun, and straightened his jacket with a tug at the lapels. "Hinkle, I'm going to stop off at your office a little later. I want to look through your files. Now, I'm going to do it, one way or the other, you can bet your ass on that. But you can make it a hell of a lot easier on yourself by cooperating with me. Because I always do what I say I'm going to do. And I always get what I want. You got that?"

Instead of answering, the sheriff looked hard at Jake, stabbing with his finger. "You watch your mouth, Rudley, or you'll come ta a bad end."

Lieutenant Wakeley slapped his open palm against the sheriff's shoulder. "Stop threatening my witness, or I might just make this official and lock you up for hampering an investigation. I can pull so many strings over your head you'll be jumping around like a puppet."

The sheriff scowled and left without a rejoinder. He plopped down in the passenger seat, the car sinking with his weight. The deputy spun his wheels on the dirt road.

"Whew, you sure are one tough son of a bitch," Cliff breathed.

"You deal with enough low-lifes, you know they're all full of shit. A shell of bravado, but yellow inside. Every once in a while, you have to let some of the shit out. Besides, I outrank him, and he knows it."

Elaine quickly rewound another roll of film. "Do you think he'll cooperate, Lieutenant?"

"Not easily. Not unless he's changed any."

"Huhn?"

"I had a run in with him before, only he doesn't remember it. Back when I first took this job. I was young then, new at it, more easily intimidated. After my daughter disappeared, I started tracing routes she could have taken home. A lot of these backwoods roads go along lakes and ponds. We've got quite a few cases of missing persons turning up years later when their cars are discovered in the water, maybe during a dry spell, or when they drain a manmade lake for maintenance. I checked every body of water big enough to hold a tricycle between every shore point and all three bridges into Philly, looking for skid marks, plowed up bushes, broken guardrails. Figured she and her man friend could have been drunk, speeding, went off the road, and drowned when their car sank. He didn't help me any then, so I sure don't expect him to help me now."

Lieutenant Wakeley turned away from the road, and gestured to the junkyard behind the house. "Sorry for the interruption, Mr. Rudley, but that's quite a car lot you've got there."

Jake did not nod, or turn around. With his solid, blank stare, he said in an even voice, " 'Bandoned autos. The county auctions 'em off, I buy 'em for spare parts."

"Well, that's great. Now, I've got a few questions I'd like to ask you . . ."

CHAPTER 15

The squeak that passed for a door chime was just loud enough for Elaine to hear. She pushed aside her notes and tape recorder, turned down the music, opened the door to the end of the safety chain, and saw two men standing outside.

"Good evening, ma'am." The taller man flashed a badge and returned it so quickly to his pocket it could have been a shooting star. "Sergeant Morris? This is Sergeant Winslow?" He ended his sentences with a curious lilt that made it sound like a question. "Lieutenant Wakeley sent us as your escort?"

Elaine tightened her bathrobe. "What? What are you talking about?"

"Lieutenant Wakeley? From homicide?"

"Yes, I know who he is."

"He sent us here to drive you in to police headquarters? Said he didn't want you out on the streets by yourself. Thought you were pretty wrung out."

"Well, he's got that right. But he didn't say anything about me coming in."

"Pardon me, ma'am, but we *did* try calling several times. Your phone's been busy."

"Oh, yes, I'm sorry. I was working, and I took it off the hook." Elaine ran her fingers through her hair, realizing how tired she was.

"Anyway, there are some things he'd like to go over with you? And he knew what kind of a strain you were under, so we're supposed to drive you in. Uh, is your husband home?"

"No, Cliff had to go to work. You know, he's missed the last couple days."

"Yes, I understand you've been busy."

"Wait a second, I'll let you in." She closed the door, released the chain, and opened it wide. "Come on in." She stepped back as the two policemen entered. "Well, I have to get dressed. You want something to drink? Coffee?"

"No thanks, ma'am."

Elaine glanced at the short, overweight sergeant. "For you?"

"No thanks."

"Well, make yourselves at home. I'll only be a minute."

"Thanks, ma'am, but we'll just wait here by the door. Police protocol, you know. We're not supposed to wander around in people's houses unless we have a warrant."

Elaine managed a grin as she retreated down the hall. "Whatever happened to police brutality and transgression of authority?"

The tall sergeant laughed. "You've been reading too many newspapers."

"Or writing them," the other added. They both laughed.

Elaine left the bedroom door open while she disrobed, pulled on slacks and a blouse, and slipped into a pair of jogging shoes. She raised her voice. "I'm not used to being treated this way by the police. That sheriff over in Jersey thinks he's God's disciple."

She heard strained laughter.

She walked quickly up the hall, ducked in the bathroom and looked at her face. She bit a piece of chapped skin off her lower lip, rubbed a tiny dollop of matter from the corner of one eye, and was ready to go.

"Just let me get my purse."

"No, hurry, ma'am."

"Uh, Brad," the shorter sergeant started, "what about transportation back?"

"Huhn? What are you talking about?"

"Well, we'll be off duty by the time the lieutenant's done with her. Suppose, well, you know how things get balled up, suppose there's nobody to bring her back?"

The tall sergeant stared at him. "Well, I guess— Gee, I don't know." He shrugged. "The lieutenant didn't say anything."

"So, why don't we bring her car along, just in case?"

"I can drive," Elaine offered. "I'm not that wrung out."

"Oh, no, we can't let you do that. The lieutenant said to drive you, and he'll be mad as heck if we don't."

Sergeant Winslow smiled obsequiously. "So why don't *you* drive her to the station, and *I'll* drive her car? That way, she can make it back on her own if there's no one around later on."

Sergeant Morris looked down at him. "Say, that sounds like a good idea." He fixed his gaze on Elaine. "Would that be okay with you, ma'am?"

"Sure. Fine. I've got the keys in my purse." Elaine was getting impatient with these two. She turned off the lights. "Shall we go?" She locked the door on the way out.

They walked down the hall and Sergeant Morris reached out a lanky arm and pressed the call button. "Now, we'll still drive you back, or whoever's on shift, but just in case . . . You know how it is in homicide, you never know when we'll get a shooting, or a suicide, or something. But if the evening is smooth, someone'll drive your car back and—"

The elevator arrived and Elaine stepped in. "I said it's okay."

Sergeant Morris punched the parking garage button. "We've got our car in the underground garage. Where are you parked?"

"Spruce Street. I can get out at the lobby and—"

"No, we'll just drive around. It's a Jeep, isn't it?"

"CJ-7, with a rag top."

The cage dropped twenty-one levels to the basement. The garage was well lit, and extended to include all three buildings of the Society Hill towers. Sergeant Morris led the way along the rows of cars toward a black station wagon waiting in the aisle.

"Got a private conveyance for you," Sergeant Morris said.

Elaine noticed the fancy chrome grill, the polished black hood, the gleaming whitewall tires. "What's it for, special occasions?"

"You could say that."

The vehicle seemed to be inordinately long, and the roof was higher than usual. She blinked when she saw the county insignia on the door, slowed down when she saw the car was a hearse, came to a dead stop when she recognized it from a picture she had taken recently.

"Sergeant, what—"

Two men appeared from behind the hearse, approaching rapidly.

"*Sergeant—*"

Both sergeants gripped her arms and propelled her forward. One of them clamped his hand over her mouth, stifling her scream. She struggled futilely, then lashed out with her feet. Her legs were caught up by the other two men, and the four of them carried her horizontally, kicking and squirming, into the open rear door.

The lid of the coffin was open. Elaine was thrown in hard. The hands on her limbs were not relaxed until a cloth was tied tightly around her mouth. Then the lid was slammed shut, and she was left screaming in the darkness. Through the thick padding she could hear muffled laughter.

She sneaked her arms upward and clawed at the overhead. The fabric tore despite her short nails. The coffin lurched. She could imagine the hearse backing up, stopping, moving forward, stopping, turning right; then she lost all sensation of motion as she frantically pounded the smooth lining, only inches from her face.

A terrible heat washed over her body. She could hardly breathe. She was smothering in the close confines, quivering with claustrophobic fear. Tears ran in continuous streams down the sides of her head and into her hair. She cried until her voice was hoarse. Finally, drained of energy, she lay still.

Eventually, she passed out.

CHAPTER 16

"Lieutenant. It seems as if we're both working late."

"That's the way it is in this business. We can't convince the criminal element to unionize, and operate on a nine-to-five basis. You got murders going on all the time, and the only way to keep up with them is to put in extra hours. Now, if they'd hire a few extra people . . ."

"It would increase my city wage tax, and it's already high enough."

"Higher from twenty floors than it is from a desk in the slums and a row home in Germantown."

"Touché. I guess I've got no right to complain, as long as I've got nose-to-the-grindstoners like you on the payroll." Cliff leaned back in the plush swivel chair, crossed his legs, and switched the telephone to his other ear. "So what made you call me here at the office?"

"I tried you at home, but kept getting a busy signal."

"The phone's off the hook, I'll bet. You know how that wife of mine is. She's as much of a workaholic as you."

"And you."

"I usually stick to a daytime routine, but losing these last two days was more than the company could stand. I've got some important litigation in process."

"Not as important as your wife, I see, or you wouldn't have taken the time off."

"Lieutenant, I know where my priorities lie. I can always

get another job, but there's not another woman like that one."

"I like to hear that. Sometimes I worry about you kids today—with broken marriages, and wife swapping, and community sex, and the lying and cheating and bickering over child support and visitation rights. Whatever happened to good old-fashioned family tradition?"

"There's still some of it around. You have to understand that the world's different today than it was, uh, in your time."

"You're treading on dangerous ground, son."

"Well, let's talk about my grandfather's time, then. Back then life really *was* simple. Not that it was necessarily better, because there was plenty of hardship, poverty, and suffering. But human values were easier to understand. People had to struggle so hard just to stay alive that a couple only ever had one goal in life: to put food on the table and keep a roof over their heads. The only thing they *had* was family. There were no other distractions. Consequently, parents had more interaction with each other and their kids grew up as part of that interaction.

"But now that society has so much to offer, there are so many avenues to take, so many inputs. We're suffering from sensory overload. We're living in a country in which individuality is being smothered. Because of the pressure of the masses, people are constantly trying to break free of the restraints of conformity and monotony. They want to be different, they want to be noticed, and it's not too difficult in a society that offers so many diversions—from skydiving to skin diving.

"And that's what makes it difficult for people to stay together. You meet someone because of a common interest, but each also has many other, divergent interests. Instead of being forced to grow together, as in the old days, couples tend to grow apart. Affluence practically forces people to seek out new experiences, entertainment, and lifestyles that his partner may not be attracted to. And usually their relationships suffer because they don't slow down long enough to analyze the importance of companionship. They don't have the sense of fulfillment that comes from intimacy and personal involvement."

"Sounds as if you've given the matter a little thought."

"Yes, well, I guess I'm a rare bird—"

"Close to extinction."

"—but I've always tried to keep my sights on a humanitarian level. It's worked for me."

"Adams, you're a fine example of the youth of today. I just wish some of the other kids thought the way you do."

"Lieutenant, I wish you'd stop thinking of me as a 'kid.' I mean, after all, you've dated women my age."

"Oh, come on. I haven't been on a date since high school. Me and the missus got married early."

"Well, I don't know what you call it nowadays, but you've been doing *something* since she passed away."

"What makes you say that?"

"Well, uh, Janice, I guess."

"*Janice?* What did she ever say that would give you that idea?"

"Well, you know, your relationship—"

"What relationship?"

"All right, call it an affair."

"Adams, what the hell are you talking about?"

"Do you want me to spell it out for you?"

"I guess you'll have to. I'm a damn good detective, but I can't figure out what the hell you mean."

Cliff sighed deeply, and changed ears again. "Have you forgotten, Lieutenant, that I know all about you and Janice?"

"No. That's what has me confused. I thought you *did* know."

Cliff paused for a moment, staring at the mouthpiece. "Lieutenant, maybe what I think I know is different from what you think I know."

"Is that supposed to make sense?"

"Okay, you asked for it." Cliff took a deep breath. "My understanding is that you and Janice were . . . sexually engaged." The dead silence on the other end of the line was numbing. "Lieutenant. Lieutenant. Are you still there?"

The voice that finally came back was a loud and gruff. "I'm here, Adams. And I'd like to know what the *fuck* you're talking about. I can't believe— I thought you of all people— Well, you goddamn son of a bitch— "

"Lieutenant, Janice told us all about her friends on the force, how many she was dating, how she—"

"Adams, she was a young woman, a bon vivant, a woman about town. Of course she dated—and more—a lot of men on the force. I knew that. But I made her promise never to tell me who. I didn't want to be put in an awkward position. But, for God's sake, Adams, you don't think we— I mean, she and I— Oh, Christ, I thought you saw the letters."

"Sure, I saw them. But I didn't *read* them. My God."

"Then maybe you should have. Then you would have known that she and I . . . well, she was like a daughter to me. A surrogate daughter. Ever since she lost her folks in that boating accident when she was in high school. I lived in Vineland then, and she was Sharon's best friend. She used to be in our house all the time. Then, when she lost her parents, when she was alone—she didn't have any brothers or sisters—well, me and the missus, we kind of took her in. She shared a room with Sharon. Was her best friend till college. Not that they became enemies, but they were growing up, each in their own way. You know how girls are.

"Then, when Sharon disappeared, well, Janice *became* our daughter. We didn't adopt her, or anything, she was too old for that. But we were family to her. She— "

Cliff lurched forward so hard his feet pounded the floor. He practically ripped his pants getting his wallet out of his rear pocket. He flipped it open and fumbled the lieutenant's business card out onto the walnut desktop. "Oh, my God. Are you Uncle Bart?"

"Who the hell did you think I was, Kriss Kringle?"

Cliff laughed out loud, a long, roaring laughter he could not contain. "Lieutenant, I don't believe it. I mean, I *do* believe it. I just can't believe the monumental misunderstanding. I thought . . . that is . . . it seemed as if . . . well, Janice used to talk about the policemen she knew—"

"Look, I knew more than I was supposed to know, because every once in a while I'd overhear one of the guys—well, you know. Or her name would crop up in a locker-room conversation. I knew she was seeing some of the men . . . intimately. And I tried not to make moral judgments about her character. Hell, she was just a young, healthy woman with an average appetite for— Well, she got around a bit. But, Adams, she was a good kid. Wouldn't hurt a fly. And she was the soul of discretion. Never went out with any married men, although God knows they tried. But to think . . . my God, I'm old enough to be her father. And I loved her like a daughter. Like my own daughter. After the missus passed on, well, Jan kind of took over for her. She was the only thing that kept me going through some tough times. Even after she moved out on her own she'd come to see me once a week without fail. Cooks a Christmas turkey for me every year. She was the last family tie I had. I got no one else."

Cliff was too choked up to speak. He heard what he thought were sobs on the other end of the line. The goose honking must be Wakeley blowing his nose. When Cliff thought sufficient time had passed, he said very softly, "Lieutenant, you'll always have me and Laine."

He heard some sniffling, then, "Adams, if you were within reach I'd punch you right in the—"

"Call me Cliff."

"Goddamn it, cut it out. I've got work to do, I don't have time for sentimentality."

"Then why did you call?"

"Christ, I don't know. I sure as hell didn't intend to pour my soul out to somebody I hardly know." Through the receiver Cliff heard papers shuffling. "Wait a minute. I'm still going through all this material you dropped on my desk. The photo lab developed some of the film Elaine shot today. Got a good pick of the sheriff holding that license plate. Well, I had it traced, and guess what?"

"It came from a stolen car."

"Worse than that. The owner *and* the car have been missing for two days. The guy supposedly left Manasquan for Philly, and never got here."

"You think the sheriff's got something to do with the disappearance?"

"I know he does. I just don't know what. He was real cagey this afternoon. You should have hung around."

"He gives me the creeps. There's something about him I don't like, and it's not just his bedside manner. Besides, Laine was about to have a conniption. She's got a gut feeling about that guy."

"It'll get guttier when she hears this. They had another fatality yesterday. In the woods."

"Oh, no."

"Yes. Naturally, the sheriff didn't want to share any information, but I badgered him until he agreed to take me out to the site. They hadn't cleaned it up yet, and God, was it a mess."

Cliff sighed. "Do I want to hear this?"

"You'd better. This was a local guy, a friend of the sheriff's. A relative. Cousin, I think. Anyway, fatso was sure upset by it. Said he'd left three kids orphans, a young wife, a live-in mother-in-law—"

"Forget all that," Cliff said. "How did he die?"

"Accident."

"Oh."

"You sound disappointed."

"No, just relieved, I guess. I thought it was something gruesome."

"Chain saw victims are always gruesome."

Cliff was silent, brooding.

"Does that make it more interesting?"

"Morbid, perhaps, but not necessarily interesting. Anyway, go on, but spare me the gory details."

"There's nothing *but* gory details. This guy was chopped up worse than suey, like somebody put him through a vegetable slicer. They had deputies out there picking up pieces and putting them together like a gingerbread man jigsaw puzzle. He—"

"Hold it!" Cliff heard the phone drop at the other end. He waited until the rattling of plastic on wood yielded to muffled grunts. "Please, spare me the clinical description. I don't want to know the guy was diced up for a Caesar salad."

"Uh, sorry. You get calloused in this job after a while."

"Just tell me how it could have been an accident."

"The guy was a lumberjack. Used to be. First he chops trees down, then he chops them up. So he's out there sawing logs for firewood, and felling saplings for fence posts. He must have been planning to do some climbing for attached deadwood, 'cause he had his chain saw clipped to his belt with a wire lanyard. Anyway, nearest we can figure he hacked down this tree and got caught in the lower branches when it hit the ground. The chain saw got ripped out of his hands, and because it was tied to his waist, it spun around and made minced meat out of him. Whoops. Sorry for the graphics. Anyway, it must have kept bouncing around like a garden hose with too much water pressure, till it ran out of gas."

Cliff found himself on the edge of his seat. "But chain saw have an automatic cutoff. As soon as you take your finger off the trigger, it shuts down."

"Clogged with wood chips and sawdust. Apparently this gut wasn't too fastidious about cleaning his tools. Makes you wonder, doesn't it. Of all the freak accidents, the pine barrens have had their fill this week. Your wife'll have a field day when she hears about it."

"I don't know. I think she's given up the idea of doing firsthand research. She's sticking to libraries and telephone interviews. You might be able to help by getting the autopsy reports. Where are they kept on file?"

"They aren't."

"What do you mean? Didn't you interrogate the medical examiner?"

"The county doesn't have a medical examiner."

"But what about Benson? He was at the station—"

"He's a coroner, not an ME."

"What's the difference? Aren't they the same thing?"

"And you a big shot lawyer."

"Corporate, not criminal. And it's been longer than I care to admit since law school."

"Excuses, excuses. Anyway, the ME examines bodies, the coroner conducts inquests. And Benson ain't no doctor. Or lawyer. He's just a high paid public clerk with some medical training. Which reminds me, you know the picture your wife took in the prep room?"

"Before her camera crapped out?"

"Yeah. Well, one of my lab men made a blowup of it—of the robe. He took it to a professor at the University of Pennsylvania. Thought the hieroglyphics might have some meaning, you know? Well, he found out the symbols are some kind of Indian scripture. You know, if some kid today spray paints a building, it's graffiti; if an Indian did it a thousand years ago, it's a pictograph. Anyway, he couldn't get a good translation, but the prof was sure it had something to do with the 'great evil spirit of the woods.' Does that sound familiar?"

"The Jersey Devil?"

"Right. Apparently the robe has some religious significance."

"Like in witchcraft?"

"Well, more in the way of ceremonies to chase away evil spirits. You know, I think this Jersey Devil cult goes way back, before the first settlers, before Columbus. I think it's a hand-me-down from ancient Indian culture. Look, I don't know anything about pre-Pilgrim redskins, but it all sounds pretty fishy to me."

"You mean, like maybe the Indians knew more than growing tobacco and planting fish heads next to cornstalks?"

"Like they smoked something in those peace pipes that raised more than their *own* spirits. They concocted ghosts and stirred up the dead and did ritual dances to make the evil spirits go back to sleep in the forest, or back into the depths of their minds."

"Well, that's not too unusual for primitives, is it?"

"I don't give a damn about primeval savages. It's today's

throwbacks that worry me. And their weird cabalistic rites. I think we've stumbled onto something that scares the shit out of me."

"Coming from you that's quite a declaration. So what do we do now?"

"You go home and take care of that wife of yours, and let me get back to work. I've got a mound of stuff I haven't gone through yet."

"Thanks, Lieu— uh, thanks, Bart. I'm about done in, anyway. I've been alone in the office for hours, and this place is as quite as a morgue. It gives me the creeps. The cleaning lady came in an hour ago and scared the pants off me."

"Just don't let her rape you. That's not my department. I'll let you know if I come up with anything."

"Thanks. And take care."

Cliff took a deep breath as he hung up. He dialed his home number and got a busy signal. He pushed back the chair, leaving the papers on his desk exactly as they were so he could pick up later where he left off. He turned off the lights and locked up the office. After a short hop on the elevator he stepped out onto the sidewalk, and was rewarded with a touch of reality as theatergoers and late-night diners strolled along center city avenues. It was a mile and a half to the river, and he always enjoyed the atmosphere, if not the actual chemical composition, of the air. It was refreshing without being fresh.

The doorman at the Towers nodded sharply, and the elevator whisked him upstairs. He was surprised to see a short, overweight man lounging around outside his door. He walked straight up to him.

"Can I help you?"

"You can if you're Clifford Adams."

"That's me."

"Mr. Adams, I'm Sergeant Winslow from homicide." He held out his badge. "Wakeley—I mean, the lieutenant, sent me around for you. Said he'd like you to come in for some more questioning."

Cliff scrunched an eye. "What?"

Winslow smiled. "I'm your escort. The lieutenant figured you two were pretty wrung out, so he sent out a private car. I get to play chauffeur for the night. But what the hell, it beats taking fingerprints off a manslaughter victim. I get enough blood and guts."

Cliff gestured with the keys in his hand. "But my wife—"

"Already gone. We asked her to lock up. I've been waiting—" The sergeant scrutinized his watch. "—half an hour, at least." He held out his hands, palms forward. "But I'm not complaining. It's light duty."

Cliff hesitated, his mind in turmoil. "That's strange. The lieutenant said . . . I mean, I thought . . ."

"I know. I can't figure out officers, either. Never did in the army. Seems like as soon as they get a commission they go crazy. Or maybe they have to be crazy first. I don't know."

Cliff put one hand up to his throat. "Look, Sergeant. I'd like to get out of this monkey suit."

"No problem. I'm not here to harass you. You're a witness, not a criminal."

Cliff opened the door and whipped the tie from around his neck. "Okay, I'll just get into some jeans and put on a clean T-shirt."

"I'll wait by the door. Police protocol, you know. We're not allowed to poke around in people's houses. Not without a search warrant."

"It's nice to know my rights won't be abused." Cliff unbuttoned his jacket as he walked along the short hallway to the bedroom. He flung it and the tie on the bed, slipped out of his shoes and pinstripe trousers, and rustled through the closet for his knock-around clothes. Loudly he said, "How long ago did the lieutenant send you?"

"I wasn't watching the clock. Maybe an hour."

Slowly and quietly, Cliff picked up the bedroom telephone. "Guess you guys deserve an easy night once in a while."

"It's a hectic job, that's for sure. People just don't appreciate it."

He kept clicking the receiver, but could not get a dial tone. He pulled on his favorite faded dungarees, snapped them around his waist. "It's a job I wouldn't want, I know that."

"Well, it's not all bad. We get pretty good bennies: hospitalization, full dental, lots of leave, and sick days. Even shift work ain't so bad once you get used to it. It's nice to be off during the day once in a while, when the stores ain't so crowded."

The phone was still dead. He banged the instrument in the palm of his hand, listened, put it down, and pulled on his hunting boots. "What about taking the job home with you?"

"Naw, you get used to it after a while. Homicides are just numbers on a report. You don't get to know any of them."

Cliff fastened the buttons and tucked in his shirt as he ambled up the hall. "Is that your in-house joke?"

The sergeant was smiling. "Every occupation's got one. To be honest, most of our work's boring. Pure drudgery. Not like on TV."

The kitchen phone was off the hook and the receiver lay on the counter. "So's legal work. There aren't many Perry Masons in this business. And they say lawyers have created more chaos than existed before God created heaven and earth."

The policeman laughed politely.

"You say you've already taken Laine?"

"Yes, Sergeant Morris—"

Cliff's fist landed in the middle of the sergeant's face, cracking knuckles and breaking bones. Winslow was propelled back against the wall. His elbow pierced right through the sheetrock and his head made a dent in the wallpaper. As he slid down like a cartoon character, Cliff jumped on him and grabbed his lapels.

"Where is she? What've you done with her?"

The sergeant's head lolled, but he brought up a fist that connected with Cliff's neck and lower jaw. Cliff fell back, gagging. Winslow reached under his jacket, and pulled out a snub-nosed revolver. Cliff kicked out, catching the fat sergeant in the midriff, and rolled forward after the gun. He caught Winslow's wrist and bent it down just as he squeezed the trigger. The report was not loud. The bullet was swallowed up by the partition.

Winslow's other fist slammed down on Cliff's temple. Cliff rolled on the carpet, keeping a death grip on the gun-wielding wrist. He twisted hard, heard a howl and felt a bone snap. The gun came free. Before he could pick it up the sergeant lunged from his sitting position, bulldozing Cliff with his round chest. The two went rolling over into an end table. The lamp crashed down on both of them.

The sergeant rolled back and right up onto his feet. Cliff scrabbled to his knees, glanced after the gun, did not see it, turned just in time to glimpse Winslow's foot headed his way. He rolled back with arms outflung, catching some of the heel on the shoulder. He used the momentum to go right over backward and up like a cat onto his feet. Winslow was already charging into him.

Cliff stepped aside, dodged the fist, grabbed a handful of shirt, and pirouetted with the short man. Winslow was spun around, but kept falling backward right through the drapes. They pulled loose from the sliding track and fell down over him like a shroud. His body kept going, unhindered by the plate glass window.

The first explosive sound was followed by a tinkle of glass and a *whoosh* of flapping material. In an instant, Sergeant Winslow was gone.

Cliff stood in the middle of the room, gasping for air, unable to comprehend what had just occurred in his own living room. His body was doused in sweat, as if he had just gotten out of a steam bath fully clothed. Particles of glass were still separating from the window frame when he heard a mild thud far below. He stared, paralyzed.

A long time later, when the cool wind hit his face like an ice pack, he stumbled backward, knocked over a chair, fell into the love seat, scrambled up and over the coffee table, and charged into the kitchen. He grabbed the handset and punched the receiver intermittently. It was not until he forced himself to hold it down for several seconds that he got a dial tone.

He got the number from Lieutenant Wakeley's card, but his hands shook so hard he kept missing the buttons. After the third try, the touch tone connected, the phone rang. And rang.

And rang.

"Come on."

After the tenth ring a strange voice growled, "Yeah, what is it?"

"Sergeant— No, Lieutenant—Lieutenant Wakeley."

"Just stepped out."

"Get him. I've got to talk with him."

"Quit your shouting, buddy."

"I have to talk with him."

"Well, he ain't here."

"When will he be back?"

"I don't know. It ain't my turn to watch him."

"How long will he be gone?"

"I said, quit your shouting."

"How long!"

"I don't know. I think he went out for a sandwich."

"I've got to talk with him. I've got to. Right away."

"Well, you ain't gonna. Now, you wanna leave a message? That I can do."

"Yes. Yes. Tell him, tell him they've got Laine. Meet me in the barrens. You got that?"

"I'm writing it down. I'll tell him as soon as he— "

"It's important. You've got to find him. You've got to!" Cliff slammed the phone in its cradle and raced for the front door. He swung it so hard it crashed against the wall and hung open. He raced down the corridor and punched the call button with frenzied haste. He spent agonizing seconds pacing in the alcove, punching the walls with his fists as if he could scare the elevator into arriving sooner.

He heard the *ding*, charged inside the cage as soon as there was room to fit between the sliding doors, punched the garage button and the door close button at the same time.

The doors took their time coming together. The cage started down. It went one floor, *dinged*, and opened its doors.

"Did you hear a funny kind of noise?"

Cliff planted an open palm against the old woman's chest and shoved. She fell backward and right down onto the floor. The last glimpse Cliff had of her was a gray bun coming loose and the round *O* of her mouth. The elevator dropped to the underground garage.

Cliff came out of the cage like a race horse sprung from the gate. The car keys were already in his hand, with the door key held between thumb and forefinger. He sped across the short aisle and did not slow down as he reached the front of the BMW. Instead of wasting time slowing for a right-angle turn, he jumped sideways right over the hood. He jackknifed his legs, planted a hand down on blue metal, and slid right over the waxed surface. As his feet hit the cement floor his hand dipped into the door handle. His body stopped dead and spun around, and the key went right into the lock. A moment later he was sitting inside.

The engine cranked right over. The seat belt alarm was still buzzing as the tires spun rubber and the car shot a short arc out of the parking spot between a Cadillac and a Continental. The BMW fishtailed between the vehicles, tires screeching all the way. Two men, looking startled, leaped out of a black station wagon parked in front of him.

One yelled, but jumped back immediately as he almost got sideswiped. The other reached for his breast and pulled something out. The window next to Cliff exploded inward, and the rear passenger window blew out. The BMW reached a bend in the garage lane and smoked around it sideways. Cliff heard two thuds against the steel body, and a whistling sound behind his head.

Coming up the ramp, he hit Spruce Street in the air with the front wheels turned. The car slammed down on the hardtop, spitting sparks and scraping metal off the under-carriage, and almost spun out of control. He twirled the leather-gripped steering wheel with more guts than precision, and managed to straighten the car in the direction of travel before doing more than banging a fender against a double-parked Mustang.

The streets were a blur. He did not remember how he reached the ramp of the Benjamin Franklin Bridge. At ninety miles per hour he passed trucks and buses and cars. Taillights passed by like rockets. He stood on the brakes as he approached the toll booth, and the tires screamed in protest. He did not look at the speedometer as he charged through the gate, but caught a glimpse of the toll collector leaping out the other side of the booth. Then he weaved and dodged the traffic until he got to Route 70. From there he travelled most of the way in the oncoming lane, passing cars like a blue streak of lightning, veering back into the flow as headlights approached, passing on the right on the narrow, stone-covered shoulder.

At 206 he took the circle on two wheels and minutes later, at over a hundred miles per hour, he was speeding along the fringes of the pine barrens. But at night the road looked so different. There were hundreds of dirt trails and offshoots. Which one did he want?

Dammit, which one?

CHAPTER 17

The coffin rocked and swayed.

Elaine pushed up against the lid and braced herself against the bumpy motion. Her eyes throbbed from crying, her fingers were torn and bleeding, she swam in a sea of perspiration. One corner hit with a crash. The padding absorbed the shock as the coffin collided with something hard.

"—the hell difference does it make? She ain't gonna perform no better anyway."

The cover cracked. Cool, pine-scented air flowed in. Garish beams of light carved cones through the night. The lid was thrown all the way back, and someone shone a flashlight into her eyes, blinding her.

"Don't look no worse for wear."

Rough hands, frigid against her skin, clamped around her arms and legs. She was hoisted out of the coffin, and carried like an eviscerated doe. She was too weak to do anything other than moan. They dropped her on the sandy ground; stones and sharp twigs stabbed her back, the pain forcing alertness into a subdued consciousness.

Heat from the adjacent fire singed her right side. The flickering yellow glow lent a devilish appearance to the ring of heavily made-up men stooping over her, pinning her hands and feet.

The sheriff's midriff obesity bulged through the folds of

the red robe tied loosely at his waist. His genitals were
overshadowed by abdominal flesh. He held a dead flashlight in front of her eyes. "Look familiar, lady? Says
'Property of the *Bulletin*' on it. Yeah, I thought ya'd
remember. Ya too smart fer yer own britches, so I'm gonna
hafta cut 'em off ya."

The blade that flashed in the light of glowing embers
gleamed like silver, and was at least a foot long. Elaine's
moan grew into a gutteral, staccato growl. She wanted to
scream, but her vocal chords would not respond. She
wriggled like a worm, but the men held her firm.

The sheriff dragged the knife along her belly. The odd
sensation tickled her skin. Then he inserted it under the
zipper, and slashed upward. Calvin was separated from
Klein. Her legs were elevated, her jogging shoes yanked
off, her jeans pulled down and over her ankles. Her socks
were caught by the tapered dungarees, and came off with
them.

The leering sheriff grabbed a fistful of silk and with one
sharp tug ripped off her sheer panties. "My, my, my. What
a purty body."

Elaine squirmed and groaned, but was held firmly
spread-eagled.

"Don'tchu worry, lady. I see ya quiverin', an' I know
whatchu want. An' I'll see ya git it."

With calculated venom he slammed a long wooden pole
into the ground between her legs. The pine shaft pinched the
skin on the inside of one thigh, causing her to cry out.

The sheriff leered down with stained teeth. "No need ta
beg. I'm gonna give it ta ya, an' a whole lot more'n what
yer usta."

Elaine rolled her eyes, beseeching the four men who
pinned her limbs to the ground. The sheriff threw down the
pole, scrunched the material of her blouse in his two,
hamlike hands, and shredded it off her body. Then he
grabbed her brassiere in the middle and tore it apart. Firm,
pear-sized breasts bobbled free.

The sheriff slapped at the erect nipples with the knife

blade. "Not as big as the udders on that other one. Hardly more'n a mouthful."

She heard the chanting, a long way off. She twisted her head and saw the procession of blazing torches streaming out of the woods. All the people, men and women alike, wore red robes untied in front, with nothing underneath. Naked feet pounded the soil to the accompaniment of skin drums. Painted faces like glaring gargoyles were contorted with mixed expressions of pain, fear, and anticipation.

"I tried ta scare ya off, lady, but chu wouldn't listen. Now yer in fer it. An' they'll never find yer Jeep inna lake."

"Hinkle, where d'ya want this guy?"

A large, still body, wrapped in red satin, was carried on a bier by four husky men.

"What the hell'd ya do ta 'im, Murdock?"

"Old man Rudley's strong as a herd of bulls. Tore into the gang like Paul Bunyon's ox. Damn near destroyed his cabin in the fight. Knocked out a wall, and quite a few teeth. Busted an arm or two in the bargain."

"Awright, quit with the excuses. His face looks like it went through a meat grinder. Is 'e alive?"

"He was still swinging a tire iron after he got hit with that two-by-four. The blood makes it seem worse'n it is. Shit, he's breathing better than the both of us."

"Well, throw some water in 'is face, for Christ's sake, an' wake 'im the hell up."

The wooden platform was laid on the ground.

"I'll do it." One of Elaine's legs was released, and Morris stood up in the firelight. He positioned himself over the inert figure, parted his robe, wrapped his fingers around his penis, and directed a flow of yellow urine into the old man's face. "I always hated the bastard."

"Hell, you wanna kill 'im with that acid o' yours."

Jake Rudley shook his head, spitting the warm droplets off his lips.

"The liquid of life."

"Don't hold it too long or you'll jerk it off." Sheriff

Hinkle shoved Morris aside, and bent low over the old man. "Hey! Rudley. Kin ya hear me?"

Parched eyelids fluttered. Jake blinked and squinted to get the ammoniated water out of his eyes.

"That's better. Well, after all these years yer finally gonna join us."

"Leave me be. Hinkle, leave me be." Jake's voice was cracked and tinged with fear. "I ain't never done nothin' to ya."

"Ya stayed outside the fold. All these years, ya scorned the cult."

"I never." Jake Rudley struggled, but his arms and legs were bound with thick cord to the wooden slats. "I din't do nothin' but mind ma own business."

"The Jersey Devil's ever'body's business."

Jake sputtered and scrunched up his face as he licked his lips. "You shoulda left it alone. It can fend for itself."

"Yeah, by feedin' off our dead. By raisin' havoc among the livin'. By roamin' the woods an' preyin' off our wimmin an' children. Ya ain't got no kinfoke, so it don't bother ya none. But some o' us gotta worry 'bout our fam'lies."

"By sacrificin' innocent people? By takin' in speeders an' tourists, an' torturin' 'em to death? Does that make sense?"

"It does when we can satisfy its hunger, an' send it inta the bowels of the earth for another seven years. Back inta the pit o' hell, where it belongs. 'Stead o' leavin' it ta haunt our backyards."

"Ya stupid bastard!" The tremor in Jake's voice was getting wilder. "Don'tcha know ya only make it stronger with each feedin'? Ya gotta kill it, man. Once an' fer all."

"An' how we gonna do that?"

"Like ya kill rats. Ya poison 'em. Ya set out bait, poisoned carcasses. I been doin' it for years, decades."

"An' it ain't worked, has it?" The sheriff sneered, hands on hips as he bent down over the prone man. "Mindin' your own business, were ya? Russ Hopkins was mindin' his own business, too, an' whad'id it git 'im?"

"That was his own fault. He 'as cuttin' down a live tree. Shoulda knowed better, 'specially *this* year."

"We'd a put somebody on the pole sooner, he wouldn't a had to worry none. But after tonight, with all this fresh meat, somehow I think things're gonna be a whole lot diff'rent."

"Hinkle, all ya gotta do is live *with* it. That's what I done. When it calls, I come a runnin'. When it wants ta be alone, I leave it. That's all ya gotta do."

"What're ya, its fuckin' playmate?"

Blood gushed over Jake's face and into his mouth, causing him to sputter. "It knows me, Hinkle. It knows who I am."

Chanters circled the seven blazing fires, torches and candelabras held high. The central fire was barely crackling, but someone was tossing in dried pine needles. It flared up suddenly, shooting flames high into the air.

"Don't care what it knows, old man. The wust part about it is, yer gonna know. We're plumb outa recruitin' powder, so yer gonna ride the broomstick with yer eyes open."

Jake screamed, terror evident in his voice. "Hinkle, ya can't do this ta me. I ain't done nuthin'."

"They done it ta Christ, din't they? An' look how famous *he* got. This ain't no diff'rent, 'cept you're goin' to appease a *real* god. That's whatchu git for shootin' your mouth off."

"Hinkle! I din't tell 'em nuthin'. Nuthin' they din't already know. An' that lieutenant—he's smart. He knows somethin's up."

"He don' know nuthin'. He's just a city flatfoot, outa his territory."

"But *it* knows. *It* knows, an' it'll git ya fer this. It'll git ya."

"Blow it oucher ass, Rudley, before I cork it up for ya." The sheriff ambled back to Elaine, picked up the wooden staff, and smiled down at her. "Lady, ya gonna git the story o' your life, 'cause yer gonna be in on the end o' this thing."

Benson ran his hand along the sacrificial log, the full moon shining down on his face out of a crystal clear sky.

Elaine hardly recognized the coroner under his varicolored makeup. "Hinkle, we going to get this show on the road?"

"Ya gettin' eager? Or scared?"

"Don't pay to play around with the Jersey Devil. I'd rather hold a pork chop in front of a pack of half-starved wolves. Let's get it the hell over with."

"Aw, ya just can't wait to shove it in, kin ya?"

The coroner checked the lashings on the A-frame. "You want to do it, it's fine with me."

"Ya can do the old man. Me, I'll take the lady." The sheriff rubbed the smooth, sanded end of the inch and a half thick pole, and laughed raucously. "Awright, tie 'er down ta a coupla stakes so she can watch the proceedin's without us havin' ta hold 'er." He bent over and stared into Elaine's fear-widened eyes. "We'll do the old man first, nice an' gentle. Then ya'll git your turn, but it'll be diff'rent. An' who knows? Maybe by then, your hubby'll be here. An' we'll have a reg'lar fam'ly shish kebab."

Sheriff Hinkle retied his robe and sauntered over to the horizontal log. "Awright, git his ass over here."

CHAPTER 18

Lieutenant Wakeley unwrapped the Italian hoagie on his desk, flattening out the white plasticized paper to catch loose onions and dripping oil. He took a large bite and, as he chewed five kinds of lunch meat and two kinds of cheese, pulled closer the pile of prints and photocopies.

The office door opened after a curt knock, and the desk sergeant walked in. "Bart, here's the rest of them pictures from the lab."

"Couldn't they make them any smaller?" The lieutenant took the wallet-sized filmstrip, shaking his head. "My eyes aren't what they used to be."

"You could try wearing glasses."

"That would make me look old and feeble."

"But you *are* old. I mean, you're getting close to retirement. You oughta think about getting outa this rat race."

The lieutenant scowled. "And do what? Watch Sunday afternoon football and eat out my stomach lining with rotgut beer? Sit around on the doorstep dodging milk bottles?"

"You could move to a better neighborhood."

"I could buy a new car, too. Burke, I don't think you understand at all. This isn't just a job, it's my life."

"It'll be your death, too, if you don't watch it. Don't you think I know why you asked for your daughter's file? That case's been closed for ten years."

"Unsolved cases are never closed."

"But what do you hope to accomplish other than torturing yourself? Face the facts, Bart. She ran away with a man, plain and simple. It happens alla the time, and you know it as well as I do."

"That's not true. I mean, I know it happens all the time. But Sharon wouldn't do that. She wasn't that kind of girl."

"She was the kind to go out with a married man, though, wasn't she?"

Wakeley came right up out of his seat. "That's enough, Burke. I don't need any of your philosophy tonight."

"You need something. What're you gonna do, camp out here again like you did on that last case?"

"Until it's solved, yes."

The desk sergeant shook his head. "Just like you've been camping out here for the last fourteen years, trying to solve a missing persons case. Bart, maybe *she* wouldn't have run off, I'll grant you that. But that guy might have abducted her, or convinced her—"

"He had a business, too. A chain of hardware stores that were making a bundle. You going to try to tell me he walked out on that?"

"He also had seven kids. And a big mortgage. And an old bag for a wife. And a sick mother-in-law. What I'm trying to tell you is he had plenty of reason to skip, to wanna start a new life. It was the simplest solution—"

The lieutenant shouted him down. "But Sharon would never go along. Forget it, will you? And just let me conduct a simple investigation."

"Bart, you're a good man, a good officer, and a good detective. But you better start facing the facts. This case has been eating out your gut ten times worse'n the alcohol you pour into it. Forget it's your daughter and look at it as a case, pure and simple. Then you'll know you shoulda stopped years ago."

"I can't forget about my daughter. Or my wife. Or *this* case, either, because it involves someone I—" Lieutenant Wakeley realized he was yelling at the top of his voice, and swinging his arms wildly. He slowly eased into his chair, and took a drink of black coffee. He dragged deeply on the cigarette that had been burning away in the ashtray, and knocked the inch-long ash on the floor. "Burke, I'm sorry. You just don't understand. You're a bachelor. You *can't* understand."

"I understand *you*. I've worked with you long enough. And dragging up old dirt isn't gonna—"

"I'm not just dragging up old dirt. This new case I'm working on—"

"And keeping secret."

"—has quite a few similarities with—you know. There's a connection here, somewhere. I'm sure of it."

"The only connection is a loose one—in your head."

"Get out of here and leave me alone, will you?"

"All right. But keep that top drawer closed." The sergeant turned and stepped across the office. He pulled open the door, but stood poised in the light. "Oh, by the way, do you know a place called Baron's?"

Wakeley ran his hand through coarse, unkempt hair. "Baron's. Baron's. Is that the sleaze joint on 64th St.?"

"You'd know better than me. You visit 'em all."

"Burke—"

"Anyway, some guy named Lane called and said you're supposed to meet him there."

"Lane? Lane who?"

"Didn't leave a first name. Said you'd know what it was about."

"I don't know any Lane. You sure it was for me?"

"That's who he asked for. Prob'ly wants you to join him in some drunken bacchanal."

"That's *enough*, Burke. When I don't show up he'll get tired of hanging around. Now get the hell out and let me work."

"Gotcha."

As soon as the door closed, Wakeley took a flask out of the top drawer and put another shot in his coffee. When he replaced the bottle, he took out a four-inch magnifying lens and passed it over the black-and-whites. Sipping, puffing,

and chewing, he studied the prints with specific attention to
background detail.

There was the old hermit, standing in front of his
junkyard. Peering past the dirty coveralls, Wakeley looked
to see if any of the other vehicles had license plates. Most
of the cars were little more than hulks, but he could tell by
the taillight configuration that the station wagon was a
Mercury. He knew about Mercuries. But there was nothing
else apparent. He put the pictures aside, filed them away in
the back of his mind, and went on to something else.

A pack of cigarettes, four cups of coffee, a pint bottle of
scotch, and half a hoagie later, he had gone through the
entire file history of both cases, had read a sizable amount
of Jersey Devil legends and word of mouth lore, had
scanned all the unpublished facts concerning the recently
exhumed bodies and remains, had studied all the photographs Elaine had taken, and had breezed through the
accounts of the hunters mysteriously torn apart in the
barrens. The only thing left was the tape-recorded accounts.
He put a microcassette into his own player and sat back to
listen, staring up at the water-stained acoustical tiles. The
voices droned on.

He listened to the sheriff bawl out four scared teenagers;
to an interview with Jake Rudley; to dictated observations
and notes; to the horrible howl that Elaine interpreted as the
call of the Jersey Devil; to her James Bond adventure in the
coroner's office, and the names and dates in the notebook.

She read them off faster than he could write, but he jotted
down the first few and let the rest go. With the tape still
running, he got up from his desk and carried the slip of
paper to the door. He opened it and called out, "Burke, can
you get on the computer and check out some old missing
persons files for me?"

The desk sergeant looked harried, with a telephone in
each hand. "Bart, I'm swamped out here. We got a
Superman suicide at the Towers. Stock market must have
plunged. It always happens that way. Guy wrapped himself
up in a cape and tried to fly off the twentieth floor."

Lieutenant Wakeley kept only one ear on the sergeant. He

did not want to miss the conversation between the sheriff and the coroner. "Yeah, well, I—" He stopped suddenly, frozen like a snowman. His mind reeled, oblivious to the clattering and ringing of the room.

"Hey, Bart. You okay?" The sergeant put down both receivers, rose slowly out of his chair. "You having a heart attack or something?"

The lieutenant gulped. His hands were shaking, and the note fluttered to the floor. He leaned against the doorjamb, his legs too weak to support him. He turned and stared into his office, at the tape recorder, his mind a montage of speeding images.

"Holy shit, Batman."

INTERLUDE 7

With its whole being, with the grass and the trees and the shrubbery, with the moon and the stars, with the very air, it sensed the coming sacrifice.

It no longer swung through the trees, or waded through cold cranberry bogs, or crept through the forest. It was the forest.

It was strong.

And it was getting stronger.

But it still needed food. It still needed energy. It had to have more. Hibernation was a debilitating process, requiring vast stores of sustenance. Before it could recede into its unconsecrated abode, before it could face the wasting away and the structural shrinkage of another cycle, it demanded an immense depository of emotional fat on which to draw.

Its stomach yearned for flesh, its black soul craved other souls.

When its stomach grumbled, the earth moved. When it flexed its muscles, the trees trembled. When its heart throbbed in anticipation, the air crackled.

It no longer merely approached the sacrificial glade, it enveloped it: from below, from above, from all around. The fires warmed it, the chanting soothed it, the pounding feet caressed it, the human oblation fed its body and soul.

But something was wrong.

Something was about to rob its fun, to spoil its supper, to ruin the homage.

Through supernatural senses it detected incursion. It felt the presence of that which did not belong, that which should not be part of these ancient rites.

This was wicked. This was sacrilege. This it would not allow. This it could not allow. It had to prevent such impiety.

That which transgressed must pay.

And dearly.

CHAPTER 19

The BMW was in a ditch, the rear wheels held off the ground by a half-rotted log jammed under the bell housing. Cliff never should have driven so fast along the darkened dirt roads, but his anxiety would not let him slow down. He was sure he was on the right trail and that he knew where he was going. Even without a map and a compass he had a natural sixth sense. It had saved him many times from having to bivouac overnight in the Maine woods.

Now, with his car stuck, his only choice was to get out and walk.

No. *Run.*

He wasted one fruitless minute rocking the car and kicking the log, then took off. He almost burned himself out after the first quarter mile; running on deep sand was a slog. He slowed down to an almost leisurely pace he knew he could keep up for miles. He was no longer a trained athlete, but long walks and constant exercise had kept him reasonably fit.

The air buzzed all around him. Mosquitoes, thirsting after blood, flitted around his ears and flew into his eyes. He slapped at them as he jogged along the darkened road.

He recognized the turnoff as soon as he saw it. At least, he thought he did. Intuition had gotten him this far, but now he was unsure of himself. He stooped and studied the deeply rutted dual tracks, gouged out by hundreds, perhaps

227

thousands, of tires. Cliff was no tracker, although he had
followed quite a few deer in his day. But he was good
enough to see that the road had been heavily traveled of
late. And off to the side, crushing grass and pine needles, he
saw the distorted remains of a Uniroyal knobby pattern like
the tread on the tires he had only recently put on the Jeep.

Breathing hard, he stumbled along the narrow offshoot.
His boots sank into the soft soil with every step, exhausting
him. When the forest thinned and the swampy lushness
gave way to higher ground that was dry and clear, Cliff
climbed out of the trail and ran along the hardened earth
under the moonlit pines.

He stopped abruptly. For a moment he simply stared, his
heart pounding hard against his sternum. Then he had to
breathe, and he let out a lungful of air and started gasping.
All around him were cars, pickup trucks, and four-wheel
drive vehicles, parked on both sides of the broadened
tree-cleared trail. He was right out in the open where it was
bright enough to read the license plates.

But nothing around him stirred. No warm engines cack-
led as the blocks cooled. No one shouted at him. There was
no sound other than the hum of insects and the sough of a
breeze whipping through the upper branches.

Cliff gulped. He looked through the windows of a beat-up
Corvair, and saw piles of discarded clothing. The adjacent
Galaxie had dresses strewn over the seats, and panties and
brassieres, and high-heeled shoes on the floor. He yanked
open the door of a Bronco, the courtesy lights flaring like a
beacon, and eased it closed enough to press in the switch.
But in that short glimpse he had seen men's dungarees and
flannel shirts and several opened makeup kits.

The forest sounds became louder and took on a cadence
like stridulating crickets. Then he heard the drum beat, the
steady thumping of fists on stretched leather. The faint
chirruping grew into a chant that was not natural, not of the
forest. For the second time in as many minutes, Cliff's
hackles rose, and a cold chill coursed along his spine.

He stood for a long time without moving, staring in the
direction from which the ancient canticle emanated, strain-

ing his eyes to see through the trees and underbrush. Then, resignedly, he put one foot in front of the other, crunched sand and twigs, crouched, and placed his other foot soundlessly between timberland debris.

He stayed off the road, ducked under low-lying branches, threaded through the brush, silent as an Indian hunter of the past, stalking. The wind was kicking up, not just waving the treetops, but whistling through the pine needles like the wail of a lost child. White puffy clouds, glowing like cotton balls in the light of the moon, whipped across the sky from the east.

Now he could make out voices, from deep bass to soprano. The drum roll quickened. Yellow lights flickered through the trees: flames waving from the tops of upheld brands. The hymns were sibilant, nonmelodious, inspiring, and creepy.

On hands and knees Cliff dashed from trunk to gnarled trunk. He crouched behind a broad bole, leaned against peeling bark, and beheld the spectacle taking place within the sacrificial clearing. Red-robed men and women romped in a wide circle around a ring of fires. Several females, breasts exposed, planted sticks and pinecones in a central, cleared area adjacent to the horizontal log lashed to the double A-frame.

There must have been over fifty participants, devilish-looking in war paint and ceremonial accouterments. Four men cut the lashes from a makeshift pallet, and raised up a large naked man who started screaming and writhing. He broke free once, but two others pounced on him and held him down while the four bearers retained their grips.

Cliff's skin crawled. The sky seemed to be alive, almost sparkling. A sensation ran through the soles of his feet that was like static electricity. His hair stood up on end. The ground seemed to vibrate in cadence with the drum beat, with the endless and tuneless chanting. He jerked his hand away from the sharp bark, his palm stinging from numerous unseen insect bites or the roughened edges of wood. The very air was palpitating.

The squirming captive shrieked in terror as they flipped

him over facedown on the log, his arms and legs weighted
by four fiendish looking devils. A fat man directed the
proceedings from one side of the log, while on the other a
taller, red-robed figure cupped his hand over the end of a
long staff as if he were smoothing or petting it.

Cliff clamped his legs together, his sphincter muscles
reacting galvanically as he anticipated what they were about
to do. He was hardly able to breathe—did not want to
breathe lest the slight intake of air alert the fiends of his
presence. He did not want to see what was happening, yet
he could not tear his eyes away from the horrible nightmare.

The pole jabbed the victim between the legs, seeking the
orifice. The screams became louder, more frantic; the
writhing became spasmodic, desperate. The rounded end of
the pole slid in. The wielder twisted and turned the shaft and
eased it into the body cavity. The prisoner let out a series of
screams that were the product of fear and pain. His whole
body pulsated against the foreign intrusion.

A harshly-painted woman knelt inside the girdle of
laid-out branches, brushed the ground, and signaled. The
screeching captive was lifted off his stomach and carried
toward her, the shaft sticking out between his legs. The
wretch was tilted, the woman guided the bottom of the
wooden pole into a hole in the ground, the man was propped
up on its end—and let go.

He stood up like stick puppet, screaming, arms clawing
and legs pumping. He was a wild, strawless scarecrow gone
mad, sinking lower with each kick, swallowing up the pole
from beneath as if by magic. The red-robed people jumped
out of the circle, while several other women touched their
torches to the dried kindling. The fire rose up around him,
not near enough to burn, just to singe.

The occult dancing resumed, the unfamiliar words rang
out in song, became a litany heralded by the squawlike
woman. The victim's wailing went on and on as he sank
lower and lower. He stretched out long legs, reached with
his toes, but could not touch the ground. He grappled with
his hands for the smooth shaft. He got his fingers around the
wood, but did not have the strength to lift himself off. His

cries grew dimmer, his gyrating slower. It took him a long time to die—geological ages, the way Cliff was counting time.

It was not until the last shriek pierced the air that Cliff became aware of the other cries, the familiar cries. It was only then he noticed the figure tied prone on the ground, her body gleaming, blond hair cascading around her head.

The clouds raced by with ever increasing speed, blocking out the moon at short, intermittent intervals. Cliff continued to cringe, straining his eyes, disbelieving, not really sure . . . not wanting to be sure. The wind blew his hair off his face. The air clapped around him like someone boxing his ears. The earth beneath his feet pulsated with a life of its own. He had the sudden feeling that he was being watched, that he was surrounded.

Something stamped the ground behind him. A snort sounded in his ear. Damp air blew against his neck. A hot, musky odor wafted into already dilated nostrils.

Cliff spun around swinging. His forearm connected with a firm, unyielding body, covered with coarse hair. He grabbed hold of slobbering, blubbery lips, felt the massive teeth with his fingers. The huge head butted his chest, slammed him against the tree, raked him with a swift, upward stroke that thumped across his ribcage like a sharp stick on a picket fence, and left searing pain.

Cliff slammed back against a pine, paralyzed with fear. His mind raced with vivid images of torture—of a torture he could not stand. He raised his fists against whatever unearthly, incarnate creature faced him, prepared to fight to the death. Prepared to die rather than be taken.

The mighty animal backed away, a dim amorphous shape in the darkness of the sudden cloud cover. Black beady eyes stared for a fraction of a second, and blinked. Then the creature leaped about and bounded off. Silhouetted against the darker pines, Cliff saw the tan fur of a whitetail buck as it leaped across the road, followed by three small does. If it had had a full set of antlers he would have been gutted like a Christmas turkey. As it was, the pedicels, in the first flush of growth, had torn the skin and left him bleeding, but alive.

Without knowing if he had cried out, Cliff whirled toward the revolting liturgy. None of the bowing, praying figures looked up from their ritual. They seemed intent on their unholy purpose.

Cliff knew what he had to do. But there were so many, and they were so strong, and he was so helpless. He watched in agony. Then, he took the only option that, in his fear, was open to him.

He ran away.

INTERLUDE 8

She *should not be there*.

She *was the mother*.

Memories clamored out of the deep recesses of its mind, once repressed but now so vivid. Before it had been adopted by the earth, by the pines, by the barrens, before it had flown away to live by itself in the obscurity of the forest, before it had devoured dead, decomposing flesh, there had been one who had nurtured it at her breast.

She had been like this one: cooing of voice, soft and warm of body, flaxen of hair—or was it white with age? It had looked up to her, for she had borne it through a difficult time, had sacrificed herself so that it could survive, let it suckle at her breast even as her milk dried up and she languished from starvation.

She had cared for it, she had reached out with her heart, she had given it—love.

She had not cared what it looked like, she had not been abhorred by its deformed body and its awesome powers. It had belonged to her, and when she left this world it was never owned again. Even mother earth merely suffered its existence, begrudged its control, relinquished the forces of nature reluctantly, only under its command.

There was constant battle between them, always a conflict: between life and death, between food and hunger, between desire and resentment. Always it had conquered, always it had subdued.

But always it had wondered. Why?

Why did it continue this useless death? What purpose did it serve? Why could it not give up this painful existence for the sanctity of thoughtlessness, for the pleasure of dissolution? And suddenly it knew.

It was incomplete. It needed to carry on in another way, in a way which only she could help.

It sent feelers through the air, tentacles through the earth. It caressed her the way she of old had caressed it. With its supernatural powers, unbeknownst to her, it slipped again into her body, suffused itself into her soul, let out the longing within its groin. And through its senses, it knew.

She was with seed—perhaps its seed. And they were going to release her as they did the old one. They were about to feed it the anguish and the body of the only one since time immemorial who had shown it compassion.

They were about to destroy a sacred mother.

NO!

CHAPTER 20

Cliff ran as if the devil himself was after him: over logs, around trees, under low, clutching branches. Chased by the wind, he charged through the pine forest like it was a high-speed obstacle course. He broke through the entangling brush, tripped and fell headlong, and rolled up still running. Nothing was going to prevent him from getting away from the awful spectacle taking place in the glade. Nothing. He reached the roadway and charged along the rutted track, kicking up sand like a dual bucket ditch digger.

He arrived at the woodland parking area completely exhausted and unable to stop. He ran into a pickup truck, hands outthrust, banged into the fender, and leaned over the hood, retching. He slid down the metal, fingernails clawing, and turned as he sat in the sand, using the vehicle as a backrest.

He cried out loud. He could not help himself. He leaned forward and muffled his face in his hands, wiping the gushing tears from his face. When he tried to uncross his legs, he found he was shaking so hard that his muscles refused to respond. His hands trembled violently. He was not in control of his body. Or his mind.

He was so wrung out that even the ground seemed to vibrate in sympathy, and the truck rattled with his sobs. It was several minutes before he was able to climb to his feet. He worked his palms along the quarter panel until he reached the tailgate. Then he leaned one-handed as he passed behind the truck bed, lurched for the next truck. Beyond this was a car. Like a drunk, he stumbled from one vehicle to another.

Then he saw the CJ-7, a ragtop. Elaine's.

He looked around quickly, guiltily. The wind was howling, the harbinger of a storm on the way. The sand swirled around his feet as if washed by waves on the beach. He leaped for the canvas door, whipped it open, jumped behind the steering wheel into the bucket seat.

The key was still in the ignition.

He turned it. The engine cranked over immediately. He revved it up and fed power to the six cylinders. The 232-cubic-inch block was well tuned. He found reverse, let out the clutch, threw his arm over the seat so he could see behind him—and froze.

On the cargo deck was a long, leather case. Tenderly, almost lovingly, Cliff reached out and touched it, first with his fingertips, then with his whole hand. He eased off the gas pedal, and slipped the transmission into neutral. He brought the case between the seats and cradled it in his lap. Slowly, he pulled down the zipper and exposed the eight-millimeter Mauser.

Behind the seat was an army surplus ammunition can. He snapped open the lid and dumped its contents on the carpeted floor. There were two full magazines and several boxes of shells. Mentally, he wrestled with himself. Fresh thoughts leaped the synapses of his brain—scary thoughts. He cuddled one of the sleek, dull black magazines in his palm. The metal was cool and calming. He could feel the power held within.

He slammed the magazine into the breech, pulled back the bolt, and inserted a round. He released the safety as he aimed down the long barrel out the unzipped passenger window.

Cliff swallowed hard. His hips arched off the seat, and he had a sudden urge to urinate. He lay down the deer rifle between the seats, climbed outside, hunched away from the wind, and relieved himself on the ground. When he sat back down he was still shaking, still sweating, still terrified by his own resolve. Involuntarily, he squeezed his cheeks tightly together.

Without turning on the headlights he backed onto the dirt trail, sand spitting out from under the front wheels as the transfer case shifted power to the front differential. Cliff was slammed back against the seat as he jammed on the brakes, banged into first, and took off toward the sacrificial glade in one deft motion. He steered the jeep into the maw of the tunnel that was an old wagon trail lined with stout pines. Strong gusts from the brewing storm walloped against the canvas top and sides. Kicked up by the knobby off-road tires, sand rattled off the steel chassis.

As soon as he saw the fires through the trees, he ground to a halt. The engine idled smoothly, with hardly a sound. The worshipers were intent on their deed, praying with hands and torches upheld, in a wide circle around the barkless log. Another figure was held down where the large man had been before. Cliff could make out only white skin and long hair. Several people made reverse obeisance toward the still figure that sagged on the upright pole, others watched the ceremony about to take place. They were seemingly oblivious to the whipping treetops and dark, thundering skies. Rain pelted against the windshield.

Cliff took a deep breath. Then another. He shook all over. It was not going to work. He could not force himself to do it.

All around him the woods was in motion. The storm whipped the trees about in sudden fury. Branches beat against the fenders with nerve-racking intensity. Large trunks swayed.

He threw the transmission into reverse, backed away slowly, quietly. He had not been noticed, so he still had a chance to escape. The Jeep stopped on its own. The engine was still whining, but the vehicle would not move. His spine tingling, he pressed down on the gas pedal.

All four tires spun, gouging holes in the sand. The Jeep remained stuck. Cliff stuck his head out the window and looked back. A pine log blocked the path—the very path he had just driven along—as if it had been placed there to prevent his retreat. But no, it must have just toppled from its shallow bed. As a distant thunderbolt lighted the clouds, he saw stones and dirt still cascading from exposed roots.

The trunk was too fat for the Jeep to climb over. Nor could he bulldoze it out of the way, for the base and the upper branches were inextricably intertwined with the surrounding trees. It was an old tree, and rotten. Perhaps he could smash through the soft wood.

He rolled forward a few feet, slipped into reverse, and rode back until the rear bumper slammed against the bark. Splintered chips flew into the air, but the log moved only a few inches. He repeated the procedure, heard the satisfying crack of wood, saw the trunk snap in the middle. He rammed it again, and again. He had to get out of here before he was spotted by those maniacs.

Once more, and he felt sure the tree would split in two. But when he dropped the clutch he heard a sickening grind in the transmission. The gear shift lever jumped out of place, the engine roared in neutral. Rain slewed through the window, dampening his clothes and the side of his face. He tried again to put the Jeep into reverse, but knew before he did that it would not go in. The reverse had been blown.

Now he could only go forward.

The storm was howling now, a raging cacophony that drowned out the crude carnal chanting. In the glow of smoking, rain-drenched fires, Cliff watched the strange posturing ceremony, saw the human sacrament held down face upward, observed the wooden stake begin its final plunge between pink, pearly legs, heard the awful scream that presaged the penultimate moment of impalement.

It was more than he could bear.

And it was more than *she* could survive.

Cliff gunned the engine and dropped the clutch. At three thousand rpms the Jeep nearly vaulted off the ground. Deep, crosshatched treads grabbed at the loose soil, spat it out in four churning rooster tails. The Jeep fishtailed as it roared forward, a crazed steel juggernaut on the way to hell.

The four-by-four rolled over a small sapling, charged

through a barrier of thorny bullbriars, and roared into
the clearing. Cliff turned on the high beams and leaned
on the horn; the light and the raucous blast of sound stopped
the satanic ritual in midstride.

Startled faces looked up, jaws dropped. Some shielded
their eyes against the bright intrusion. Cliff paid them no
mind, but steered for an opening between two fires. The
jeep bounced from side to side as the tires dropped into
shallow depressions. He jerked the wheel sharply from side
to side to keep his heading. The outer fringe of worshipers
scattered just as a .ton of angry steel raced through the
blazing circle.

Flames licked the sidewalls and quarter panels as Cliff
swerved desperately to miss an old woman. The Jeep
skidded until he got both hands on the wheel and corrected
his course. He aimed for the altar where four startled men
were still holding down his wife by her arms and legs.

He rounded the central fire pit with its grisly, motionless
manikin, carving an arc that made the Jeep reel at an
awkward angle. A rock crashed through the windshield,
high and on the far side. Somebody yanked an axe out of the
altar's cross brace and swung it wildly as the Jeep approached. Cliff veered off, avoiding the sharpened,
tempered steel, and bounded over a hillock that tossed the
Jeep in the air, first the front, then the rear. He stood on
the brakes, and brought the vehicle to a halt just inside the
opposite fire ring.

The ceremony was completely routed by now, and the
robed participants were dodging all over the grassy clearing, screaming and shouting invectives.

He felt the heat from the flames, saw the paint on the
wheel well begin to bubble. He threw the stick shift into
reverse. Nothing happened and he remembered the blown
gear. Switching to forward again, he popped the clutch and
lurched away just as a maddened mob reached the opposite
side. One man tried to jump in the passenger door. He clung
on as Cliff took off, was dragged for several seconds, then
screamed as his legs hit a log and he was knocked free.

Unbelievably, Elaine was still being held in place,

although her supporters were crouched close under the horizontal log. Her limbs were being bent unnaturally. She found her voice. Cliff headed for her tormentors.

The axe man jumped out threateningly at the same time a knife slashed through the window. Cliff felt the cut on his arm, saw a leering, painted face, struggled to maintain control while avoiding the long-handled axe, dodged the central fire pit, and slammed head-on into a robed figure he had not noticed. The chromed bumper caught the body at the knees. The man folded over the hood and hung precariously, arms outflung. As the Jeep dropped into a gully and banged up the other side, the silent figure was tossed upward like a matador gored by a charging bull. He slid along the waxed hood. The fiendishly painted face smashed against the windshield, blocking Cliff's view. The glass splintered and crystal fingers tore through the skin and held the face like so many claws.

Cliff slammed on the brakes before he crashed into the rain-swept forest. As the tires gouged deep troughs in the wet soil, the limp body slid off the hood like a broken rag doll. Glass shards in the nostrils ripped off the nose, which stayed in the windshield for a moment before falling through the shattered hole, bouncing off the steering column, and landing inert upon the floorboards.

Cliff ignored the ghastly remnant, tried to back up, realized again that he had no reverse, and drove the Jeep over the body by straddling it with the wheels. A pole slammed against the side of his head, but most of the force was absorbed by the window frame. Cliff recognized the slender coroner from Elaine's pictures. He spun the wheel and floored the accelerator, turning the Jeep practically within its own length.

The mob was closing in on him, and unavoidably he sideswiped two of the cultists. Their screams were drowned out by a peal of thunder. Cliff hunched over the steering wheel, half senseless from the stab wound on the shoulder and the knock on the temple. His vision blurred as he went into a swoon. He ducked rocks and bits of wood thrown by a knot of whooping women. He swerved again and headed the Jeep straight for the A-frame. There were people in his way, but now he could not think clearly enough to care.

He had only one goal, and that was to save Elaine. If he had to knock off a few pawns to check his mate, so be it.

He ran over three gawking worshipers, grinding them and their red vestments under the oversized tires. The Jeep bounded over the bodies, crushing bone and flattening flesh, and dashed alongside the sacrificial log. He scraped off the two men holding down Elaine's left side.

One woman disappeared under the steel chassis, then a man got wrapped up in the right front wheel. Another was still on his knees, praying, when the left fender collided with his head, spinning him around and cleaving open his skull like a burst watermelon.

Cliff spun the wheel just before reaching the fire ring, and skidded to a halt facing back into the glade. He saw Elaine slide off the trunk and hit the ground, free but motionless. He hit the gas and the Jeep rumbled forward. He steered for Hinkle, but the overweight sheriff ducked and rolled under the log. The other two who had been holding down his wife scrabbled frantically. Cliff managed to run over the legs of one, crushing them, and was rewarded by a loud scream.

He cut the steering wheel sharply, and spun the Jeep in a sand-spitting rotary. The vehicle slid sideways through a fire pit, bounced, and knocked down three scrambling people. He churned up the ground, temporarily losing control of the vehicle. The Jeep caught up with an old woman and ran straight over her, lurching sickeningly into the air as it rolled over the folded body.

"Git him!"

A flaming brand ricochetted off the hood. Cliff kept turning wildly, randomly, chasing after fleeing worshipers with red robes flapping in the wind. He felt heat near his head, looked up, and saw the canvas roof afire. He ran down a waving man, then headed for the trees as flames spread through the material.

He stood it as long as he could, until the whole roof was ablaze. He slewed to a stop, grabbed the rifle and ammunition can, and rolled out the door. He had thought his premeditated attack would turn into a complete rout. Instead, the entire contingent of the cult was closing in on him.

Cliff waved the Mauser over his head. "Get back or I'll shoot!"

If anyone heard him, they paid his threats no mind. He jammed the wooden stock into his shoulder, and fired into the air. The report was swallowed up by a bolt of lightning striking the forest nearby. He wiped rainwater off his forehead and out of his eyes. He fired again, coincidentally at the same time as another thunderbolt struck.

Zombielike, they kept coming.

Cliff fired three rapid-fire shots into the ground between him and the advancing horde. None of them so much as faltered. They continued their ancient chant, as if the gun and the threat of death had no reality to them.

"I'll kill you!"

Cliff leveled the rifle at the leading man. He had grown up shooting squirrels and groundhogs, rabbits and muskrats. He had drowned a sick, diseased cat. He had killed deer at point-blank range. And once he had bagged a moose along the shores of the Allagash. But he had never shot a human being, had never aimed a weapon at a fellow man.

But as those spindly arms reached out for him he lowered the barrel and discharged the weapon into the man's leg. The old geezer collapsed, groaning. But the woman behind him stepped right over the injured man, grabbing for the rifle. Cliff slugged her in the ribcage, knocking her aside. He heard the cracking of bone, the gasp of air escaping her lungs.

Cliff screamed as another man clutched his shoulder. He swung the rifle in a broad arc. The thick stock crashed into the worshiper's skull. Blood and teeth flew out of his mouth.

"You fucking lunatics," he shouted.

He put the rifle up to his shoulder, sighted quickly, squeezed the trigger. The weapon exploded, and a glazed-eyed man flew backward violently with a gaping hole in his shoulder. Cliff worked the bolt, ejected the shell, and chambered another round. He aimed and squeezed. A short woman with sagging breasts fell back with her arm broken in half.

He fired again and again and again, each shot the knell of a human body suffering abuse. A torch arced in the air, landed next to him. With practiced ease Cliff shot the man who had thrown it. These people were nothing more than wild animals who deserved to be slaughtered—who, by their slow approach, were asking for the release of death.

Cliff changed magazines and continued the massacre. He had always thought he did not have the capacity to kill. Now, he did not have the time to aim to wound. Nor did he have the will. Like an automaton he fired into the mass, trying to stop them any way he could. If it meant death, then they deserved it.

The magazine was empty. He ripped open a cardboard box and loaded bullets one at a time. He fired and killed; pulled the bolt, loaded, and fired. And still they kept coming, a mindless horde, repeating the primitive words of their satanic rite.

They were on top of him. He swung the rifle like a bat, fracturing a man's jaw. An old woman grabbed his face, stuck bony fingers up his nostrils. He lashed out with his elbow, caught her in the solar plexus, and knocked her down. He pulled up the rifle and slashed at another robed figure. Someone caught his arm, a body fell against his legs, a man jumped on his head. He was borne down to the ground by the sheer weight of numbers.

Kicking and clawing, they dragged him away from the burning Jeep. He had killed and maimed a couple dozen sloe-eyed chanters, but there were too many left for him to fight. He felt his clothes being ripped off, felt the rain on his naked chest. He was lifted bodily and carried toward the sacrificial altar. He was flipped over and slammed belly down on the barkless log.

He craned his neck and saw Elaine's fear-crazed eyes only inches from his own. She babbled incoherently. Someone thwacked him in the rear and his testicles screamed with pain. He struggled against the four men holding his limbs, but to no avail.

For a moment the lightning flashes stopped and the wind eased off as if the storm were gathering its forces. The glade was engulfed by an eerie, sepulcral silence. A nauseating odor fumed up out of the ground as if mounds of rotting vegetation and decaying animal matter were suddenly exposed.

Sheriff Hinkle, retying his loose robe around a bent erection, stooped alongside him, leering frantically. "Mister, ya sure created a lot more fodder for the altar. But chu an' the lady're gonna be the first to feed the Almighty. I'm gonna give ya the shaft like ya never got it before."

Cliff took a last look at his wife before squeezing his eyes shut. He tried to make it all go away, as if this awful scene were not really happening, as if it were part of a nightmare from which he would soon awake. But he could not block out the pain, could not close his ears to Elaine's dreadful moaning.

He heard the drums, and the chanting—not as loud as before, and not as many voices. But the requiem was more frightening than ever. His abdominal muscles quivered, his sphincter clamped tightly. He knew what was coming, only this time it was going to be worse, much worse.

The sheriff grabbed Cliff's hair, twisted his head to the side. "Looka here, mister. Look what I got fer ya."

He rubbed clear jelly on the rounded end of the pole that was as thick as a newel post. He laughed in tune with the chanters. Lightning arced in the clouds, shedding a preternatural brightness that flashed across the landscape with startling clarity. The injured people lay huddled together off to one side. The rest walked in a circle inside the ring of fires, supplicating.

"This ain't no rectal thermometer."

A sudden gust of wind nearly blew off the sheriff's robe. The sixty-foot pines raged, whipping like blades of grass in a gale. The rain pelted down with a fury. The ground rumbled and the sheriff was nearly knocked off his feet. He stumbled back for balance, was caught by Benson.

Hinkle laughed like a crazy person. "I ain't as good as the cor'ner, so this could hurt a mite."

"Stop bragging, and just get on with it. We got hurt people to take care of." The coroner squinted up at the dark clouds. "I don't like the looks of this storm."

All attempt at ceremony ceased as the uninjured worshipers aided the wounded. Moans of pain came from every direction. Only a small knot of people were participating in the sacrifice. The rest were helping the lame to their feet, or preparing makeshift stretchers. The police photographer shouted orders and offered medical assistance.

"Murdock'll take care of 'em. Right now our biggest problem's the Jersey Devil." Sheriff Hinkle leered down at Cliff, licking his lips with a fat tongue. "Ready or not, here it comes."

The pole rubbed along Cliff's inner thigh, teasingly. It jabbed his anus, retreated, jabbed again. Cliff tried not to cry out. He squirmed futilely, actually picking one man up off the ground with his strong right arm before the painted cultist got a better purchase. The slimy pole felt again for the anal opening, centered on the tender orifice, started to push through into the rectum. Cliff let out a cry as his whole body stiffened.

The A-frame lashing snapped with a loud retort. One pair of crossed saplings fell away, and the heavy sacrificial log collapsed at that end.

"What the devil."

Cliff landed hard on his scrotum, groaned, and rolled away clutching his groin as he was let go. Suddenly freed, with all eight of the holders down, he scrambled to his feet, kicked one man in the jaw with the side of his naked foot, scooped up Elaine, a limp doll, and dragged her away.

The Jeep's gasoline tank exploded with a roar, lifting the rear of the vehicle straight up in the air and over the front bumper. As it somersaulted forward like a child's toy, the blazing four-by-four crashed down on the roll bar, pivoted for a moment, then tilted crazily, shooting flames in all directions.

Cliff was knocked under the other, upright A-frame, with

Elaine on top of him. The sheriff was bowled over by the
log as the untied end sideslipped. The rain pelted down like
grapeshot, stinging. The very earth wallowed, like the deck
of a small boat in a choppy sea. The air was electrifying,
seemingly coruscating with a life of its own. The trees
glowed with Saint Elmo's fire, like ghostly, fringed mono-
liths.

The glade was filled with a caterwauling that was louder
than a thousand hoot owls.

The untended fires raged out of control as if suddenly
doused with gasoline. Flames raced up the sacrificial shaft
and ignited Jake Rudley's horribly contorted body. It
glowed for a moment, a scintillating caricature in human
form, then flashed like a Fourth of July sparkler. The stench
of roasted flesh was nauseating.

From near the burning wreckage of the Jeep, the spilled
bullets cooked off with sharp, intermittent bangs. A bolt of
lightning blew out the base of a tall pine, burned a track to
the top, and split the timber in half. It fell into the clearing
and crushed two worshipers under its trunk and spreading
branches.

Jake's body burst into a long plume of smoke and fire that
coalesced in the air above the rapidly dissolving head. The
thick, dark smudge billowed into a roiling apparition with
fantastic, ever-changing features. Flames darted out of the
smoldering blackness, giving it the appearance of a face
with a flickering, darting tongue and cruel eyes that glowed
like embers.

"Ohmigod."

What was left of the prostrating cult got to their feet, and
backed away from the swirling spectre. Another lightning
bolt struck at the opposite side of the clearing, another pine
tree fell among a group of fleeing worshipers. Cliff stood
up, but the ground shook and rumbled so hard it was
impossible to stay upright. He drew Elaine back under the
tripod formed by the log and the A-frame. Thunder roared
in continuous tempo.

Despite the torrential downpour, the two fallen trees
caught fire. The sky was alive with bursts of lightning, the

dark forboding clouds flaring up like pocket incendiary bombs. Hurricane winds drove the rain practically parallel to the ground. Cliff protected Elaine as best he could from the watery onslaught, and cowered on the ground. The surface soil was rippling: concentric rings spreading out from the central fire as if a boulder had been dropped in the middle of a pond.

The seething black cloud above the blazing effigy took on house-sized proportions. It was a grotesque head whose neck rotated in a continuous arc, whose evil eyes scintillated like burning rubies, whose tongue stabbed out like hot lava.

The crippled were left where they lay. The remaining cultists ran screaming from the fuming atmospheric phantom. The ground shuddered and convulsed, and those that reached the forest disappeared under pine trees that toppled like dominoes, ripped out of the sandy soil by the roots. The whole forest seemed to be collapsing.

A bright ball of light burst from the soil, the pent up energy of electron accumulation, completely immolating the crying, running mob that was caught in the open glade beyond the ring of fires. Tatters of red material fluttered to the ground like confetti, along with bits and pieces of flesh and the white stubs of bone: a gruesome ticker tape parade.

The man who had been holding Cliff's arm stood up and raced for the road. As he passed the burning Jeep a secondary explosion sent sheet-metal shrapnel sailing across the clearing. His body was severed in half so fast that his legs and hips remained standing for several eerie seconds after his trunk toppled headfirst to the ground.

A woman screamed, gathered her robe around her, and ran out of the path of a crashing tree. Detonating bullets exploded in her face, shearing it off her head. As she spun around, Cliff saw blood gush out of the throat, saw the gray sponge that was her brain slip loose from her skull.

Another man stood up and was instantly struck by lightning. His body was split asunder like a bisected tree. Both charred, smoldering halves fell away in opposite directions.

Two young women crawling past the fire ring suddenly disappeared when the ground opened up beneath them and the giant, quivering maw of the earth swallowed them at a gulp. The sidewalls clashed together with a bang and a puff of dust, and there was nothing to show where they had gone. The land undulated like a carpet being shaken.

A whirlwind swept through the area, churning up dirt and debris like a giant vacuum cleaner. A group of red-robed people, arms and legs gesticulating wildly, were picked up by the twister and flung into the air. One was dashed against a tree, torn to pieces as his body was shredded by needle-sharp branches. It rained blood and gore. One was slammed into the ground so hard his body came apart at the seams. The rest were tossed out of sight.

The lightning flashes ceased, the rain abated, the earth became still, the fires died out. Nothing moved, not a body stirred. A deep, dreadful, ominous silence ensued.

The stars came out and twinkled.

Cliff poked up his head cautiously, as a turtle confronts the world from its shell. His naked body was soaked, and gravel clung to him tenaciously. Wet leaves, twigs, and pine needles covered the ground like a soggy blanket. For a moment, all he could hear was the gentle susurration of his own breathing.

Then he heard a crack like a rifle shot. The pole that held up the nearly consumed form of Jake Rudley snapped at the base and fell over. The corpse landed on its back with the arms bent at the elbows, facing the placid sky, supplicating.

Elaine whimpered, barely audible at first, then louder, until Cliff calmed her by clamping her to his broad chest and wrapping his arms around her shivering body. He rubbed his hands over her drenched hair, kissed the top of her head.

"It's all right, honey. It's all over now. It's all over."

She continued to shake and sob. "No . . . no . . ." She pressed her naked body tighter against Cliff's.

"You're safe now."

"My insides hurt. As if I've been . . . raped. By a dry . . . by a bottlebrush."

Cliff kissed her eyes, her cheeks, her lips. "It's all right, honey. I'm sore, too. We're both pretty wrung—"

A twig snapped. A cold ice pick threaded its way through

Cliff's backbone. He jerked around, saw the obese body of the sheriff skulking toward them. Hinkle's smile was anything but pleasant. He raised his right hand, pointing. A shaft of moonlight speared through low, dissolving clouds and glistened off blued steel.

"Din't think ya were gonna git away scot-free, didja?"

Elaine went wild, sobbing and clamoring in Cliff's arm, sinking against him for protection.

"Ain't gonna do no good cryin'."

Cliff stared at the gun, at the crazy gleam in the sheriff's eyes. He knew there was no bargaining, no pleading for mercy, and no way to outrun those deadly, speeding projectiles or to reach the sheriff before he could fire. He clutched Elaine tighter and waited for the inevitable.

The sheriff slowly, very deliberately, stretched out his thumb, cocked the revolver, and aimed the pistol directly at Cliff's bruised forehead. Cliff refused to blink, refused to back down at this final moment.

A shot rang out. Cliff blinked automatically, and Elaine convulsed in his arms. He opened his eyes, felt for a wound on her body, saw the sheriff twisted sideways, saw the gun fly out of the chubby hand. Elaine pushed back, stared at Cliff for a moment, then redirected her gaze toward the sheriff. The lawman looked dumbfounded at the blood gushing from his forearm, raised faraway eyes past Cliff and Elaine.

"Hinkle, if you believe in this Jersey Devil bullshit you better start praying for salvation, 'cause your ass-kicking days are over."

"Bart!" Cliff yelled.

The lieutenant was wet and disheveled, but his gun arm was steady as a rock. "Sorry for being so slow. I finally put the pieces together—a giant jigsaw puzzle that kept me stymied for fourteen years."

The sheriff clutched his wrist, trying to stem the flow of blood from his shattered hand. *"You!"*

"That's right. Me. The city slicker you thought you could fool." Lieutenant Wakeley marched into the flickering orange cone of light from the central fire. He was smiling smugly. "It took me a long time to catch on to what you've got going on here."

"I don't know what chu know, or what chu *think* ya know," the sheriff bragged, "but it'll never hold up in court. Nobody's gonna believe *this*."

"*Court!* Who the hell said anything about court, you slimy bastard?" Wakeley raised the sights of his gun and fired again. Hinkle's knee burst apart in a torrent of blood and bone, and the sheriff collapsed bawling to the soggy soil. "You don't think I'm going to let you get to trial, do you? Hell, I'm not going to give you any more chance than you gave my daughter."

Whimpering, the sheriff crawled away. "You got no proof."

"I got all the proof I need." The lieutenant tapped his head. "Right here." Then he tapped the pistol. "And I got the jury right here. And inside are seven executioners."

Hinkle rolled over on his side, groveling. "Stop it, Wakeley! You can't do this."

"The hell I can't." He shot again, into the fleshy part of the sheriff's thigh.

Sheriff Hinkle grunted. He struggled up onto his hands and one knee, but could not go anywhere.

"I'm not going to let you off easy." Lieutenant Wakeley ran after the sheriff, grabbed the red satin material, and ripped it off the corpulent body. "I want to see you suffer." He pulled back his leg, and jammed the toe of his muddy wingtip between those fat, ugly legs.

Hinkle screamed, his body reacting galvanically. A bright red spot of blood drained from his flesh-covered orifice. Lieutenant Wakeley wasted no time in directing his gun toward the bull's-eye. He pulled the trigger and a .38-caliber slug drove right up into the sheriff's intestines. Hinkle screamed again, his body jiggling on the ground like a battery-operated Tonka toy out of control.

Turning, the lieutenant holstered his gun. "Well, that ought to finish him off in a couple of minutes." He stood silently, watching the clawing, whimpering man squirm like a beached whale. In his wild gyrations, he finally came to rest next to the scorched, smoking body of Jake Rudley. "Guess I oughta call the mammal-stranding center. You kids okay?"

Cliff reached out, grabbed the angled log, and pulled himself upright. Elaine, stuck to him like a leech, came up with him.

"Honey, are you all right?"

She had stopped crying, but her voice was cracked and hoarse. "Ye-ye-yes. I'm . . . okay. Cold."

"Here, you better put this on." Lieutenant Wakeley held out the sheriff's robe, and wrapped it around her mud-spackled form. "Wait a minute, Cliff. I'll get one for you."

"If you can hold Laine, I'll try to find my clothes." He had to unclench her fists to break away from her.

"Don't go . . ."

Cliff hugged her again. "Just hold onto Uncle Bart for a moment. You'll be okay." He eased her into Wakeley's embrace, disentangled himself from her arms, and stepped back. He located his pants and shirt among the debris, and pulled on the wet things. "Don't know if they'll keep me warm, though." He flashed a weak smile. "I see you got my message."

The lieutenant kept his arm around Elaine, offering comfort as well as support. "A little garbled, but I eventually figured it out. The real giveaway was that tape from the coroner's. Seems as if he kept a list of the people they've been—" His upper lips curled as he looked at the hideous remains of Jake Rudley, still cooking slowly in the orange embers. "—cremating. It'll probably solve most of the local missing-persons cases over the last half century, maybe longer."

"You mean, you checked up on some of them and found—"

"No, not yet. Didn't have time. That's just a hunch. But the last name on the list gave it all away. It was . . ." The lieutenant swallowed hard. "It was . . . Sharon's man-friend. And the date jived as well. Those bodies dug up last week . . . if they hadn't been cremated, they might have proved—"

"Don't," Cliff interrupted. "Don't even think about it. You'll never know for sure. And you're better off *not* knowing."

The lieutenant shivered, as if a sudden winter chill had descended on him. "Yeah, I guess you're right. Still, as a detective . . ."

Elaine wiped her eyes with the back of her hand. "You've still got the Jersey Devil to find." Her voice cracked, but she was speaking more clearly now. She broke away from the lieutenant and sidled up against her husband. "And now you've seen what it can do."

Lieutenant Wakeley laughed right out loud. "Come on, Laine."

He strode over to where Sheriff Hinkle lay next to the fire. His fat form had rolled into the outer coals. With his knees tucked up under his body he looked like a starched, stuffed pig. The only thing missing was the apple. "Hell, you don't really believe in all that Jersey Devil crap, do you? Those are just stories to frighten children and gullible adults. There's a logical explanation for every—"

The pine barrens howled.

It was a high-pitched, atonal caterwauling that vibrated in the air like the siren calling Ulysses. Beyond the smoking Jeep, the woods lit up with a piercing white glow that quickly staggered from side to side. The sound grew louder for half a minute, then faded rapidly and died with a sudden chirp. The sea nymph called no more. The forest grew preternaturally dark.

From the opposite side came a crunching sound, and the rasping of a giant bellows. All eyes turned to the oncoming phantom. It stopped at the treeline—Or had it been there all the time?—a stunted, rotten tree trunk which in the darkness, and in vivid imagination, had taken human form. Elaine shivered in Cliff's arms, and Cliff felt his sphincter contract. He tightened his grip on his wife.

"What the hell—" The lieutenant was cut off by the thrashing of brush near the Jeep.

"Oh, Cliff, it's coming back."

Cliff redirected his attention to the smoldering four-by-four. A thick black cloud wafted sideways, close to the ground, and hung there without even the slightest breeze to blow it away. Slowly, gradually, the inky patch of smoke roiled toward them. The front of it was dimly illuminated by the barely-burning central fire.

Twin yellow orbs appeared, like eyeballs shooting beams of light. A broad, amorphous gray mass moved out of the cloud. It seemed to Cliff that it rolled across the ground, its feet obscured by the smoke. The head was large and bulbous. The trunk had limbs too far apart to be normal. The legs were huge, elephantine, and they moved in an odd manner: first from the middle, then independently from each side.

Cliff found himself shaking in tandem with Elaine. He could not believe this was happening, could not believe this was real.

Incredibly, the monster started separating, like a single cell dividing through mitosis. The gray mass widened, the eyes got farther apart. The legs split into two pairs. And where before there had been two arms, now there were four. The odd-shaped head became two adjacent, inverted, wide-rimmed soup bowls. Then both creatures charged.

There was a shout of *"Get him!"* a rushing of two uniformed policemen. Deputy Hopper, gun in one hand and flashlight in the other, ran straight for Lieutenant Wakeley. The startled lieutenant raised his gun just as Hopper threw him a body block. They crashed to the ground in a heap. A gun went off, loud in the pervading silence. Both men lay still, clasped in each other's arms.

The lump in Cliff's throat threatened to choke him. Elaine had jumped once, but otherwise stood still within his clutch.

Another shot rang out.

A swishing sound was followed by a long-handled axe cleaving a log next to the lieutenant's head. A painted, red-robed figure staggered forward into the dim firelight. Cliff barely recognized the tortured, bloody features of the coroner. He collapsed in a heap and lay still.

With agonizing slowness, the pair on the ground began to move.

Hopper pushed himself up to his knees. "Lieutenant, are you all right?"

Wakeley shook his head as he struggled up to one elbow. "Hell, no, I'm not all right. You scared the living hell out of me."

Deputy Bridger, smoking gun still trained on the fallen coroner, took a step forward. "Sorry for the alarm, Lieutenant, but Benson was about to scalp you with a fire axe."

"Well, under the circumstances, I'll let it slide." Wakeley got to his feet with Hopper's help and brushed himself off. "And you ought to be damn careful when you come at somebody with a gun. If I'd been myself, I'd have shot you."

Hopper smirked nervously. "Sorry, sir. I wasn't thinking."

The lieutenant rolled his shoulders as he pulled out his lapel and slid the gun into his shoulder holster. "Yeah, well, apparently, neither was I. Some police officer. I froze up when I should have acted instinctively. I'm getting too old for this business."

Stiff lipped, Bridger jerked his chin at Cliff. "You two okay?"

Cliff ran his hand up and down Elaine's arm. "I'll let you know when my heart starts beating."

"We'd a got here sooner, but there's trees down all over the place. Couldn't get the car any closer." He swung his hand in the general direction from which they had come. "Looks like that tornado took out quite a few people, too."

Elaine spoke up tremulously. "I didn't know they had tornadoes in this part of the country."

"It's pretty rare," Bridger allowed. "A low pressure area and a hot offshore breeze'll do it. Not usually this violent."

"We can talk about the weather some other time," Wakeley said. "What I want to know is, what're you two doing here in the first place?" He nodded at Hopper. "And how come you're on my side today?"

Hopper's lips quivered. He glanced around the clearing at

the carnage, at the dying fire, at the charred remains, at Hinkle's body. "The sheriff, he . . . he . . . he was involved in something nasty . . . something—"

Bridger interrupted. "Hell, I knew he was on the take. I knew he was looking out for himself. Didn't seem any different from any other lawman. But I didn't know nothing about this. But when he sneaked in the office with that paper bag . . . He locked it up in the safe, but soon's he left I opened it up. Watched him once to get the combination. I couldn't believe what I found . . ."

When he faltered, Hopper said, "It had some clothes in it. And a camera. I took the film to a private lab in Cherry Hill. A buddy of mine. It was a special emulsion, he said. Some kind of invisible red. But the pictures . . . It was this parade, these people with robes. Holding torches. In the glade. I was through here the other evening. Scared the hell out of some fishermen with my siren. They didn't have licenses—"

"And the clothes . . . Well, they belonged to the newspaper lady." Bridger stole a look at Elaine. "The other one. She'd been in to see me the other night. She was lookin' for the sheriff. I recognized the outfit. That's why I gave the film to Hopper."

"I was scared to death to come in here, after seeing those pictures. But the fire tower reported a lightning strike, said the woods were ablaze. Goddamn, I was scared."

Bridger humphed. "I wasn't taking no chances, what with the goings on at these festivals. I knew some of them were in cahoots, but not how many. So, I called for reinforcements. Got five volunteer fire departments converging on this place from all sides. Called the Stateys and told 'em we were chasin' a gang that robbed a coupla stores, and needed backup. Got the FBI on the phone and made up a story 'bout stumbling onto a drug ring making a payoff. Then I told the National Guard we had flooding from the storm and we had stranded folks to rescue. Hell, we got half the state mobilized and headed this way."

Hopper was excited, his fear gone. "Nobody'll get away, unless he can climb into a hole and swim through the ground. We saw Murdock vamoosing out of here, all spruced up like a Halloween goblin. Hit him with the searchlight, but he kept hightailing. Don't matter. Them trick-or-treaters won't get far."

The lieutenant nodded wryly. "Man, I got to give you credit. When you put out a call for help, you don't fuck around. Bridger, you're gonna make a good sheriff someday. Maybe tomorrow. But one word of advice: every lawman ain't on the take. It's the few bad apples that get all the publicity."

Bridger smiled. "I'll remember that, sir. Well, what say we get you folks back to the car. You look pretty cold, ma'am. And what with all these official agencies out on a false alarm, I got some fancy explaining to do."

"I'll back you," Lieutenant Wakeley said. "You just might have blown the lid on the biggest secret society since the Hell Fire Club. And a damn sight more dangerous. And this little lady here's got all the evidence to substantiate the claims."

Elaine's jaw dropped and she waved her hand at the surrounding destruction. "Lieutenant, the cult may be exposed, even exterminated. But how do you explain all this?"

Lieutenant Wakeley's grin was patronal, but bordered on patronizing. "Earth tremors. Seismic activity. Heard it all on the radio just before I got here. Five point six on the Richter scale. Worse earthquake Jersey ever had, and the epicenter was right here in the barrens. Was knocking houses down all over the place. Hell, no, there's no such thing as the Jersey Devil. Or God, either. Just a bunch of sick, sadistic people who—"

Cliff heard a loud pop, saw sparks shoot into the air. He could not help but jump. Elaine cringed against him. The sheriff's body burst into flames, roaring and crackling. The stench of burnt hair and flesh filled the air.

Lieutenant Wakeley approached the conflagration warily. "It's a bed of hot coals. These jokers must have spread some ceremonial ointment on their bodies. Something flammable."

"Lieutenant, stop making excuses. Stop ignoring your senses," Elaine shouted. "What about that ball of lightning? What about that storm?"

"An offshore squall that turned inland. Believe me, Laine, there's a logical explanation for everything."

"No! I don't care what you say, or what kind of deductions you make. Something's living out here in the pines. Something . . . not natural. Something that I don't want to know about."

The lieutenant stared into the flames consuming the sheriff's body. "Well, there is one thing . . ."

He paused for a moment, and looked up, first at Cliff, then at Elaine. "You remember those canine carcasses you brought in for analysis? Well, I got a report from the forensic lab. They performed an examination of the dentition on the gnawed bones." Lieutenant Wakeley swallowed, and returned his gaze to the rampant human bonfire.

Cliff tightened his grip on Elaine. "And?"

The lieutenant sneered. "Whatever chewed up those dogs—was human."

EPILOGUE

Once, when it was mortal, it had a human mother.

Its mother brought it to life, nurtured it, gave it love, begged for protection from the powers that had sired it. That protection came in the form of death, a timeless death, an endless death, a death from which there was no worldly escape. And so it went on in lifeless continuance.

They killed her.

The men came and they killed her.

It did not understand how, or why. But it watched and it saw what they did to her. It saw them press her down over the log. It saw them bare her buttocks. It saw them part their robes and pull out their stiffened, fleshy rods: rods that looked like sticks but were somehow attached. It saw how they penetrated her writhing body, how they plugged her up when the blood began to flow, how they took turns as she screamed, and did it again, and again, over and over, even as she gave in, in futility, until she could take no more and she became still, and the men could not rouse her and they left her for dead, bleeding.

Then it had come out of its corner, crawled to her breast, sucked on nipples that had nothing to offer. Her body was limp, her arms and legs rigid. She did not move, she did not respond, she did not hold her arms out to it.

It was hungry.

It was lonely.

Its stomach growled in pain, its heart in anger. She was the only one who could feed it, the only one who could love it.

They were gone, and with them they took all that was life to it. And so it died—not the ultimate death of mortals, but the resignation of the loss of life, of everything it had to live for.

There was no quelling the ache in its chest or the throbbing in its belly.

It sucked on her nipples until they became soft. Then it chewed, tearing off tiny bits of flesh. It was not milk, but it was food. It was all she had to offer. It went back for more, gnawed at the breast, devoured one, then the other. It stripped off the skin and gobbled it down. Underneath, it found more nourishment. It sucked up the organs, gulped down the lungs, swallowed the heart.

It discovered a new kind of existence.

It ranged through the pine barrens, growing, maturing, gaining in strength, increasing its vitality. It reigned terror on the land. Soon it was respected, revered, omnipotent, everlasting.

Then she came and shattered its heart, brought out from the deep recesses of its mind the sadness, the loneliness, the uncontrollable hatred harbored within.

But she also brought out the yearning, the little lost child. She was a woman, a mother-to-be. She offered those same feelings its mother had, with provision, without requital, as a person, as a lover, as a parent.

And they were going to take all that away.

It had to prevent such travesty. It drew all its powers from the earth, from the pines, from the sky. And it made them pay for their sacrilege. It saved her from mindless oblivion.

And in doing so, saved itself.

It was free, freer than it had been its whole death. It had atoned, it had avenged its past, exonerated its existence. Now it no longer had to cling to that dreadful mortality. Its purpose had been fulfilled, its immortality abolished.

At last, it could die the ultimate death of eternity.

It lay down on the still wet earth, spread itself out, slunk into the mud, let itself be absorbed by the elements. Its body was evaporating, its mind dissipating. It watched for the last time the stars twinkling and the moon shining. It was returning to its mother, its dream over, its death discharged. It no longer had a purpose, it no longer had a will. Comfortably, exquisitely, satiated with death and torture, for the last time, in final ecstasy, it closed its eyes on the world.

Seven years later, they opened.